D0511688

Jackie French
Pennies
for Hitler

BAINTE DEN STOC

WITHDRAWN FROM
DÚN LAOGHAIRE-RATHDOWN COUNTY
LIBRARY STOCK

 Angus&Robertson
An imprint of HarperCollins*Publishers*

On page 280 is reproduced a condensed version of a letter sent by Prime Minister John Curtin to Australian schoolchildren on 30 September 1942. The letter later appeared in various publications.

Angus&Robertson
An imprint of HarperCollins*Publishers*, Australia

First published in Australia in 2012
by HarperCollins*Publishers* Australia Pty Limited
ABN 36 009 913 517
harpercollins.com.au

Copyright © Jackie French 2012

The right of Jackie French to be identified as the author of this work has been asserted by her under the *Copyright Amendment (Moral Rights) Act 2000*.

This work is copyright. Apart from any use as permitted under the *Copyright Act 1968*, no part may be reproduced, copied, scanned, stored in a retrieval system, recorded, or transmitted, in any form or by any means, without the prior written permission of the publisher.

HarperCollins*Publishers*
Level 13, 201 Elizabeth Street, Sydney NSW 2000, Australia
Unit D1, 63 Apollo Drive, Rosedale, Auckland 0632, New Zealand
A 53, Sector 57, Noida, UP, India
77–85 Fulham Palace Road, London W6 8JB, United Kingdom
2 Bloor Street East, 20th floor, Toronto, Ontario M4W 1A8, Canada
10 East 53rd Street, New York NY 10022, USA

National Library of Australia Cataloguing-in-Publication data:

French, Jackie.
    Pennies for Hitler / Jackie French.
    ISBN: 978 0 7322 9209 6 (pbk.)
    For children.
A823.3

Cover design by Jane Waterhouse, HarperCollins Design Studio
Cover images: Boy © Ocean/Corbis; St Paul's Cathedral © Corbis;
background images by shutterstock.com
Typeset in Sabon 10/15pt by Kirby Jones

To the magicians of Monkey Baa Theatre for Young People — Eva, Sandie, Tim and all the cast and crew — who have taken Hitler's Daughter *on so many kinds of journeys to so many audiences, with love and gratitude*

Some stories have no true beginnings. Perhaps this story was born ten thousand years ago, when a hungry man on a hilltop saw strangers wandering down his valley.

'Enemies are coming!' he cried. His tribe picked up their spears.

That afternoon there was blood on the grass.

Hatred is contagious. Fear is too. When things are bad it is good to have someone else to blame.

This part of the story begins with a boy.

Chapter 1

There were cream cakes for tea the afternoon they killed Georg's father.

He had been happy that morning, too excited to concentrate as he wound the tape measure around Johann's head. All the other boys in his class at the Adolf Hitler Schule measured their friends' heads too. 'The Rektor will give a speech to the graduating students,' Georg whispered. 'And then there will be cakes for afternoon tea.'

'With whipped cream?' whispered Johann enviously.

Georg nodded. This was the first year he had been allowed to go to the graduation ceremony at Papa's University, and Mutti had promised him there would be cream cakes.

'I wish I could have the afternoon off school and eat cream cakes,' whispered Johann.

Georg grinned as he wrote down how wide and how long his friend's head was. It was good to have an important father who was a professor at the University.

I

'Silence at the back there!' called Herr Doktor Schöner. Herr Doktor Schöner was new. The older boys said he had been one of the earliest members of the Nazi Party, years ago, with the Führer. Now he taught at their school! 'Has everyone finished measuring?'

The boys nodded.

'Georg, collect the answers, *bitte*, and bring them to me.'

Georg collected the sheets of paper, then took them up to the desk on the platform under the blackboard and the big photo of the Führer.

'Thank you,' said Herr Doktor Schöner. 'Sit down, Georg. Now, can anyone tell me why the shape of the head is important?'

Georg had already read the whole Racial Studies textbook. He put up his hand.

'Georg?'

'Because different races have different head shapes.'

'Yes. Good,' said Herr Doktor Schöner enthusiastically. 'Some races have small, narrow heads. That is why they are stupid. Some races have round heads. They are slow, and cowardly. But the pure German Aryan head ...' Herr Doktor Schöner stared around the class, as though he is judging all our heads, thought Georg, suddenly nervous. 'The Aryan head is wide, but long too. Those with Aryan brains are not only most intelligent, but also natural leaders.'

A boy put up his hand. 'Are all Germans natural leaders?'

Of course not, thought Georg, just as Herr Doktor Schöner said: 'Of course not. Sadly, some German people married foreigners.' Like Mutti married Papa, thought Georg. The prickle of unease grew. 'Some Germans are only part Aryan. Even if they have blond hair and blue eyes, their heads may not be the right shape. That is why we must make the Aryan race

2

pure again. The Untermensch, the inferiors — those who are not as intelligent, or who are blind or lame, as well as, of course, Jews — must not be allowed to breed.'

He flicked through the boys' answers. 'Now, let us see what your heads say about all of you.'

Georg tried not to wriggle in his seat. Papa was English! What if Georg's head shape was inferior?

Even as he thought it Herr Doktor Schöner lifted up his head from the papers. 'Georg, would you come out to the front?'

Georg stood. The stares of his classmates as he walked to the front seemed as heavy as the weights they lifted in the gymnasium.

'Look at this boy,' said Herr Doktor Schöner. 'Look at him carefully. What do you see?'

The class was silent. Georg tried not to let his fear show. Papa couldn't be inferior. He was a Herr Professor even if he was English!

'A perfect Aryan head!' cried Herr Doktor Schöner.

Georg glanced at him. Herr Doktor Schöner must not know Papa was English! But the English King's family was German. Englanders had German ancestors. Papa must have German ancestors too.

He was a perfect Aryan! He felt like bouncing on his toes. But he stayed standing straight and firm, like the German soldiers Herr Doktor Schöner said they must be like.

'A perfect Aryan holds himself upright,' said Herr Doktor Schöner. 'He is brave, and in command.' Georg was glad he hadn't bounced. 'You may sit down, Georg. Now, can anyone tell me how you recognise a *Jude*?'

Johann put up his hand. 'A *Jude* has a long nose, and black hair and eyes. They slouch and —'

3

The bell rang along the corridor. Racial Studies was over. Georg grinned. No more school till tomorrow!

~∭◎

There was a crowd around the big newspaper barrel on the footpath as he came out of school. There always was, these days. The newspaper barrel had the pages of *Der Stürmer* pasted on it every day, so even those who couldn't afford to buy a copy could see the great things the Führer was doing.

Georg craned his head to see the pages through the crowd. There was a big photo of the Führer reviewing his troops — thousands and thousands of them with their arms held out in salute. Georg could almost hear their cry: '*Heil*, Hitler! *Heil*, Hitler!'

Georg wished he had been in the crowd to shout and salute too.

Their house was only two streets from the Adolf Hitler Schule. It had been the Rainer Maria Rilke Schule until last year, when the name had been changed to honour the Führer. Papa had been annoyed. Papa loved poetry, and Rilke had been a great German poet, one of those Papa taught about at the University.

The trees along the street were budding spring green above him. A lark sang its bright violin-like song as he opened the front gate. Daffodils nodded yellow heads as he opened the door.

He sniffed. Lamb stew with dumplings for lunch. Down in the kitchen he could hear Lotte singing. Tante Gudrun said good servants shouldn't sing. But Papa laughed and said, 'Let her have her fun.'

Tante Gudrun had snorted. 'That is how you English do things, I suppose.'

Georg thought Papa's ideas better than Tante Gudrun's. And Papa was a good German now. He had lived here for fifteen years, ever since he had come as a student and fallen in love with Mutti.

Tante Gudrun had pig's eyes. Papa had pretended to be cross when Georg said that, but Georg could see that he was laughing inside, and Mutti too.

What if Tante Gudrun really did have pig's eyes? Georg grinned. Maybe an evil witch had passed a pigsty one day and turned the pigs into women. One woman kept her piggy eyes. One had piggy feet so she always had to keep her shoes on ...

'*Röslein, röslein, röslein rot,*' sang Lotte in the kitchen.

Mutti and Papa were already sitting at the table in the dining room. Georg kissed Mutti's cheek — it smelled of flowers — then Papa's, warm and smooth. Drops of water glistened on the butter in its crystal bowl on the table. The cherry jam gleamed next to the hot rolls. 'Good day, Papa, Mutti.'

'And good day to you,' said Papa in English. The newspaper lay next to him, still folded.

Georg glanced down at it.

'Papa?'

'Mmm?' said Papa.

'Will the Führer be at the graduation?'

Papa laughed. 'Of course not.'

'Why not?'

Papa grinned. 'Our mighty leader has better things to do than come to graduations.'

'Shh.' Mutti gave a swift look towards the kitchen door. 'Lotte will hear you.'

5

Papa reached across and picked up Mutti's hand; he kissed it. 'Somehow I don't think Herr Hitler will send me to a labour camp just for calling him a mighty leader.'

'I think that —' began Mutti, then stopped as Lotte came in with the lamb stew.

Georg waited for Mutti to eat first, then lifted his fork.

There were letters on the table too. The postman must have just been. Georg craned to look at the handwriting as he chewed his lamb. One for Mutti from her friend in the Black Forest and one for Papa from his sister, Aunt Miriam, in England. He wished someone would send him a letter.

He selected a roll with poppy seeds and watched the butter melt into the white bread. He reached for the cherry jam.

'One spoonful,' said Mutti, not even looking up from her letter.

'Two,' offered Georg.

'One.'

'Two, because it's a special day. Like Weihnachten.'

Mutti laughed and looked at Papa. 'What do you think? Is graduation day as special as Christmas?'

Papa looked up from Aunt Miriam's letter. 'Getting those students to graduation is special enough. Some of them think about nothing but politics these days. Smashing shopkeepers' windows, beating up old men for the crime of being Jewish.'

'Shhh,' said Mutti again, with a glance towards the kitchen.

Georg spread his two spoonfuls of cherry jam. Papa didn't understand about the Jews. It was the Jews' fault Germany had been so poor till the Führer took control. Herr Doktor Schöner had explained it at school. The Jews controlled the banks. They poisoned the Vaterland and made it weak just by living among them. The Jews killed babies for their secret ceremonies; and they poisoned the wells in villages.

Sometimes Mutti laughed when Papa didn't even know what had been in the newspaper last week. She said that he was still living back in Goethe's time, or Schiller's. They were more of the German poets Papa loved.

Suddenly Papa slammed the letter on the table. Georg looked up in shock. Papa was never angry.

'Darling, what is it?' asked Mutti.

Papa held up a square of newspaper. 'Miriam. She has the kindness,' Papa made the word sound bitter, 'to send me an advertisement for a job at Oxford. A tutorship!'

'But you're a professor!' said Georg. As though Papa would want a tutor's job. And in England!

'She means well,' said Mutti. She cast a quick look at Georg. 'My love, perhaps she has a point. Maybe you should take a year's leave. We could go to England till things settle down here.'

'No. There's no point in discussing it any more,' said Papa. 'This is my home now. Your home. Georg's.' He slapped his napkin down onto the polished table, stood up and strode from the room.

Georg heard his footsteps hard on the stairs.

'You may clear up now,' said Mutti steadily, as Lotte peered from the kitchen. 'Yes, Georg, you had better go and get dressed.'

Georg nodded. Papa's anger cast a chill over the house. He hadn't even told Papa how he had the most Aryan head in the whole class either.

He hesitated outside Mutti and Papa's bedroom door, then knocked. 'Papa?'

Papa opened the door. 'Yes?' He was smiling again. 'Have you come to see me tie my bow tie?'

He hadn't: he'd just wanted to see if Papa was still angry. But he nodded. He sat on the bed next to Papa's freshly ironed long

7

black academic gown as Papa took the tie from its case and circled it around his collar.

'I'm sorry I shouted,' Papa said abruptly.

'Papa, why does Aunt Miriam want us to live in England? Is she lonely?'

Papa chuckled. 'Miriam? Not her. No, she's worried for us, that's all.'

'Why?'

'Kristallnacht,' said Papa shortly.

Kristallnacht had been the big celebration when the Brown Shirts had risen up against the Jews, burning their houses, smashing their shops, painting the big yellow Star of David on their doors so they couldn't pretend to be like everyone else.

Kristallnacht had been nearly six months earlier. It had been dangerous to be on the streets then, with so many bands of angry youths roaming around. But now the Führer and his Brown Shirts had the Jewish problem under control. Aunt Miriam is silly, thought Georg.

'We wouldn't ever go and live in England, would we?' Everyone knew the English were cowards, hiding across the Channel. They had only won the Great War because the American Jews had paid for lots of guns.

But now Germany had the greatest army ever seen. One day, said Herr Doktor Schöner, Germany's Third Reich — its Third Great Empire — would take over the whole world. Every boy in every country would salute the German flag: would raise their arm and yell, 'Heil, Hitler!'

This was the best time ever to be a German.

Papa sat on the bed next to him. 'You don't want to live in England?'

'No,' said Georg. They had visited England only once, last year, to see Aunt Miriam. London had been grey; it was not beautiful like the silver dappled lake where they usually went for their summer holiday. Georg wondered what sort of head shape the Englanders had. He would have to ask Herr Doktor Schöner.

'I don't want to go back to England either. Miriam doesn't understand.' Papa could almost have been speaking to himself. 'A poet is above politics. Politicians come and go.'

'Even the Führer?'

'Even the Führer. But the words of the great poets last forever.'

'Tell me a poem,' said Georg. Poems were for bedtime, to make the sweet dreams come. But suddenly he wanted a poem now.

Papa looked at him in surprise, then nodded. 'One poem and that's all,' he said, as he did every night when Georg wanted 'just one more'. Perhaps Papa understood that Georg wanted a poem to make him feel safe, just like he did when he snuggled up in bed, to drive away thoughts of Papa's sudden anger at the table.

Papa smiled at Georg and took his hand.

> '*Über allen Gipfeln*
> *Ist Ruh,*
> *In allen Wipfeln*
> *Spürest du*
> *Kaum einen Hauch;*
> *Die Vögelein schweigen im Walde.*
> *Warte nur, balde*
> *Ruhest du auch.*'

Georg took a deep breath. Papa was right. The great poets' words did have power, long after their authors had died. He felt the peace of the poem seep through him.

'Was that by Goethe, Papa?'

Papa nodded. '*Wandrers Nachtlied II*.' He began to translate it, his voice as soft as a cloud.

> '*Above every hilltop*
> *Is peace.*
> *Quiet touches the treetops,*
> *The breeze hardly breathes*
> *Through the leaves;*
> *The tiny birds are silent in the forest.*
> *Wait …*
> *Soon you'll be at rest too.*'

Chapter 2

The sense of peace lasted as Georg took off his Lederhosen, the brown leather trousers that Tante Gudrun had given him last year for his tenth birthday. 'So he will look like a proper German boy,' she had said pointedly to Papa.

As he grew older Mutti would soak the Lederhosen in hot water. The hot wet leather would stretch when he put them on, so his Lederhosen would get bigger as he did. Georg hoped he would grow soon. He was the shortest boy in the class. But at least he had the most Aryan head.

He still hadn't told Papa and Mutti! After the graduation, he thought, while we are eating cream cakes. Papa could tell the other Herr Professors. They would congratulate Papa on having a perfect Aryan son.

Downstairs he heard the door shut as Papa left for the University. He and Mutti would meet him at the Hall.

Georg put on his new trousers, rubbing his shoes to make them shine, tying his bow tie just like Papa's. He went downstairs. Lotte was singing again in the kitchen.

'You look so handsome,' Mutti said. Her dress was like spring flowers. She arranged her fox fur across her shoulders.

Georg bounced on his toes. 'Hurry up! We'll be late!'

Mutti smiled. 'No, we won't.'

'Will there be ice cream as well as cakes?'

'No ice cream, I think.'

'Why not?'

Mutti laughed. 'Today is for the University students. Ice cream might drip on their gowns.'

She took Georg's hand as they walked out the door. Like all their tables and bookshelves, it smelled of lemon polish. The daffodils smiled at them from the garden, nodding their heads in the spring breeze. The rosebuds were swelling. *Röslein rot*, red roses, just like in Lotte's song.

He would never see them again.

Papa waited for them in the echoing foyer of the University. All the buildings in the University looked like they had been made for giants. Stone faces with tongues poking out or long hooked noses stared down from the tops of the buildings around the quadrangle.

Papa said the stone heads were called gargoyles. Georg liked the one with round cheeks best. The others made him shiver — a fascinated shiver as though the gargoyles knew something that the small humans below them did not. Sometimes he imagined that when all the people were gone at night the gargoyles made faces at each other and yelled insults across the grass.

Papa kissed Mutti's cheek and patted Georg on the back. 'You look very fine,' he said. 'I've reserved you seats in the front row.'

He led the way up, up, up the two flights of broad stone stairs and through the big wooden doorway into the Hall.

The Hall was full of women sitting in silk dresses, and hats like Mutti's, with a sprinkling of proud fathers too.

Georg stared out the long windows at the tops of the trees outside, then up at the dragons and knights with swords painted on the ceiling. He had hoped the Hall might have a clock where a knight chased a dragon when the clock struck the hour, like the one down in the quadrangle, but there was only a portrait of the Führer on the wall by the stage.

Georg wondered what the Führer was doing today. It would be something grand. Already he had reclaimed Austria and the Sudetenland for Germany; and Czechoslovakia again; and pushed the arrogant French from the Vaterland. Georg thought of the soldiers in the newspaper. Maybe even now they were marching into Poland to free the Germans in Danzig. Herr Doktor Schöner said that Danzig was a German town, even though it was in Poland. Soon the Führer would free Danzig too …

Mutti sat next to Frau Doktor Hansmeyer, who smelled of peppermint drops. Georg wriggled onto the chair next to her. His legs dangled. He hoped he would start growing soon.

'I'll see you later,' said Papa softly. Then he was gone, his black academic gown swishing around his trouser legs.

Georg watched the students stand in a line in their new black robes. The University orchestra began to play. *Gliddle, gliddle, gliddle* went the violins. *Boom PAH* went the tuba.

The University lecturers strode in, the Rektor in his red robe, the Herr Doktors and Professors in their black. Papa looked straight ahead till he was level with Georg and Mutti, then turned and winked as he passed.

The lecturers sat in a row on the stage as the music stopped.

The Rektor gave a speech. It was interesting at first, but went on too long.

A tall student with blond hair got up to speak. It was a long speech too.

'We also serve who do not fight with guns!' The student's voice was fierce and proud. His blue eyes were as bright as the sky. 'Our swords are words. We fight with pen and page. Even here, in the still heart of learning, we keep faith with our fathers and with destiny …'

Georg looked at the paintings on the ceiling. Who was the knight? Why did he have to fight the dragon?

Maybe the dragon had been stealing sheep. The villagers were starving! They implored the knight to save them, to kill the hungry dragon …

The story began to weave itself. The dragon roared. The trees burst into flame … No, that wouldn't work. The knight would roast in his armour and his horse might run away.

Georg started the story over. This time Hitler was the knight, but on a tank instead of a horse, just like the photo in the paper when the Führer entered Prague. A tank would be better against a dragon than a horse …

At last the student sat down. One by one the students came onto the stage to get their scrolls and to shake the Rektor's hand. The students shook Papa's hand too. Papa looked important up there on the stage.

The last student bowed and smiled, and took his scroll.

Cream cakes at last, thought Georg.

The orchestra began to play the national anthem. Up on the stage the Herr Doktors and Professors stood to leave.

Suddenly the tall student who had spoken earlier ran up onto the stage again. He gazed at the audience and began to sing. '*Deutschland, Deutschland über alles ...*'

The crowd muttered, startled. Georg wondered if the Rektor would order the student to be quiet.

Down below the stage a small group of students stood apart. Now they sang too. One by one the crowd began to sing as well. Georg smiled. It must be all right to sing then. Georg joined in; he'd learned the words at school. '*Deutschland, Deutschland über alles in der Welt ...*'

Germany, Germany above all others in the world.

All at once the students' song changed. Georg strained to understand the words.

'*Juden 'raus! Juden 'raus!*'

Jews out! Jews out!

The audience's singing straggled away. They sat, confused.

'*Juden 'raus! Juden 'raus!*'

Jews? Georg looked around. There weren't any Jews here. Jews weren't allowed to teach, not even in schools. They couldn't go to University.

The group's song was a chant now. Young men in their black robes — blond hair, brown hair, black hair, some with glasses, one with a moustache — the same intent look on all their faces.

The crowd grew silent. Even the orchestra stopped playing. No one moved or murmured. It was as though they had been turned into gargoyles too.

'*Juden 'raus! Juden 'raus!*'

Suddenly a man at the back of the Hall joined in the chant. '*Juden 'raus! Juden 'raus!*' Others in the audience yelled too. The sound echoed across the Hall.

'*Juden 'raus! Juden 'raus!*'

The tall student ran down the steps. 'Now!' he yelled.

The small group of students began to march. They marched like schoolboys marching into class. Left right, left right, they marched.

'*Sieg heil! Sieg heil!*' the students shouted as they passed the photo of the Führer. They saluted, their arms held out. '*Sieg heil! Sieg heil!*'

The tall student yelled another order. Two of his group grabbed one of the other students by the elbows.

The young man struggled. His friends tried to pull him back. The band of students linked arms, a wall of black-robed shadows impossible to pass. The two students dragged the young man across the room towards the windows. The chant was even louder now.

'*Juden 'raus!*'

Someone screamed at the back of the Hall. Mutti leaped up and looked around. All the adults scrambled to their feet too. Georg climbed up on the chair to see.

'Mutti ... Mutti, what's happening?' Was the student a Jew? Was that why the other students were dragging him away? But he didn't look Jewish. He didn't even have a long nose. There couldn't be any Jews here!

'Stop them!' cried Mutti.

The students stopped at the windows. Suddenly the student vanished, flung out the window by the strong young arms of those who had been his friends.

His shriek was swallowed in the yells of the crowd.

Georg thought he heard a thud far down on the ground. The Hall was filled with noise. Noise and hate, he thought, still staring at the students.

The student executioners smiled, as though they had done good work. Their friends were already dragging a second victim towards the window.

'No!' screamed the young man. The scream went on and on, as though it was a song. *Neeeiiinnnn* ...

'My God. My God,' whispered Mutti. She gazed up at Papa on the stage, her gloved fingers twisting in anguish.

Most of the audience seemed dazed too. Only Papa moved.

'For pity's sake, stop them!' yelled Papa, reverting to English in his anger.

He ran down the steps from the stage, his face white. 'Someone help me!' he yelled, in German now.

Three of the students broke from their group. But they didn't help. They grabbed Papa's arms. Papa wrenched himself around. 'Do something!' he appealed to the Rektor.

The Rektor stood, uncertain. He glanced at the photo of the Führer. He shook his head.

The two executioners lifted the second victim up to the window. '*Juden 'raus!*' they screamed, their voices high in triumph.

'No! I'm not a Jew!' the young man yelled.

One of the executioners laughed.

'*Nein!*' The young man screamed. He tried to grasp the window sill as they thrust him through the opening. For a moment Georg could hear the scream outside too. Then it was gone.

Suddenly Papa ducked, forcing his arms free. He ran across the Hall, towards the students at the window.

'Why in heaven's name are you doing this?' he began, his voice so furious it rose above the chant.

They will stop now, thought Georg dazedly. Papa will tell them there are no Jews here. He will explain how poets are above politics ...

The student with bright blue eyes, eyes like the sky in summer, bent to grab Papa's legs. Papa fell down between the black robes of the students.

'He is a Jew too!' yelled the student. 'He tried to hide, but the truth is out! Our Herr Professor is a Jew!'

'*Jude! Jude! Jude!*' It was as though the students had only one voice now.

Mutti screamed. The scream went on and on. She managed two steps towards Papa but Frau Doktor Hansmeyer grabbed her arm. Mutti shook it off but someone else held her too. She struggled and her hat fell off.

'Papa!' Georg jumped off his chair. He was lost in trousered legs and skirts. He couldn't see. Someone grabbed his wrist.

He heard Papa yell, 'Marlene!' That was Mutti's name. Papa called, 'Marlene, save Georg!' and then more faintly, '*Ich liebe dich.*' I love you.

Georg strained to see between legs and skirts. What was happening to Papa?

'Mutti!' he yelled. 'Mutti!' He couldn't even see her now. The orchestra played again, as though they tried to drown out the yells.

Suddenly Mutti wrenched his wrist from the grip of whoever held it. She lifted him up. Georg was much too big to be carried, but Mutti carried him down the Hall, stumbling in her high-heeled shoes.

Georg tried to look back, to see what had happened to Papa. They had to help him! But Mutti pressed his face hard into her shoulder. She made a strange, harsh noise that might have been a sob.

Down the wide stone stairs, worn with hundreds of years of students' feet. Down, down. Behind them people yelled. Someone called, 'Frau Doktor Marks!'

Were they trying to help them? Perhaps they had rescued Papa. Perhaps the Hall was orderly again.

Georg looked back up the stairs. A young man stood there in a black student robe. 'You have a little Jew rat, Frau Doktor Marks! How does it feel to have a Jew rat for a child?'

For a moment Georg thought the boy was going to follow them down the stairs. But he vanished back into the Hall. The screams had stopped. The crowd was singing again now.

Mutti staggered against the stairwell. She put him down, and wrenched off her shoes.

'Run,' she whispered. 'As fast as you can, Georg.' She took his hand, holding her shoes in her other hand. Georg glanced up the stairs again. But no one watched them now.

They ran, down the stairs, into the foyer. The cream cakes had been set out on the white-clothed tables, and the coffee urn. The women in white aprons stared at Mutti's feet in their torn stockings, at the running boy and woman with no shoes and hat.

Mutti pulled him out the door.

People ran towards them across the stone paving of the quadrangle. Georg felt snow fingers of terror down his back. But the people weren't chasing them. They kneeled by the bodies crumpled beneath the window. Blood gleamed on the green grass and cobblestones. The bodies looked like scarecrows blown over in the wind.

'Papa,' he cried. 'Where is Papa?'

No, Papa couldn't be in that crumple of black robes and broken bodies. He would have made the students let him go. He would be running after them.

'We have to wait for Papa!'

Mutti jerked his hand. 'Run,' she panted. Her hair was loose from its pins. 'Georg, run!'

The gargoyles stared down, grinning and poking out their tongues.

Mutti dragged him across the quadrangle and down into the street. She slipped her shoes back on, then pulled Georg towards the tram stop, gripping his hand like she would never let it go. Georg's mind felt like ice.

How many bodies lay in that puddle of black and blood?

Had one of them been Papa's?

Chapter 3

The tram clattered towards them on its tracks. Mutti didn't seem to notice the wind that whipped her skirts as she glanced back towards the University. Her face was as blank as its stone.

Papa would come soon, Georg told himself. He had to come soon.

The tram stopped in front of them with a creak and a clang. Mutti hauled him up the steps, onto a hard wooden seat. She didn't let go of Georg's hand even on the tram, though he wasn't a little boy now whose hand had to be held in case he fell off. But Georg didn't pull it away.

Mutti didn't speak to the conductor either, just handed him money for their tickets. She gazed out as though looking at something Georg couldn't see.

They got out at the stop before Tante Gudrun's house.

The wind pushed at Mutti's skirts again. It smelled of flowers, of summer to come. Georg wished the wind would go away. If the wind stopped there might be peace, like in Papa's poem. He would hear Papa's voice: '*Quiet touches the treetops ...*'

Mutti still didn't speak as she hurried him across the road and down the footpath, through Tante Gudrun's neat white-painted gate, along the path between the yellow daffodils. Mutti pulled the door bell over and over, as though the noise could make up for the words she couldn't speak.

At last Tante opened the door; she was wearing her navy-blue silk dress. Tante's house always smelled of turnips, which was strange, because Georg had never eaten turnips there. Perhaps the servant ate them in the kitchen.

Tante stared at Mutti's face, her messy hair. Mutti's face looked set in stone, like someone had decided to make a gargoyle pretty. 'Marlene? What is it?'

Mutti shoved past Tante, into the hall with its soft flowered carpet. She opened the door of Tante's living room. 'Stay in here,' she said to Georg in English. 'Promise? Don't move.'

Georg was so relieved that she could speak he nodded, even though he wanted to yell at her, to ask about Papa, about the Jews. To ask, 'What's happening? When can we see Papa?'

Instead he waited. He sat on the brocade sofa and looked at the flowered carpet. He thought of Papa, of blood and gargoyles. He thought of the bodies on the grass, then forced the thought away. He tried to make his mind empty, to stop the pain. He tried to find a story, any story. The stories were all gone. Even the rest of the words of Papa's last poem seemed frozen somewhere he couldn't reach.

Now and then he heard voices from the kitchen. At last he moved closer to the door, to listen.

'Please, Gudrun,' Mutti kept pleading. There was a mumble and then, 'Please help us.'

Perhaps Mutti wanted Tante Gudrun to ask Onkel Klaus to take his motor to the University to fetch Papa. Papa wouldn't know that they were here. He'd worry. Mutti should telephone Lotte so that she could tell Papa where they were when he came home again ...

He remembered the students' laughter as the young man screamed. Pictures of the bodies seeped into his mind again. He tried to push them out but they seeped back. Bodies and blood, black student robes, red blood, white faces on green grass. The young men's faces and —

He thrust his fist into his mouth to stop from crying out. Papa's face all bloody on one side, the other side the skin all white, the eye staring towards them as though it couldn't see, would never see again.

It couldn't be Papa. It was someone else! It had to be! But if it were ... then Onkel Klaus could take Papa to the hospital. The doktors would make him better. They'd bandage up his head so you couldn't see the red, just like they'd bandaged up Georg's foot when he had cut it at the lake.

'Your foot has gone white!' Papa had joked. 'Poor Georg, one pink foot and one white.' They'd laugh at Papa's white head and Lotte would bring in stewed pears with cream ...

The students must know it was all a mistake now. Papa was not a Jew. He was their teacher. A teacher should be respected. They'd say that they were sorry. The tall student would beg Papa's pardon.

He tried to tell himself the dragon story again. Stories made time pass. But the world of stories had vanished from his brain.

There was a series of clicks outside the door as someone pressed the phone to get the operator. He heard Mutti's voice, fast and urgent. Was she calling the University, to speak to Papa or the Rektor? Was she calling their house to talk to Lotte?

He couldn't make out the words. He had never heard Mutti speak like that, as though a shell of iron suddenly covered her, each sound tight and hard.

Mutti put the receiver down. She opened the door, stepped into the room, then shut the door carefully. He ran to her and she held him close. For a second he was afraid that she'd *feel* hard and stiff too. But she felt just the same.

'Mutti, what's happening?' He spoke English, because Papa might be hurt and so it seemed right to speak his language now.

'The brave Aryan Super-race is getting rid of the unclean.' Her voice was flat.

She wasn't crying, so he couldn't cry either. Her face looked like it hurt not to cry. 'I don't understand.'

'There is nothing to understand. Just hate. Just stupidity. How can you make the stupid see sense?'

'Mutti, please.'

'The students have been going through the records, to see if anyone at the University was Jewish.'

'Because Jews aren't allowed in the University?'

She shut her eyes for a second, then opened them and nodded. 'Some of the staff and students think that anyone who had a Jewish grandfather or even great-grandmother must be a Jew too. They think one Jewish ancestor taints your blood. They believe lies because they want them to be true. They think the Nazi Party will give them good jobs after what they did today. And you know the worst?' Mutti clasped her hands together, almost as if she was praying. 'They are right.'

Georg let the last question out. He tried to make his voice strong but it came out as a whisper. 'Why did they call Papa a Jew?'

Mutti took a breath. Her face still looked as cold as the stone of the University.

'Your father's grandfather was Jewish. To them that makes your father Jewish too.' She clenched her fists like Georg did at the dentist's, as though the next words hurt almost too much to say. 'It means they think *you* are a Jew.'

'I am not a Jew!'

'To them you are.'

'No! We measured our heads in class today. I have an Aryan head. A perfect Aryan head! Herr Doktor Schöner said so.'

'Your teacher is wrong. You can't tell what race people are by their head size.'

Georg stared at her numbly. Herr Doktor Schöner was a clever man. Mutti was just a mother, not a scholar. The Adolf Hitler Schule wouldn't let Herr Doktor Schöner teach things that were wrong.

There are no Jews in our family, thought Georg desperately. Jews killed babies. They poisoned wells. How could you suddenly be a Jew? But the students had yelled, '*Jude! Jude!*' as they grabbed Papa. The student had called him a 'little Jew rat'.

'Do they think that you are a —' he stumbled over the word '— Jew too?'

'Perhaps, because I married your father.'

Could you catch being Jewish, like you caught the flu? It didn't make sense. Nothing made sense. Today was broken. His life was broken. Later the shattered pieces might come together. 'When can we see Papa? Will he be all right?'

She answered neither question. 'Georg, you must be brave. Can you do that?'

He didn't know. He nodded anyway. 'Did — did they hurt Papa?'

'Yes,' said Mutti. That word was iron too.

He wanted to ask how badly Papa was hurt. But his mouth wouldn't make the words. Instead he whispered, 'Where is he?'

'Georg … I can't answer that. I have no time to explain. You have to get to England: to Aunt Miriam. Now! As soon as we can get you there. You will be safe in England.'

Papa had promised they weren't going to England. But somehow he knew that this morning and this afternoon were different worlds. 'We can't go to England till Papa is well.'

'Georg, please. For Papa's sake.'

Mutti shut her eyes, then opened them again, as though what was inside her head hurt too much to see. 'For my sake. For Papa's sake. Miriam was right. She has been right all along. We should have left a year ago. Now,' she took a breath, 'we need you to be safe. That's what your father said —'

Mutti's voice stopped, like her clockwork had run down. She clenched her fists again. Georg could see her nails cut into her palms, as though one pain made another easier to bear. When she spoke again her voice was like the wireless, clipped and remote.

'The Nazis won't let Jews leave Germany without permission these days. We can't risk trying to get it now, in case they are looking for us after what happened today. Even if I managed to leave Germany the English government might not let me in. They won't let many Jewish refugees into England. And now I too would be a refugee.'

'But we went there last year —'

'Last year I was with Papa.' Mutti's voice almost broke on the word. 'But you have an English passport. If you can get out of Germany you can go to Aunt Miriam in England. But it will be hard to get you out. If I try to come with you they might catch us both.'

'I have to go without you? Without Papa?'

'We will come when we can.' Her voice held truth; but it held other things too.

'I want to go home!' The words burst from him.

'It's not safe.'

He stared at her. How could home not be safe? Unless the students were there. They knew where Papa lived.

'Georg? Will you go to England? Please?'

Mutti had never spoken like that before. Grown-ups said: 'Do this, do that.' It was an order, even if they added 'please'. This was the first thing Mutti had ever asked of him. Her voice pleaded, and her eyes.

'Yes,' said Georg.

He felt her relax a little beside him.

'When do I have to go?'

'Soon. Some … friends are coming. I don't know them well.'

'But you said they are friends?'

'Friends are people who help you.' Her voice was bitter now. 'They help people like us. They will get you out of Germany. I phoned them. They said they will be here soon.' She held him close.

'Mutti? I'm hungry.'

She almost smiled at that. 'Tante will give you food.' Her voice twisted. 'She will do that, at least.'

Chapter 4

The 'friend' was a woman with fat cheeks, like the good gargoyle's, and fat ankles too, in thick brown stockings. Mutti opened the door for her. Tante had vanished, for some reason, after bringing him soup and cold pork and bread.

The woman looked Georg up and down. 'He's small. That's good. But can he lie still for hours? Not make a sound?'

'Georg has great self-control,' said Mutti. 'Please, Frau ...' She hesitated. 'I'm sorry, I do not know your name.'

'You can't tell the SS or Gestapo what you do not know.' The fat woman stared at Georg again. 'There is a chance to get him out of the country on the train tonight. After tonight, I do not know.'

'Tonight then,' said Mutti. Her voice was iron again, as though every one of her bones was cold.

For the first time the woman spoke to Georg. She kneeled down and looked him in the eyes. Her breath smelled of caraway seeds. 'Well, boy? Can you lie still in the dark for many hours? For a whole night? Not move at all? Not speak or cry or make a sound?'

Not move or make a sound for a whole night? He didn't know. How could you know if you had never tried? He could stay still for half an hour, when he and his friends played hide and seek. But for a night?

If he said yes he would have to go to England, to Aunt Miriam, who he hardly knew. Go with strangers, no Mutti and no Papa.

Mutti's eyes were bright; Georg imagined there were tears behind them that she couldn't cry. He remembered Papa's words, screamed above the roar of the crowd: 'Marlene, save Georg!'

Mutti's eyes said 'please'.

This was all he could do for Papa now.

The fat woman gripped his arm. 'Look at me, boy! If you move or make a noise the Nazis will find you. They may kill you. If you move or cry the people who are taking you may die as well. They risk their lives for you. Can you stay still for that?'

'Yes,' said Georg.

The woman stood. 'I think you can too.' Then to Mutti, 'Do you have a suitcase?'

'I don't know if it is safe to go back to get his clothes —' began Mutti.

'Not for his clothes. For him.'

—⁕—

Mutti fetched one of Onkel Klaus's suitcases from the attic. She didn't ask Tante. Georg thought she didn't care if Tante wanted her to have it or not. He hadn't heard Tante's voice since she had brought his food, or the servant's either. Were they still here?

It was dark outside now. Mutti slipped out the front door, leaving him with the woman. The woman didn't talk to him. She sat, as though she needed all her spare time to think.

Georg looked around the room, at Tante's china dogs on the mantelpiece, at the cushions she had embroidered, the gaslight hissing on the wall.

Perhaps, he thought, Papa will be at home. Perhaps he wasn't hurt at all; maybe he landed on something soft. When Mutti comes back he will be with her. He will find a way that we can all go to England together, like a holiday.

He shivered. No one had come to light the tiled stove, despite the evening's chill. What if the students were waiting at home? What if they grabbed Mutti, carried her upstairs and then forced the window open? What if …

The door opened. It was Mutti, alone. She had his coat, and clean underwear and his passport too — the one he had shown the guard when they went on holiday last summer.

'So,' said the woman. 'We will begin.'

He was hungry again. He was thirsty too. But the woman would not let him drink. He could not get out to use the toilet once he was in the suitcase. He must pretend he wasn't there.

The suitcase had holes now, small holes so he could breathe. The coat was tucked into it to muffle any sound in case he moved.

He stared at it, unable to quite believe what was happening, that Mutti could send him to strangers, alone, so far away.

That he was supposed to hide in this.

'Can you do it?' asked the woman.

He glanced at Mutti and saw the hope frozen on her face. 'Yes,' he whispered again.

Mutti reached out a finger and stroked his cheek. It was as though she couldn't bear to hug him. 'Thank you,' she whispered. 'For saving my son.' But she didn't look at the woman. Instead she stared at Georg, as though she was trying to record his face, every expression and every move, to store it up for later.

'He is one of many,' said the woman. 'We do what we can. For every one we get out of Germany a thousand are trapped here.'

Georg wondered if the woman really saw him, except as a package. One of a thousand. Would she even remember his name?

He gave a cry and flung himself at Mutti. At last he felt her arms warm about him. 'I love you,' she whispered. 'Always remember that. Do this for me. For Papa. More than anything on earth, we love you. We want you to be safe. Know that forever.' She kissed him. 'Be happy. We will come to you when we can.'

He clung to her.

The woman coughed. 'It is time.'

Mutti tensed, then pushed him away, towards the suitcase.

Chapter 5

At first he didn't think that he would fit. His legs stuck out over the rim of the suitcase. His body clenched in panic. He didn't want to do this, but he couldn't fail either. He curled his legs close to his body, then closer still. I am a snail, he thought. The suitcase is my shell.

'*Gut*,' said the woman. She tucked his underwear between him and the walls of the suitcase, then laid his coat on top of him. 'The cloth will muffle small noises you make,' she said. 'But not much.'

He nodded, a tiny movement in case she thought he couldn't lie still. He could only see Mutti with one eye now. He stared at her, trying not to blink, not to lose a second.

The lid came down. The world was black, not light.

'Do not speak until it is open again,' said the woman. He heard the click as it was latched down.

He wanted to call out 'Goodbye' to Mutti. He wanted to say he loved her too. Why hadn't he said that before? But if he called out now he would break his promise. If he spoke now the woman might take him out and say he couldn't go.

He listened for another word from Mutti. But there was nothing. Perhaps she thought if she spoke he might answer back. He tried to imagine her, standing there, in her flowered dress. He wondered if she would let herself cry properly now.

It was dark. Too dark. He couldn't breathe.

He couldn't bear it: the dark; the lack of air. He imagined his fist breaking through the case into the light. Then he felt a tiny breeze from the holes, which were near his face. He thought of Papa and of Mutti's face.

Maybe if he did this impossible thing it would be all right. If he could lie still and quiet the whole night then Papa would be safe again; Mutti would be free to come to England too.

He felt the suitcase being lifted up. At least he faced up, not down. He couldn't have borne being carried face down. The clothes cushioned him as he lay still.

Muffled voices. He could just make out words from Mutti: 'Take good care of him.'

'We risk our lives each time we do this. We take all the care we can.'

The suitcase moved. It bumped a little up and down, and back and forth. The woman must be strong, to lift him and the big case too.

Out the door, he thought. He heard the click of the garden gate. He tried to listen for Mutti's footsteps on the path too. But there was only the *click, click* of the woman's heels.

Mutti was gone.

Panic seized him. He was floating in a world of black, with nothing to hold onto. Nothing that he knew behind him, a strange new world ahead. He couldn't do this! He couldn't!

And yet he knew he could. He could do this: he *would* do this and it would all be all right.

He shut his eyes. It was silly, because the world inside the case was black anyway, but it helped. He shut out the click of footsteps and remembered Papa's words instead, the poem after lunch. How had it gone again?

> *'Über allen Gipfeln …*
> *Quiet touches the treetops,*
> *The breeze hardly breathes*
> *Through the leaves;*
> *The tiny birds are silent in the forest.*
> *Wait …*
> *Soon you'll be at rest too.'*

Georg imagined Papa's hand in his, imagined Mutti with him.

And he knew that wherever she was — back at Tante's, or out in the street going to find Papa — she was with him too, thinking of him, hoping for him, trying to send her warmth to him so he wasn't alone. Know that forever, she'd said.

Papa's voice whispered in the suitcase: *'Soon you'll be at rest too.'*

~𝕸☉

The suitcase moved back and forth, back and forth. It made him feel sick a bit, till he forced himself not to think of his tummy, but to listen for Papa's voice in his memory. He heard the sound of a tram.

The suitcase clunked on a floor, and he heard the tram sound underneath him now. *Clunkaclunka clunkaclack.*

The ticket collector called. The tram stopped, then started. Four stops. Five.

The suitcase was lifted again. He heard the mutter of a crowd.

34

He had a sudden urge to yell, to scream, 'I hate you! I hate you all! You have made me a Jew.'

He didn't.

The suitcase bumped back and forth. He heard the hiss of steam and the clanking of an engine.

Train station, he thought. And then: I have to move.

His arm cramped — or had it been cramped before? His knees screamed. If he didn't move the pain would grow, his leg would get stiffer and stiffer till it cracked. He had to move! He had to breathe fresh air!

If he moved in this crowd then they would find him. The faces would peer down at him, yell, '*Juden! Juden 'raus!*'

If he moved then he would die.

The poem's peace had vanished. Mutti and Papa had disappeared too. Finally, he tried twitching one finger at a time, and then a toe.

It took a long time to move each one, and then he began again. First toe, second toe, third toe … first finger, second, third. He kept his lips pressed together hard so he couldn't make a noise.

The suitcase clunked onto another floor. A man's voice said, 'Let me put that big case up on the shelf for you.'

'So kind,' said a woman's voice — not the woman from Tante's house. This one sounded young.

He felt himself and the case fly through the air and land, *thunk*. He grunted with surprise, then clenched, wondering if anyone had heard.

Someone laughed nearby. The young woman said something. The man answered back.

No one had heard.

He lay in pain and silence till the train began to move.

Chapter 6

He thought he slept. Perhaps time simply went away.

He woke to agony — his knees, his elbows, even his neck. He couldn't breathe! Where was he? He blinked, trying frantically to see, then remembered where he was.

The suitcase. The cries of '*Juden 'raus!*' Papa and the bodies on the grass ...

His body screamed for air. For a second he thought he really had screamed. He *mustn't*.

He lifted his head slightly and sniffed at the holes. He could see light through them dimly now. As long as the light was there, he had air too. He tried moving his toes and fingers again, moving his knees and elbows just a tiny bit. It helped, or maybe it just took his mind away from the pain.

How long had he been here? Please, please, he thought, let me have slept most of the night. The woman had said he had to be still for a night. Please, let it be nearly over now.

The train clunked below him. *A-hugachug, a-hugachug.*

How long did it take to get to England? Four days when they had gone on holiday, but they had stopped each night on the way and visited the museums that Papa liked. Papa ... Had Mutti found Papa now? Or was he —

For the first time he let himself think the word. Was Papa dead?

They may kill you, the woman had said. The people who are taking you may die as well. This was a world where being dead was possible.

Please, don't let him be dead, thought Georg. Please, let us all be alive.

He couldn't stay in the case for four days. You died if you didn't eat or drink, didn't you? They wouldn't carry him in the suitcase just to let him die.

Maybe the fat woman hated Jews. Maybe it was a trick! He would die here in the dark, die with no food, no water. Die like Papa.

He clenched his fists, then when the action didn't rock the suitcase clenched them over and over, wriggling his toes too. It would be silly to go to all the trouble of carrying a boy in a suitcase if you only wanted him dead. He wasn't going to die and Papa wasn't going to die and Mutti wasn't going to die either.

The fat woman had told the truth. She said he had to stay in the suitcase for one night. He could do that.

How far did a train go in one night? Out of Germany? He should have asked. Would she have told him more if he had asked? What you do not know you can't tell.

A-hugachug, a-hugachug went the train around him. There were no other noises. He wondered if everyone was asleep.

Not morning then. Maybe a long way till morning. Hours before he could move again, breathe fresh air, drink water —

cool fresh water. His throat hurt, as though he'd been crying. Could you cry in your sleep? He bit his lip. If he had cried in his sleep someone might have heard him. But he'd have felt the case move if someone had opened it and found him inside.

He was still safe. But he couldn't sleep again. Couldn't risk sleep. If he was found then the Gestapo would know that Mutti was trying to get him out of Germany. If she hid her Jewish son then she must be a Jew too. If he was found it wouldn't just be the women who carried the suitcase who would be punished.

He tried to think of a story. One of his favourite ones. The story in which he had a big dog called Bruno … no, that story had Mutti and Papa in it. The story about the Führer and the dragon.

Not the Führer. The Führer wouldn't be in any of his stories now. The Führer would never be in the story of a *Jude*.

His stories had all vanished. Were they back home?

The train shuddered and muttered around the suitcase.

At last he slept again.

The light was brighter through the holes when he woke up. Again he panicked for a moment, then remembered where he was and realised that once again he must have slept without making a noise, or not one anyone had heard.

The pain was worse. The whole world was pain. He was half grateful for it. The body could only understand so much pain. When his body hurt this much the things he didn't want to think about, the things he had to think about, didn't hurt as much. He heard voices below him: a child called out somewhere; a baby cried. The pain had become part of him.

A man's voice barked something. He froze. It was an official's voice; it was an order. Was it the Gestapo?

He tried to not even breathe. He waited for the jerk of the suitcase.

Could he run if they opened it? If he jumped up and ran away he could hide. If they didn't find him they'd never know he was Mutti's son. She would not get into trouble for smuggling out her son. But would his cramped, frozen muscles let him run?

Where could he hide on a train? Under the seat? But people would see him. They'd tell the Gestapo officers, 'The Jew is under the seat.' In the toilet? But they'd look there. You always checked behind the toilet door in hide and seek, and there was always some silly kid hiding there because he hadn't found a better place to hide.

But there was nowhere else. Not on a train. And suddenly he knew what he would have to do.

He must open the door. Must face the rushing darkness and jump out into it. He would die — that's what happened when you jumped off a train. But perhaps no one would find his body till Mutti was safe. If he put his passport down the toilet before he jumped no one would know who he was ...

'Passports!' The order came again, but this time he understood the word.

Passports. You showed your passport when you came into another country. They must be leaving Germany. He was safe.

No, not yet. He tried to remember last year's holiday. They had shown their passports long before the border. He remembered Papa pointing out the guardhouse as they passed. Mutti had been wearing a hat with flowers. She laughed and said, 'We are in France now.' Georg had stared out the window but the land didn't look any different from Germany: the same plots of cabbages; the same cows in fields. Even the trees had been the same, and the old women in their black skirts and ragged headscarves carrying rocks or potatoes in their filthy aprons, their ankles thick and knotted from years of fetching and carrying.

He shouldn't have thought of the toilet. Even though he hadn't drunk anything for hours and hours, he still needed to go. He pressed his legs together. The need got worse and worse then, slowly, somehow, it went away.

He tried to remember the holiday again. Not the holiday last Easter down at the lake. He would remember every second of that trip, just as it had been — Mutti laughing in her summer dress, her bare arms brown and Papa without his Herr Professor face, laughing too, in white flannels carrying the picnic basket, stopping to kiss Mutti's neck so she blushed and whispered to him, but looked happy too.

'You are a Rhine maiden,' said Papa to Mutti. 'You are a siren who has captured me, a poor Englishman. How can a poet escape the song of a Rhine maiden? One glimpse of her gold hair and he is lost!'

'Mutti has brown hair,' said Georg.

Papa laughed. 'In the sunlight it is gold. And in my heart. *In meinem Herzen bist du gold.*' He lifted up the picnic basket. 'Who is ready for lunch?'

Mutti spread the picnic blanket, and Papa opened the basket. There was cold chicken and a flask of tea and two bottles of lemonade. No, don't think of lemonade.

The thin taste of past happiness fled. Would he fit in a picnic basket?

Don't think of that either. Don't think of baskets or cases or you'll scream. Don't think of Papa or Mutti; don't think at all;

just wait for it to go away — for everything to go away. Count to a hundred and then you can scream.

Eins, zwei, drei … hundert. He bit his lip and began to count again. *Hundert. Zweihundert. Tausend …* One more thousand and then he really would scream. *Eins, zwei …*

The train stopped.

He waited for the suitcase to be lifted down. But although the voices went further and further away, it didn't move.

Had they forgotten him? Would he stay here locked away for days and days?

Maybe they were too scared to let him out, in case someone saw them and told the Gestapo. Maybe they had left him here thinking, 'He is a clever boy. He will work out that he has to get out himself, find his own way to England. We are rid of him now.'

I will count to ten thousand, thought Georg. If no one comes then I will try to get out.

But how? The suitcase was made of strong thick leather. He couldn't kick through leather. Maybe if he scratched with his fingernails long enough he could make a hole, and then a bigger hole. Maybe if he yelled someone would come.

No, if he yelled whoever heard him might call the French police. They might tell the German police who would tell the SS who would know that Mutti had tried to smuggle her son out.

He would have to wait till it was quiet, till it might be safe to sneak away.

How long? he thought desperately. Pain no longer mattered, nor did thirst. It was as though he was fading into the darkness of the suitcase. If he didn't move or make a sound soon he would vanish. There would be no Georg to escape at all.

The suitcase moved down through the air. There was a very gentle thump, and then a clicking sound that he realised meant he was on a trolley.

He didn't know if he felt relief or anguish that the journey was still going. Dreaming of getting out made it worse. Dreaming of freedom made it worse too.

Think about the movement, he told himself. Up and down and back and forth, then down, *clunk*. A whistle, a man's yell. The suitcase moved again. The suitcase was on a trolley, rolling along the platform.

He tried to listen to the voices all around. Were they speaking German or French or English? He knew a few words of French. Or were they speaking Dutch, perhaps? You could get to England from Holland, and Belgium too, even Poland perhaps. Why hadn't he asked? Why hadn't they told him?

What you do not know you can't tell.

Up again, and back and forth, the sound of cars, the suitcase thudding onto something soft and then an urgent voice: 'See if he's all right.'

The lid opened.

Chapter 7

The light hurt. His body hurt. He tried to see, to move. He thought, I have gone blind. And then, I am crippled too. But then his eyes began to see.

He tried frantically to work out what he was seeing. Was he really safe or should he run? If French — or Dutch or Belgian — police found a boy in a suitcase they might send him back to Germany. The French didn't like Jews either. The Dutch? He didn't know.

A young woman's face peered down at him. She had blonde hair in plaits tied up about her head. She was not the police. 'Thank God. He is fine,' she said to a man with a grey beard.

They were in a car, on the back seat. The young woman began to massage his arms with gentle fingers. The pain made him whimper but he tried not to cry out. 'Don't worry,' she said. 'You are safe now. Safe.'

'Are we in England?' he managed to say.

'No. In France. England soon. But you are safe here.'

The man with the beard lifted him out of the suitcase and helped him move his limbs to lie flat out on the car seat, his head in the young woman's lap.

She smiled down at him. 'You were very brave,' she said. 'And now you're safe.'

─❦◎

Her name was Fräulein Schmidt. The man was her brother, Herr Schmidt. Later he was to think that perhaps those weren't their real names — what you do not know you can't tell. Schmidt was the most common name there was. But for now the names fitted. They were enough.

Fräulein Schmidt gave him water. He hadn't known his throat hurt till he drank it. She gave him a small fresh roll with sausage. He ate because his belly said that he was hungry, but it tasted of dust.

He looked out the car window at the France that looked like home: shops that might be German shops except for the signs in French; cars that might be German cars on the road.

It was morning. Somehow he knew it was *early* morning; there was something about the long shadows, the freshness of the light. It was as though last night had stretched till it was a thousand nights long. It had been a thousand nights. Somehow he knew that as long as he lived that night would still take up years inside his brain.

Now he knew that 'nothing' — seeing nothing, never moving, all sounds muffled — was the most frightening thing in all the world.

Herr Schmidt got into the driver's seat. He drove them to a hotel and when they arrived he took out Georg's suitcase and another from the boot. Then he drove away, leaving just Georg and the Fräulein to go into the hotel, and stand by the reception desk.

His legs trembled. His hands did too, until he clenched them so they steadied. He wouldn't cry.

'My little brother is tired from the journey,' said the Fräulein to the receptionist. He understood her, even though she spoke in French. 'Georg is good at languages,' Papa had said. 'He is good at everything,' said Mutti. 'A scholar like his father,' and she'd kissed his hair.

The receptionist handed the Fräulein a key.

The room was small, with striped wallpaper and lace curtains. It looked French, though he couldn't have said why. There was a bed with a lacy frilled cover for the Fräulein and a trundle bed to pull out for him to sleep on too. He was glad he was to sleep in her room tonight. He'd had too much of being in the dark, alone.

They ate up there — cups of hot chocolate, fresh bread rolls. She let him dunk the bread into the chocolate, and didn't correct him when some dripped onto his shirt. He wanted to sleep, but she shook her head. 'If you sleep now you won't sleep well tonight.' Something in her voice also seemed to say, 'You need to be too tired to be scared. If you are tired you won't cry for your mother tonight and make people notice us.'

Later they walked to a park, a young woman and a boy, no one special to notice. He didn't pat the statues, or even stare at the fountain frothing into the lake. Fräulein Schmidt bought him an ice cream, a big scoop held between two wafer biscuits, asking for it in French. He knew without her telling him that he was not to speak when anyone could hear him. No one must notice a German boy and a Fräulein. No one must notice them at all.

People spoke French all around them. He watched the pigeons bob and sway as they trotted around on the grass. They looked like the pigeons from back home, despite the French voices all around. He shut his eyes and said to Mutti, I'm watching pigeons. I'm safe. Where are you?

There was no answer.

He waited till they were back at the hotel to ask, 'Could we telephone home, please? I want to speak to Mutti.'

Fräulein Schmidt shook her head.

'Tante Gudrun's then,' he said desperately. 'I know the number. She will know where Mutti is.'

Fräulein Schmidt put her arm around him. For a moment he wished he really was her little brother and that she would be there always, at least till Mutti came.

'I'm sorry,' said Fräulein Schmidt softly. 'I don't know your mother. I don't even know her name — or your surname either. Shh,' she added, placing a finger to her lips. 'Don't tell me. If … if I am ever caught the Gestapo might hurt me till I give them names. If I don't know your mother's name then I can't say anything that might hurt her. Do you understand?'

No, thought Georg, I don't understand. He understood the words, but not how a world could crack and move, like there'd been an earthquake but not in the ground: all around instead. But he said, 'Yes, I understand.'

Fräulein Schmidt smiled. 'You will have to be brave again. You can be brave, can't you? You have been so brave so far.'

Georg made himself nod. He wondered what Johann was doing now, and his other friends at school. But they were not his friends now. They had been friends with the boy they thought he was. They would not be friends with a Jew.

'Good,' said Fräulein Schmidt. 'Now, will we try *pommes frites*? And roast chicken too.'

Chapter 8

FRANCE

She left him at the gangplank of the ferry to England the next afternoon. She hadn't told Georg before they reached the wharf that she'd leave him there. She had even taken her suitcase, just like she was going to England too.

For the first time he felt betrayed. Fräulein Schmidt had said that he was brave. Did she think he would cry like a baby because she said she had to leave him now?

'If the German border guards see "England" many times on my passport they will be suspicious.'

'Have you taken other boys to England?'

She pretended she didn't hear. 'You have got your book? Your sandwiches?'

He nodded. The book was an English book, about English children, by a man called Arthur Ransome. It had taken a while to find a shop with English books, but he needed to read the language well now.

'You are lucky,' she said softly. 'You have an English passport. So many have nowhere they can go even if they escape. No

47

country that will take them in.' She bent down and hugged him. 'Good luck,' she said. 'Your aunt will be waiting for you.'

'You're sure?'

'Yes. My ... brother ... telegraphed her. She telegraphed back. Your aunt will be at Dover when you arrive. She lives in London, yes?'

'Yes. She works for a person in the English government.'

'That sounds good. She will take care of you.' Fräulein Schmidt hugged him again, then pushed him gently towards the gangplank, carrying his suitcase. 'Goodbye, Georg. Good luck.'

He wanted to throw the suitcase in the oily sea. He wanted to kick it, destroy it and all its memories. But it held all he owned now. It was a thread that linked him back to Mutti.

He showed the man his ticket, then ran to the rail to see if the Fräulein was still there.

She was. She waited till the ferry hooted, and began to sail away. She waved and he waved back. She was still there when the ferry turned as it sailed out of the harbour.

He ran to the other side of the ferry, but by the time he had got there she was gone.

Chapter 9

ENGLAND

Aunt Miriam wore navy blue, and a look of annoyance and something else he didn't understand, but she managed to smile and kiss him on the cheek before she held him at arm's length. 'You're filthy.'

He thought of the ice-cream stains on his shirt. 'I'm sorry. I have no other clothes.'

'Well, that can be remedied. Is that your only suitcase?'

'Yes.'

'The porter will take it.' She hesitated. 'You are very welcome, George.'

'My name is Georg,' he reminded her.

'It's George now.' She bent and said quietly, 'I will explain when we get home. Come, or we will miss the train.'

⟨⟨⟩⟩

England looked wet. It was still grey too. Herr Doktor Schöner back at school said the English were weak; and they had only won the Great War because of the Americans.

School, thought Georg. He had almost lost track of days. It was Monday now. His friends would be at school. Although not his friends now. He should have been at school, reading about the English, not sitting here among them.

The Englishmen in the train carriage did not look weak. There were two men in dark suits and bowler hats reading newspapers, one at each window, like they were twins, but one was old and one was young, and they did not seem to know each other. Then there were Aunt Miriam and Georg. Aunt Miriam did not speak either, until the guard called out that dinner was being served in the First Class dining car.

Aunt Miriam stood up and said, 'Come on, George.'

He didn't think that he was hungry, but he was. The soup was tomato, very red. The meat was grey lamb slices in grey gravy, on thick white plates, with crisp-skinned roast potatoes and soggy Brussels sprouts. He ate it all, even the Brussels sprouts, though Mutti would have whispered, 'You only need eat one.'

After that there were prunes and custard, which he ate as well, even though he didn't like prunes, or custard either. Then Aunt Miriam took his hand and led him back into their carriage, where the men still read their papers. It was good to feel the warmth of someone's hand. He was sorry when she let go.

It was night by the time the train rattled into Victoria Station. It smelled of soot and steam. He remembered it a bit, from last year. That was where Mutti bought a magazine, wearing her green scarf. That was where Papa tipped the porter who wheeled their luggage on his trolley, just like this porter was carrying his suitcase now.

He wished he had left the suitcase behind. He hated even to touch it. Aunt Miriam led him through the crowds, into a taxi. The porter put his suitcase in the boot. Aunt Miriam reached out a hand to give him money, then tapped the glass between them and the driver to tell him to drive on.

Another journey, thought Georg. It was as though the world was all journeys now. There would never be any place to stop. But at least he was in fresh air now. He thought of the suitcase in the boot and shuddered. At least he had never been in the suitcase *and* a boot.

Or had he? Did he really know where the case had been when he'd been inside?

'What's wrong?' asked Aunt Miriam.

'Nothing.' How could he say that even being in a car again made him remember how the world had shrunk to darkness and a suitcase ride? Or that he wanted the taxi to stop, to let him out, so he could stand in the fresh air and just be still?

He couldn't say that. Be brave, the Fräulein had said. Brave had nothing to do with it now. He simply was, that was all. He was a package and would travel till he wasn't sent any further.

But it only took a few minutes to get to the tall building called a 'block of flats' where Aunt Miriam lived. She paid the taxi, then took his hand as a man came out of the revolving doors.

'Good evening, Wilkins,' she said, as he picked up Georg's suitcase. 'This is my nephew, George. His mother's train has been delayed so he is staying with me for a few hours. Will you show her up when she arrives?'

'Yes, Miss Marks.'

'Thank you, Wilkins. Say "Good evening", George.'

'Good evening,' said Georg, bewildered. Was Mutti really coming soon? Hope bit into the darkness that clung to him, but not much. If Mutti had really been so close the Fräulein would have said. She would have joined him on the ferry, or at least they would have waited for her at Dover.

He followed Aunt Miriam into the lift, and waited till the lift-man had taken them up to the third floor and Aunt Miriam had unlocked the door of her flat.

He had been to this flat only once, the year before, with Mutti and Papa. It looked just the same with the queer sofa and chairs, the Persian carpet, the big clock. Aunt Miriam began to take off her hat and coat and gloves.

'Aunt Miriam, Mutti isn't really coming tonight, is she?'

Aunt Miriam sighed. 'No. But the doorman will be off duty in an hour. I had to say something. Children are not allowed to live in this building.'

Georg blinked. 'Why not?'

'Children make noise.'

'I will be quiet.' He had a sudden terror that Aunt Miriam too would tell him to leave, would put him on another train to the unknown.

Aunt Miriam sank onto the sofa. She took his hand. 'Georg ... George, this has been so sudden. I tried to get your father to leave Germany. I told him what might happen, but he wouldn't listen. He was lost in the past with his precious Goethe, just as he has always been. He never saw things as they really are, never even wanted to see them —' She stopped, clamping her lips together as though she wanted to say more. 'Never mind that now,' she said at last. 'We have to make the best of this. We will have to pretend you don't live here for a while.'

'But people will be seeing me —'

'Say "will see me". That is the correct construction. You have to speak proper English, George. It's important.'

'Will see me,' said Georg tiredly. 'People will see me.'

'Not if you're careful. Children can visit here and there are three different doormen. They won't notice if you come in and don't go out, as long as you don't go in and out too often. I'll try to get another flat as soon as I can, but I may not have time for a while. Work is so busy now. I often have to work late.'

She patted him, a bit awkwardly. 'I've never had much to do with children. Will you be all right here by yourself?'

'*Ja*. I mean "yes",' he said, suddenly overwhelmed with weariness. He seemed to have been saying yes a lot, when really he meant no. An idea drifted into his mind. The children in his new book had gone to boarding school. He had never thought of boarding school before, but they seemed to like it.

'Aunt Miriam, could I go to boarding school? That way I will not be living here except for holidays. Maybe by then Mutti and Papa will come.'

For a second he thought Aunt Miriam was going to cry. Her face screwed up and she took a handkerchief from her pocket. 'I ... I don't know when they'll be here. And school ... School is out of the question for a while.'

'Why?' It wasn't as though he wanted to go to school, or even boarding school. He just wanted to find a place to stop, a space till Mutti and Papa reappeared. Somehow, no matter what thoughts lingered in the darkness of his mind, they had to find him, they had to be together once again. 'Is it because I am Jewish?'

'What? No, not at all.' She seemed to be trying to choose her words. 'It is because you are German. George,' she emphasised the new name, 'England and Germany will be at war again soon. Everyone knows it's going to happen. We just don't know when.'

Georg nodded. At school everyone said there'd be a war soon too, even if Papa had refused to listen when Mutti tried to talk about it. Another war — a bigger one than just invading Austria or Czechoslovakia. A war with England.

And this time Germany would win.

'My job is ... sensitive,' said Aunt Miriam. 'If people knew I had a German nephew living with me, that my German sister-in-law might arrive soon, it might not look good.'

'You could lose your job?'

'It's more than that, George. When war is declared any Germans may be put in prison camps till it's over.'

'The English put children in prison?'

'George, I just don't know what will happen. I don't really know your status here. I haven't had a chance to find out. I didn't expect any of this. You have to be patient while I do my best. I have to be careful what I ask.' She took another breath. 'You'll have a holiday for a while. Listen to the wireless and practise saying English words. Your English is remarkably good but there's still an accent. Maybe in a few months you can go to school.'

She sighed, then gave him a clumsy hug. She didn't seem to know how long a hug should last. 'So much can happen in a few months these days.'

Or in a few days, thought Georg as he hugged her back.

'Come,' said Aunt Miriam. 'I will show you to your room.'

Chapter 10

LONDON, MAY 1939

He found the library the third week he was in London.

Aunt Miriam had bought him new clothes, taking his German garments with her one Saturday morning, to show the shopman the sizes.

She returned with two pairs of trousers, shirts, pyjamas, socks and underwear, even a mackintosh and Wellington boots. Georg thanked her. She was trying to be kind. But they both knew she was right when she said she didn't know much about children.

Mostly she had left for work when he woke up. His body craved sleep now. In dreams he was back in Germany. Only sometimes the dreams still had yells of '*Juden 'raus*' and blood in them.

Each day when he woke he kept his eyes shut, hoping that when he opened them he'd be in his room in Alfhausen, the wooden shutters closed against the morning light, the lark singing in the garden. Downstairs Lotte would warm the rolls, singing of roses.

Instead he woke to the blank walls of Aunt Miriam's spare room. It still looked like a spare room, not a boy's. There were no photographs, not even any clothes in the cupboard. The flats were 'serviced'. Each morning he had to pack his clothes away in the hated suitcase and put it up on the wardrobe, and strip his bed sheets too, so that the maid who came in to clean each afternoon didn't guess a boy stayed here.

It was strange how an empty flat seemed noisier than one with people in it. When Aunt Miriam was at work he heard every creak of the floorboards from the people above; he heard every gurgle of the pipes. It was strange at first hearing a flush and knowing a stranger had gone to the toilet.

The telephone stared at him from its wooden pedestal. Sometimes he almost picked it up, and asked the operator to put through an international call, just like Papa did at Weihnachten when he called Aunt Miriam to wish her a merry Christmas. Surely telephone systems were the same in England. All he had to do was pick the receiver up and book a call and, in half an hour or even less, the phone would ring and the operator would say, 'Your call is through,' or whatever English operators said.

He didn't. Partly it was because phone calls were expensive, and he didn't want to anger Aunt Miriam. But mostly it was because he was afraid that if he called a number in Germany the Gestapo might know somehow that a Jewish boy was calling.

If only Mutti would ring him! But when the phone rang it was only Aunt Miriam's friends, or once her boss from work, asking where she had left a file. Georg never answered the phone, even if Aunt Miriam was in another room, not even when he learned that the English also said 'Hello' to answer the phone, just like at home. People might ask questions if a boy answered Aunt Miriam's phone, especially a boy with a German accent.

He made himself toast for breakfast, for it seemed there were no bakers with fresh rolls here, or perhaps the maid didn't go and fetch them, as Lotte did at home. It was funny to make bread hard, instead of eating it soft and fresh, but that was what the English did, so Georg did now too. He spread his toast with strawberry jam — Aunt Miriam had marmalade, which he had never eaten before, and didn't like. She asked him what jam he liked best, just as she had asked what else he liked to eat too, what fruit, and did he like milk to drink and was he old enough to drink tea. He wished he could listen to the wireless while he ate breakfast. The flat wouldn't seem so empty with a human voice. But the programmes didn't start till ten o'clock.

Each afternoon the doorman brought up groceries when the maid came to clean and make Aunt Miriam's bed. Georg checked the kitchen clock to tell when he had to slip down the back stairs, trying to find a moment to cross the foyer before letting himself out into the street when the doorman was talking to a delivery boy, or reading his paper.

It didn't matter if someone saw him sometimes. Aunt Miriam had told the doormen that her sister had moved nearby and that her nephew would be visiting often. She said that he had been ill with scarlet fever and so was away from school. As long as a boy wasn't living in the building, and was quiet, it seemed no one would mind.

At first he wandered the streets and looked in shop windows. Aunt Miriam had given him money, though she hadn't said what he should spend it on, or how long it had to last. On the fourth day he found a park two streets away. He watched the nannies pushing the prams there and, later, the children walk home from school. Sometimes the children laughed together or played games. It was hard to watch them then.

He tried not to think of Johann these days. There had been a Jewish boy at school three years before. Georg and Johann and the other boys had thrown rotten apples at him one lunchtime. The Fräulein had stopped the row, then told the Jewish boy he had better go home.

He hadn't come to school again.

Georg still didn't understand how he could be Jewish — how Papa could be and Aunt Miriam too. Papa never killed babies. He wasn't even rich, as Jews were supposed to be.

Could ... could the Führer be wrong, and Jews weren't all evil? Or was he different from other Jews, and Papa and Aunt Miriam too, because they were only a little bit Jewish, so it didn't count?

If the Führer was wrong about Jews perhaps he was wrong about other things. About the English being weak and cowardly, about the French being arrogant and treacherous, about Americans being ruled by Jews and bankers.

Maybe Germany didn't even have the right to rule the world. If the Nazis did conquer the world then Jews would be hunted everywhere. And if they weren't bad then what about the gypsies? Maybe even black people weren't Untermensch, subhuman, at all. He vaguely remembered someone saying that in Berlin a black man from America won lots of running medals, and the Führer had had to shake his hand. A black man who was stronger and faster than the Aryan Super-race of Germans ... Had he read it somewhere? No, it wouldn't have been in the paper. Perhaps Papa had told him.

Sometimes, as he walked the streets, he thought he saw Papa's face, or Mutti's flowered dress. He knew it wouldn't be them, not really — they would have telephoned Aunt Miriam as soon as they landed in England. But it was good to pretend, just for a while, to follow them, trying not to catch up too soon, to delay the rush of disappointment when he saw a stranger standing in front of him with Papa's hair or Mutti's scarf.

It was hard sometimes, to fill in the afternoon.

In the park was a small café that sold tiny ice creams for the English coin, a penny. He began to buy a penny ice cream every day, learning about English money and English coins. He copied the way one of the nannies said, 'An ice cream, please,' so that his words wouldn't sound like he had an accent.

The library was across the park. He discovered it by accident, following some boys who had been playing catch with a ball. He told himself he followed them to see what English children did, in case they were different from German ones, but mostly it was because he had nothing else to do — not until Saturday afternoon, when Aunt Miriam would take him to a film, or Sunday, when they would go to church, have lunch in a restaurant and then go to a museum. Museums and films were educational, Aunt Miriam said. They would help him be more English.

He looked up at the library building nervously. Were strangers allowed inside? You had to show your card at the University library before you were allowed in. But then a woman carrying a baby walked up the stairs and right past the woman at the desk inside without showing anything. He followed her. He could always apologise and leave if someone stopped him.

No one did. The woman at the desk even smiled a welcome at him, before looking back at the books she was stamping. He stood in the foyer and looked around.

It was tiny. The only library he knew back home was the big one at the University, with walls and walls of index files, and quiet tables for students to study at.

This one was only two rooms: one for 'Adults' on one side of the foyer and one with a sign that said 'Children'. The tall shelves of books were just like at the University. He slipped inside.

One wall had big shelves, with books for little kids. But the other shelves had proper books, with lots of words. English words — but that was good. They'd help him to seem really English.

He picked a book off the shelves, another of the Arthur Ransome adventures, and sat at a table with it. He had only read two chapters when the woman from the desk came up to him.

He froze, hunting for English words to apologise. Perhaps the library was for students of a certain school, or children from certain families. Would she call the police? Why hadn't she stopped him before?

But she just smiled at him. 'Library's closing, dear. Would you like to take that out?'

It took a moment to work out that she meant he could borrow the book. He shook his head cautiously.

'You're not a library member, are you? You get your mum to bring you down tomorrow and sign you up. It's only threepence a week. Then you can take out four books at a time.'

He nodded, hoping an aunt would do. Threepence was only three pennies. It would have to be Saturday, when Aunt Miriam wasn't working. He hoped they were open on Saturdays. He didn't want to risk his accent being recognised by trying to ask.

He put the book back on the shelf, with the Rs, exactly where it had been before. Papa (his heart clenched a little) had shown him how libraries worked. Alphabetical order seemed the same in England as at home. The lady smiled at him as he left.

He went to the library every afternoon that week, as soon as he had eaten the lunch that Aunt Miriam had left for him. (She told

60

the maid that she had guests to dinner often now, to explain the extra food.) The librarian smiled at him every time he came in.

Aunt Miriam was tired when she came home from work. It was usually late, long after Georg had eaten his English dinner of baked beans on toast that he could make himself, or shepherd's pie to heat in the oven left by the maid.

He waited till Saturday morning, till Aunt Miriam had woken late and showered, and was frying sausages for breakfast. They weren't like German sausages — they were coarse beef sausages, bland and fatty, instead of pork — but the smell made him homesick just the same. He made sure any tears were gone before Aunt Miriam put the sausages on the plates, with a fried egg each and bread fried in the sausage fat.

'Aunt Miriam?'

'Yes?' said Aunt Miriam absently, frowning down at the newspaper headlines. Georg glanced at the newspaper. *Hitler Tears Up Naval Treaty with Britain.*

'May I be a member of the library across the park? It is three pennies a week.'

'Threepence, not three pennies. Yes, of course.'

'The librarian said I should bring my mother. Will an aunt do?'

'I should imagine so,' said Aunt Miriam, her eyes on the paper. She took a forkful of sausage and dipped it in the egg yolk. 'We'll go down after breakfast.'

'Aunt Miriam?'

She looked up at the new note in his voice. 'Yes, George?'

The words fell over each other in their hurry to get out. 'May we put a phone call through to home? Or to Tante Gudrun? I ... I hoped Mutti would ring me but she hasn't. I want to know how Papa is. I want to write to them. Please can I write to them? I ...'

Aunt Miriam waited till he had finished. She looked at the sausage, then put her fork down. 'George, I wanted to talk to you this morning. I need to tell you ...'

'Tell me what?' asked Georg.

'A letter came from your Aunt Gudrun yesterday. I wrote to her as soon as you arrived to let her know you were here safe and well. I was careful not to mention you by name. I said "a package".'

I am a package, thought Georg.

'I wrote to your mother at your home address too, but my letter came back yesterday as well. It had been opened, but not by your mother, I think. Don't worry. I was careful what I wrote to her too. Things ... things are not good in Germany.'

'But Mutti? What did Tante say about Mutti and Papa?'

'Your aunt says that your house, all your father's property, has been confiscated. That means the government owns it now,' she added when she saw Georg didn't understand.

'Our house? Why? It's ours!'

'Because they say your father is Jewish.'

'But he isn't! Jews are different. Everyone knows that,' he said cautiously, because he was no longer sure, but wanted to hear what Aunt Miriam would say. Aunt Miriam knew things, like who was the President of America and why it was really called the United States.

'Did your parents tell you that Jews were different?' asked Aunt Miriam quietly.

'No. Papa said I was too young to understand.' Grown-ups told you that when they were afraid that you *would* understand, thought Georg. But he didn't say that to Aunt Miriam. 'Papa said I wasn't to listen when people talked about Jews.'

'As though if you don't listen it doesn't matter.' Aunt Miriam shook her head. 'George, by the Nazi system your father is Jewish. I tried to tell him, to warn him, but he said that he knew the German people better than I did. The land of Goethe and Schiller, he said.' She shook her head again. 'Your father could never see that people can be both good and bad, that a land can have beauty as well as evil.'

'You think Germany is evil?'

Aunt Miriam sighed. 'I don't suppose Germany is any more evil than any other country, though I could never say that in public. There are fools in this country too, but just now Germany has one for a leader.'

'No! The Führer isn't ...' Georg hesitated.

'The Führer is a tiny little man who wants to be a big one,' said Aunt Miriam evenly. 'And he wants to make his country bigger too. Germany was in a bad way when he came to power. And he's done good things — bringing the nation together again. But to do that he blamed all the hardships on the Jews, creating hatred and fear, to give communists and fascists and every unemployed peasant a common enemy. The Jews. Sometimes it's as though hatred spreads like the flu. One person gets it, then another and another.'

'You are a Jew.' Georg made it a statement, not a question.

'No. But Herr Hitler would call me one. My grandfather — your father's grandfather — was Jewish. He stopped practising his religion when I was a little girl and your father was still a baby. My mother is a Gentile — non-Jew — just like yours; and for practising Jews that means we are Gentiles too. But to Hitler you are still a Jew.'

'I am not!'

'To the Nazis you would be Jewish,' said Aunt Miriam wearily.

Georg was silent. It didn't make sense. But so much didn't make sense these days. Did any of it ever make sense? he wondered. Had the world changed, or had he just realised parts of it were stupid and wicked?

His mind came back to the most important thing. 'Our home is gone?'

'Not gone. But it isn't yours now. All your father's money, everything he and your mother owned, it's all been taken by the government.'

'Then where is Mutti now?' But he knew the answer even as he asked it.

'I don't know. Your Aunt Gudrun doesn't know, or if she does she won't tell me. She says her sister has vanished and that she has brought shame on the family by marrying a Jew.'

'No!'

'I'm sorry,' said Aunt Miriam simply. 'If it helps, I think perhaps your aunt knew someone would open and read her letter before it got to me. A Nazi, who might use her words to try to find your mother, or put your aunt in prison if she helped her. Perhaps Gudrun has helped your mother to somewhere safe.'

Georg remembered how Tante Gudrun had vanished on that awful day. Perhaps, he thought.

'I ... I am sure your mother is safe,' said Aunt Miriam. 'She acted quickly to get you out. She'll make good decisions now. But I don't know where to write to her. We have to wait till she sends us a letter. Maybe the Nazis will let her leave.'

'I will write to Hitler. Hitler will make things right. He can order them to let Mutti come here, and —'

'George, Hitler is the one who hates the Jews.'

'But ...' His world was breaking into pieces. All the things he had been so sure of — his home, his parents, the glory of the Führer — it wasn't just that they were no longer there for him. It was as though they never had been — not as he had thought they were.

'Why?' It had seemed to make sense when he had thought that Jews were evil.

'I don't know why. Maybe it's because things were so very bad in Germany after the last war. Maybe when things are bad it helps to have someone to hate.'

Georg thought about that. 'Then if you make people happy the hate would go away?'

'Yes. No. It isn't simple. I just don't know.'

Georg thought about giving Hitler a penny ice cream between two wafers. Hitler would eat it and smile …

No, a penny ice cream had only given him a penny's worth of happiness. It hadn't covered up the pain. A penny ice cream wouldn't be enough for Hitler either.

'Aunt Miriam, did the letter say how Papa is?' He watched her to see her reaction.

Aunt Miriam's face went carefully blank. 'No. I'm sorry. Gudrun didn't mention your father. She … she asked me not to contact her again.'

'Will you?'

Aunt Miriam stared at him, then down at the newspaper. 'I don't know,' she said at last. 'I think if she knew something we should know Gudrun would tell us, despite what she says. Maybe your mother will find some way to get a letter to us.'

There is something you're not saying, thought Georg. It was what he hadn't been thinking too. Dead, he thought. You won't say maybe Papa is dead. I won't say it either. If we say the word aloud or think of it too often it might be true.

'I have some other news.' Aunt Miriam tried to smile. 'I have spoken to the building supervisor. They've agreed that in the circumstances you may stay here.'

'The circumstances?' He could leave his clothes in the cupboard. The hated suitcase could be put out of sight under his bed.

'I told them the truth. Part of the truth. That your mother is abroad and can't get back just now. I said she was Swiss though, not German. You must remember that if anyone asks you. It will explain your accent too. George, we will be at war with Germany soon. There is a lot of anger against Germans now.'

He stared. War happened somewhere else, in Prague or the Sudetenland or Spain.

'I just want you to be prepared,' said Aunt Miriam. She stood up, and scraped her congealed sausages into the bin. 'Let's go to this library and then we can have a good lunch somewhere and feed the swans.'

Chapter 11

MAY TO DECEMBER 1939

The year crept on.

Summer brought long days, longer than at home, and twilights that stretched forever. Sometimes it even brought blue skies. There were tomatoes in the shops and strawberries that brought a sweet pang of home, and lettuces. Summer school holidays began, with children in the streets holding hands with their parents. Sometimes the group of boys played ball in the park. They asked Georg to join in once.

It was fun, being with other boys again. But the boys left for their tea without even telling him their names and for some reason they never came back to the park.

Part of him missed having friends. Mostly he tried not to think about what he missed, in case it all came tumbling in.

No letter came from Germany; no telephone call either. Every day when he came back from the library he hoped Mutti might be sitting in the foyer, waiting, in her flowered dress and the green coat. But she never was.

The library was the heart of his days now. Aunt Miriam had

told the lady — the librarian — that same story she had told people in the building: that he had been sick and was still not strong enough for school, and that his Swiss mother was abroad and could not return. He thought he sounded more English now. He listened to the wireless, mouthing the words, as soon as it came on in the morning and at night while he was waiting for Aunt Miriam to come home.

Sometimes they were hard words for a German boy to repeat. The English on the wireless spoke of the Nazi menace, the German threat. Sometimes they spoke of the treacherous Hun.

That's me, thought Georg. I am the Hun.

He read Aunt Miriam's newspaper too. There were things that were hard to understand, even when Aunt Miriam explained them; they were frightening too.

The government was giving 'Anderson' air-raid shelters to everyone in London and other cities that could be bombed. There was a photo and a diagram of the shelters, to help people work out how to put them together. The shelters were made of corrugated iron and looked no bigger than a bed. People had to bury them in their gardens, so they could hide in them when the bombs fell. Corrugated iron wouldn't stop a bomb but, if you were lucky, the dirt you piled on top of it might.

We have no garden, thought Georg. Where will we go if bombs come?

Mutti had sent him to England — so *far* — to be safe, but the newspaper made it sound as if there was no safety, not even here.

In May the paper said Hitler and Mussolini of Italy had signed a pact, to say that they would fight together if there was war.

He looked at a map of the world in the library that day, and stared at the pink splodges all over it. Canada, Australia, India,

Burma, so much of Africa. It was hard to understand. England had the biggest empire on earth — there was more pink than any other colour. How could it be in danger, even from Germany and Italy combined? Of course Germany had the Führer, while England only had Mr Chamberlain, whose voice was as dry as English toast. The German army and navy were the biggest in the world. German soldiers were the best in the world too. He hesitated at that. Were they really? Or was that what he'd been told? Were they the best like Jews were bad?

He asked Aunt Miriam that night. She sighed and slipped her shoes off as she sat down on the sofa. 'Get me a cup of tea, George, there's a lamb.' The days in her office were even longer now.

He made the tea carefully, one spoonful for Aunt Miriam and one for the pot, taking the pot to the kettle and not the other way around, so the water would be hot when it poured onto the leaves. He was proud to be able to make tea now. Adults in Germany drank coffee, but he had never made it; he never went into the kitchen except when Lotte was making Kugelhopf and let him lick out the bowl.

Aunt Miriam sipped the tea gratefully, then dunked in her Garibaldi biscuit. The English ate biscuits from packets, bought at the shop, instead of cakes made at home. At least Aunt Miriam did.

At last she spoke. 'People say the sun never sets on the British Empire, and that's true enough.' She smiled briefly. 'Yes, it is the biggest in the world. But we don't have nearly as many soldiers as Germany. Nowhere near as many aeroplanes or ships, and certainly nothing as massive as Germany's battleship, the *Bismarck*. Germany has been preparing for this war for ten years; and England has done nothing in that time.'

'Nothing?'

She shrugged. 'Not enough then. England hoped to negotiate a way to avoid a war. I hoped too. But lately, well, war is coming for us whether we want it or not. If we don't fight we will be ruled by Hitler and his Brown Shirts.'

People who hate Jews, thought Georg, but he didn't say it.

'But England will win? The empire will fight too?'

'The empire will fight.' She shook her head. 'However, the empire isn't like it looks on the map, George. India has millions of people but very few soldiers, even though they're good ones. Australia looks big but it's mostly desert and there aren't a lot of people. Canada too has more forests and lakes than people. Africa — well, Germany has colonies there as well.'

'So Germany might win a war,' said Georg slowly.

Aunt Miriam shut her eyes. Her face was hollowed with weariness. 'I studied history at Oxford. Your father studied his poets. He studied dreams and words. I studied what people did and tried to understand why. Countries that begin wars rarely win them, George. Maybe because greed stops them seeing situations clearly. And maybe because only a certain sort of madman leads his country to invade another.'

'But Hitler has already won in Czechoslovakia, in Austria ...' Though the Austrians didn't fight back, he thought.

Aunt Miriam opened her eyes. 'I didn't say victory would be quick. Or easy. Ten years, a hundred ... but we'll win, George. We won last time, despite the odds. We'll win again.' Her smile looked almost sad. 'Or perhaps I am like your father too. Perhaps I only see the patterns in history that tell me what I want to see: that our tiny island has a chance of winning, of defeating a country determined to persecute and kill many of its own people as well as outsiders.'

Ten years of war. A hundred. He glanced out the window and down to the street. A horse was dragging a cart piled high with rubbish. A man in filthy grey clothes called out, 'Rag and bones! Bring out your rag and bones.' The cart came in the evenings after people had eaten their dinner. Aunt Miriam had let him take down the chop and roast lamb bones last week, but there were none today. The man and the cart looked so normal. So safe. It wasn't fair that the world could look safe while darkness hid around the corner.

It wasn't fair at all.

He read the newspaper every morning after that; it was usually slightly crumpled after Aunt Miriam had read it over breakfast. Ten thousand Jewish women marched through the streets of a place called Palestine to ask the English rulers to let more Jews come from Germany to Palestine. But it seemed the Führer wouldn't let them out, nor the English rulers let them in.

He wondered if they would let Mutti in to England if Papa wasn't with her. Aunt Miriam would help if she could, but he didn't ask Aunt Miriam what she thought. If he didn't know for sure then he could still hope that one day — someday — there'd be a knock, a phone call, a flowered silk dress down in the foyer.

In August Hitler and Stalin of Russia promised not to fight each other. At least that was better than Russia promising to fight England too. The newspaper that day had an article about a new type of plane too: it had been invented in Germany and was called a 'jet'. It went very fast by pushing out jets of hot gas.

For a moment Georg was proud of his country and then remembered it wasn't his country any more.

Sometimes now Aunt Miriam's women friends came round to supper. They all worked like Aunt Miriam, which disappointed him, as he hoped some might have children. The women wore skirts and jackets like Aunt Miriam did, and shoes with stumpy heels. They were women who knew things, like Aunt Miriam; and they talked about them too.

He listened when Aunt Miriam and her friends talked. He handed around cups of tea on a tray, just like Lotte had done. He bought a cake at the bakery and served it on little plates too. It wasn't as good as Lotte's Kugelhopf. The cream was thin and sweet and sort of rubbery, not like real cream at all. But Aunt Miriam's friends smiled at him, and said how lucky Aunt Miriam was to have a nephew like him.

'I know,' said Aunt Miriam. He knew she meant it too.

He sat on a stool by the door, so quiet that they mostly didn't notice him, so he could listen to them talk, to hear things that even Aunt Miriam might not tell a child.

They talked of the 'Polish crisis' and of how Hitler had offered not to fight England if the English allowed him to have the part of Poland called Danzig.

It had seemed so simple back in Germany. The Führer had to free the Danzig Germans from Polish rule! But here it wasn't simple at all.

One of Aunt Miriam's friends called Hitler 'that frightful little man'. That hurt a little too, though he wasn't quite sure why.

The library was better. The stories there were far away: boys battled boa constrictors in the jungles; and a girl called Dorothy was swept up in a tornado and taken to a land called Oz.

He took to going to the library earlier and earlier each day. It was shut at lunchtime, but one day when he was about to leave the librarian asked if he would like to share her sandwiches. They were cheese and pickle, and she gave him a cup of milky tea, the first that he had drunk. He didn't like it much, but drank it to be polite.

Her name was Mrs Huntley. She told him about her daughter, quite grown up now. She and her husband had gone to Australia, the big pink splodge on the bottom of the world, 'where there are lots of butterflies, dear, and it's hot even in winter. They like it there, but it's a dreadful long way away. I never get to see the grandbabies at all. They send me photographs, of course, but it isn't the same.'

Next day he brought his sandwiches down to the library, and hoped she would ask him to stay again. She did. She had made an apple teacake, and they had a slice each for lunch and for tea as well, before she closed the library to go home to make her husband's supper.

Now if there was no one else in the library who needed their books stamped Mrs Huntley would take him around the shelves and show him books that he might like, even books in the 'Adults' room. A book on keeping bees, which was most interesting, one called *Birds of the Marshes* and one on keeping hens too. Georg thought he would like to keep hens. Or a dog. A dog that he could hug for warmth and comfort. A dog would curl up on the sofa with him, on the long nights while he waited for Aunt Miriam to come home.

But of course it was impossible in a flat.

—❦❧◦

'I've found a place for you at the Gresham School,' said Aunt Miriam one Saturday. It was omelettes for breakfast — a supper dish at home but something the English ate in the morning instead — with grilled summer tomatoes and toast with jam.

'It's a good school — a bus ride away, but better than the local. Your English is good enough to pass muster now.' She smiled at him, the abstracted smile that was the only kind she had these days. 'You've done very well, all on your own. I'm proud of you. We'll go and buy your school uniform today.'

It was a nice uniform: grey flannel pants, a dark blue blazer and a dark blue cap. He was glad now it was a day school, not a boarding school. He'd be able to see Mrs Huntley after school and there'd still be weekends with Aunt Miriam.

He put the clothes on in the evenings, alone in the flat waiting for Aunt Miriam to return. He looked in the mirror and tried to imagine himself doing maths and playing cricket with his friends. An English boy with English friends.

The chance of school vanished.

The Gresham School announced that in August it would evacuate all its students to High Martin Manor, in the country, away from any bombs that might fall on London.

'I think it best,' said Aunt Miriam carefully, 'if you don't go away with the school to the country. Not when you don't know anyone.'

Not till I've proved I can fit in, thought Georg. Not till no one would suspect that I am German.

The uniform hung lonely in the cupboard. He had worn it so couldn't send it back. He guessed that if he ever wore a school uniform he'd have grown out of this one.

He knew now just how much having a German nephew living with her might hurt Aunt Miriam too. Having an English father and an English passport made him English only as long as he sounded right.

He worked even harder on his accent. He read the newspaper over and over, so he'd know English things. He tried to imagine himself doing the things the children did in his English storybooks: sailing boats and building fires and playing at the seaside. But what was a sandcastle? Could you really build a whole giant castle out of sand?

—◈◎—

They called it Operation Pied Piper in the newspaper. Over three short days three and a half million children had to leave England's cities — cities, like London and Manchester and Liverpool, that might be bombed. They were taken by train or buses or even trucks west to Wales or to villages far from the coast.

'Do I have to go?' asked Georg.

'Parents don't have to send their children. But children need to be safe.'

'Will you send me?'

She bit her lip. 'I haven't decided. Do you want to go?'

'No.' It wasn't just that he was scared that strangers might find out he was German and put him in a camp behind barbed wire. Aunt Miriam and her flat and Mrs Huntley's library were the only safe things he knew. Aunt Miriam mightn't know much about children, but she was his.

She nodded slowly. 'Very well. But if … if things get bad you may have to leave then. And …' She hesitated. 'I shouldn't tell you this, George. Don't repeat it.'

Who would I tell it to? he wondered. To Mrs Huntley? To Mutti, in my dreams?

'My office may be transferred out of London. Its work is too important to be lost to bombs.'

'Where would we go?'

'No one's told me. No one has said anything official yet. Somewhere in the country: that's all. Somewhere that doesn't look like it would be worth a bomb.'

A cottage, thought Georg. That's where his books said people lived in the English countryside. No one would think of bombing cottages. He imagined packing the dreaded suitcase again; it would be worth it to go to a cottage in the country. In books cottages had roses around the door. *Röslein, röslein, röslein rot* ... Maybe they could have some hens. He might even be allowed a dog.

He watched from afar as the children assembled in the park, one of the nearly two thousand assembly points just in London. He didn't want to get too close in case someone thought he was one of them and accidentally took him too.

The children had a suitcase each — smaller than his, like a school bag — and brown labels around their necks on pieces of string. Some of them were crying. The little ones held the big ones' hands.

Mothers huddled in clusters at the other end of the park. There were few men. Even today, the men had to work, though their children were being taken away. The organisers didn't allow the mothers too near. Some of the women covered their faces with their hands as though they couldn't watch.

Mutti would have watched, thought Georg. Mutti looked at me till the suitcase closed. He knew in his heart she had watched the suitcase as it was carried down the path and down the street.

She would have followed it to the station if she hadn't been afraid that someone would see her and wonder about the suitcase with him inside.

It began to rain: a cold grey drizzle like the clouds had simply melted onto the ground.

Buses drew up, long buses with hungry mouths like lions that swallowed the children one by one. Every time a bus drew away fewer children were left behind.

A woman screamed. She fell to the ground, sobbing. She still sobbed as two older women helped her away.

At last there were no more buses. The organisers herded the remaining children into two lines, each couple holding each other's hand. They began to march, left right, left right, across the road then down towards the train station.

The mothers followed.

The buses had been cool and silent. It was different with the hiss and chuff of trains. The children clambered into the carriages. They leaned out, their cardboard labels dangling. They waved and shouted — at their mothers, at the porters, at children who hadn't yet boarded. It was almost like a holiday was coming, not a war.

The mothers waved too, coming nearer now the official guardians were on the trains.

'You be a good girl now?'

'You write as soon as you get there, you hear?'

'No mucking up! You behave yourself, or I'll come down and give you what for.'

'And change your vest every night and don't forget to take that medicine ...'

No one said 'I love you'. No one said 'I'll miss you' or 'My world will crack when you are gone'. No one said 'I don't think I can bear this, but I will'.

He hadn't said those words either. For the first time he wondered if they even needed to be said.

He waited till the last train had vanished down the line, till the last mother had shoved her damp handkerchief in her pocket and trudged slowly out of the station, before he left too and went back to the flat, silent till he turned the wireless on.

He was listening to the wireless one evening, repeating the phrases the announcer said, when there was a knock at the door. He started — no one had ever knocked at the door when he had been there alone before. The maid had her own key, Aunt Miriam's friends only came when she was there, and the doorman downstairs took deliveries.

The doorman must have allowed whoever this was up.

For a second his heart seemed to rip in two. It was Mutti! Or Mutti *and* Papa ...

He opened the door.

A tall man stood there, with long, thin legs like a grasshopper's and grey hair under his tin hat. He peered down at Georg. 'Good evening, laddie. I'm Captain Hawkins, air-raid warden. Can I speak to your mummy or daddy?'

'My aunt isn't at home,' said Georg carefully.

'What? Oh, yes, the doorman told me. You're —' he looked at the list '— Marks, George and his aunt, Marks, Miriam. Well, you'll do, laddie.' He reached into a box, out of sight in the corridor, and pulled out two strange bundles. 'Gas masks,' he said.

'Gas masks?' repeated Georg. For a moment he thought it might be a reference to his own name, Marks.

'To put on if there is a poison gas raid,' said Captain Hawkins patiently. 'The Jerries sent poison gas down on us in great big canisters in the last war. I was in France. Chaps coughed up blood —' He saw the expression on Georg's face and stopped. 'Well, just you make sure you put yours on if you hear the siren, and you give your auntie hers too. Can you do that?'

'Yes,' said Georg.

'Right, see how I do it? Suck in your breath, then hold the mask in front of your face and pull the straps over your head as far as they will go.'

Captain Hawkins's face vanished in the gas mask. He looked even more like an insect now: a strange, evil insect. He pulled the mask off and became human again.

'Now you try it. Make sure you don't twist the straps now.'

Georg took the thing and placed it over his face. It felt peculiar and stiff and he couldn't see very much. It smelled horrible too. This is meant to make me feel safe, he thought. Safe from gas, like the shelters are to keep us safe from bombs.

He didn't feel safe at all.

～✿◎

One day there was no newspaper when Georg got up and wandered out into the kitchen. He looked in the bin, in case Aunt Miriam had used it to wrap scraps, then in the living room, but it was nowhere.

Aunt Miriam must have taken it to work, he thought. He missed it. The newspaper had news from Germany every day now. It wasn't news he liked to read, but at least he could see his homeland's name in print and know that it was still there.

79

Somehow seeing the word 'Germany' made it possible that Mutti was safe, and Papa too.

But the library received newspapers every day. He waited until the old lady with the yellow headscarf who came in every morning to read it had finished with it; and the old man with the pipe too. Mrs Huntley didn't mind if he went into the 'Adults' room these days. She knew he liked the magazines, the books on animals and the encyclopaedias that only the Adults section had.

He sat in one of the shabby leather chairs, still warm where the pipe man had sat on it, and began to read: comics first, and then a leaf through the pages looking for German news.

It was on page six. He read it, then read it again. The paper began to shake. He saw it was caused by his hands trembling and put the whole thing down.

So this was why Aunt Miriam had taken the newspaper away today. Not because she needed it, or wanted to read it on her way to work.

She had taken it to stop him reading this.

The Jews in Germany were being put in places called concentration camps where they had to work to help Germany win the war. They were tortured there — whipped and beaten with sticks. Hitler himself had ordered the floggings.

Georg tried to keep his eyes wide open, to stare at the people passing outside the window, at the dog on a lead walking along the street. Anything ... anything to keep the pictures from his head.

Papa, his back red with blood, just like the blood on his head ...

No! He couldn't think that! He couldn't!

Mutti, screaming in pain ...

80

No! Now he was gone, and Papa ... now Papa *might* be gone, Mutti must be safe. No one would think she was Jewish now. He tried not to think of her huddled by a barbed-wire fence in a camp and crying.

No, Mutti wouldn't cry. She hadn't cried when they hurt Papa. She hadn't let the tears fall for her son, at least not when he could see. Mutti wouldn't ever cry because of Hitler.

Now Hitler might be coming here.

—⁂◎

Georg was at the library the day the war arrived.

No other young people used the Children's room now. Occasionally he saw other children in the distance: even a mob of boys once. A few families must have kept their children home, like him. But none of those left in this part of London used the library.

Mrs Huntley smiled at him when he arrived. She had assumed that he wasn't to be evacuated because of the illness Aunt Miriam had told her about. But today she seemed distracted.

The streets were emptier than he had ever seen them. It wasn't just that the children had vanished. Most of the adults had gone somewhere too. Were grown-ups also leaving London now? But Aunt Miriam would have told him if they were, and he didn't like to ask Mrs Huntley. Mrs Huntley knew how to find a book about polar bears, but he thought she didn't understand the world outside like Aunt Miriam did.

He found a book, an old *Boy's Own Annual* he hadn't seen before. It told him how to build an underwater spear gun. It didn't seem like something you could use in a pond, but maybe if he ever went to the seaside like children in the books —

Someone yelled outside. The sound of cheering echoed from down the street. Mrs Huntley ran outside and into the tea-shop next door.

Georg stared. Mrs Huntley had never left the library during the day before. A minute later she was back. She slipped back behind her desk, hunched up with her cardigan wrapped round her as if she was cold.

He approached her quietly. 'Are you all right? Why are they cheering?'

She looked at him, her face wet. 'It's war, dear,' she said flatly. 'Mr Chamberlain says we're at war.'

'With Germany?'

There didn't seem anyone else to be at war with, other than Germany's friends of course. Mrs Huntley nodded. 'My Ernest was in the last war.' She added in an almost whisper, 'Lost his leg on the Somme.'

Georg had a vision of a man waking up one morning and not remembering where he had left his leg, hopping about in the fields looking for it. He thought of grey-faced, legless men, sitting on street corners, their shabby hats on the footpath beside them, hoping for coins. No, he thought, Mr Huntley lives in a house, with Mrs Huntley.

'Gassed him too. He's still up most nights, choking and gasping, trying to get some air into him. That's why I have to work here. Now we're for it again. The whole horrible mess of it —'

It was as though she suddenly saw Georg again. She gave him a tight smile. 'Don't you worry, dear. We saw the nasty Huns off last time. We'll see them off this time too.'

'Yes,' said Georg. He forced himself to add, 'We will.'

82

A week later Mrs Huntley was in tears again. 'My dog, Blondie. The papers said pets have to be put down ... All resources are needed for the war effort. Can't be wasting good food on dogs.' She wiped her eyes savagely. 'Poor old boy. I'd have shared my last crust with him, if I could. Had him near fourteen years. Hundreds of them all in a pile at the vet's: dogs and cats and a horse too.'

Georg thought, I won't be getting a dog then. Even if we go to a cottage I can't have a dog.

⁓❦◎

Planes thundered overhead, grey metal against a greyer sky: bombers or planes carrying troops to squadrons in France or Poland — no one seemed to know.

The main streets suddenly were 'one way only' — cars piled with families, dogs that had been spared being put down, suitcases, even chairs and tables tied on the roofs, rumbling out of London. Trucks trundled through the streets, taking paintings from the galleries and crates from the museums. All the treasures of London were being taken away to safety from the threat of bombs.

All of London seemed to be moving, except for them, and Mrs Huntley and the library.

But the bombs didn't come.

There were no street lights now, in case they showed the German bombers where to drop their cargo. He helped Aunt Miriam fit thick blackout curtains to every window in the flat. No crack of light that might lead the enemy up the river to London could show in the whole city. He wasn't allowed to turn a light on now unless the curtains were pulled. The nights were getting longer again, so he pulled them before he left the flat each afternoon, so he didn't have to fumble his way across to the windows in the dark when he got back.

Registration day arrived. They lined up to register at the baker's shop, the butcher's and the grocer's for the new ration books. No one knew what food would be rationed yet, but everyone knew that life would be hard.

England didn't grow enough food to feed her people, so it all needed to be rationed so everyone could get a fair share and leave enough to feed the men in the army and the navy and air force. You couldn't fight on an empty belly. Civilians — those who weren't in the army or navy or air force — would get what was left. The newspaper explained how to keep chickens for eggs or rabbits for meat or plant a vegetable garden.

Georg liked the idea of rabbits, though not the killing them or meat part. Even keeping rabbits was impossible in a flat. Maybe they could have a garden in the park. But the men were piling walls of sandbags in the park now. He supposed the soldiers could hide behind them to shoot at the enemy when they arrived.

Aunt Miriam filled the larder with cans of baked beans and canned salmon. They weren't rationed. 'If things get bad,' she said quietly. 'It's best to have something in reserve.'

Christmas was coming. Georg watched the calendar, waiting for 6 December, Nikolaustag, St Nicholas Day. But Aunt Miriam didn't remind him to put his shoes outside the front door the evening before. He waited till she was asleep, then opened their front door and checked outside in the hall, to see if other people had put their shoes outside. No one had.

He put his shoes out anyway, but next morning they were empty, not filled with oranges or nuts, not even a bunch of twigs to show that he'd been bad.

There were Christmas trees in the shop windows now. Mrs Huntley had a tree branch in the library that she had asked Georg to help decorate too, with coloured balls and tinsel instead of proper Christbaumgebäck, the special little Christmas biscuits that Mutti made in the shape of stars and lambs and tiny trees before baking them and hanging them on their Christmas tree. He would have liked a Christmas tree in their flat, like they had at home. But Aunt Miriam worked even later these days and was always tired.

People sang carols in the street, holding out collection boxes for people to drop money into, but for once he didn't try to make out the English words. They weren't *real* carols, the carols Mutti and Papa sang, just like there was no Stollen or Lebkuchen, no baby Jesus in the manger with all the animals made from bread dough in the window of the baker's, not even a bread lamb.

Somehow Georg knew there was no point hanging up a stocking on Christmas Eve. The Christkindl would not find him here. Aunt Miriam worked late, even on Christmas Eve. There was no feast of carp and potatoes.

He sat by the coal fire, which smelled sour and not of pine wood, and shut his eyes. He tried to remember Mutti's voice as she sang '*Stille nacht*', the smell of ginger and spices, the Stollen rich with butter and marzipan.

He tried to remember Papa's laughter as they tramped across the snow in the forest that the Rektor owned to gather greenery to make the Weihnachten Kranz, the wreath. Papa had found mistletoe in the woods and held it over Mutti's head and kissed her.

This was not a real Christmas. Would he ever have a proper Christmas again? Or were memories of past Christmases all he would ever have?

Even his birthday had come and gone without Aunt Miriam noticing, and he didn't even tell Mrs Huntley, in case she wondered how a boy could have a birthday without even a card from his parents. At least there were presents for Christmas. Mrs Huntley had knitted him a pullover in brown and green. He had bought her a set of handkerchiefs with H for Huntley embroidered on them.

On Christmas morning Aunt Miriam gave him new pyjamas, socks, a chess set and a new coat that was too big. He was growing fast though and, as she said, when clothes rationing came in they might not be able to get him another for a while.

He would have liked to have some toys. Of course, he was too big for toys now. But a toy on the chest of drawers would make the room seem like his, instead of a place to pause and leave the suitcase for a while. Maybe a cricket bat would be just as good. It was very English to play cricket, even if there was no one else to play with (he couldn't see Aunt Miriam playing games).

Aunt Miriam was home all Christmas Day, at least. Two of her women friends came for dinner, with a bottle of sherry, a plum pudding and a silk scarf for Aunt Miriam, and a kaleidoscope for him that showed strange patterns that changed as you looked through it, and a book about a man named Biggles — *Biggles of the Flying Squadron*.

Georg thanked them politely. He didn't say he didn't want to read the Biggles book. He had seen other books about the man named Biggles in the library. But even though he had read nearly all the books in the library now, even the ones for littlies, he'd left the Biggles ones alone. He knew from the covers that Biggles flew aeroplanes and dropped bombs. He didn't want to read stories about a war. War threaded through his whole life. Stories were the only place that he could escape from war.

All day he hoped the phone would ring. Papa always called Aunt Miriam at Christmas. Surely, wherever Mutti was — and Papa, he added, ignoring the whispered question that always came now when he thought of Papa — she would find a way to call today.

But no call came.

It was only later, after the crackers had been pulled, the funny hats put on, the goose eaten (not suckling pig like at home), the plum pudding lit and eaten, just like the one Mutti had made for Papa every year — it was only later snuggled down in bed in his new pyjamas, listening to Aunt Miriam talking seriously to her friends — it was only then that he allowed himself to cry: deep gulping sobs that almost rocked the bed.

No presents or even a card from Germany. Not even something from Tante Gudrun. Of course he hadn't expected it, not during a war. Mutti couldn't come now till the war was over. No letters or cards could come either. He knew that, but —

'George?' Aunt Miriam sat heavily on the bed. She patted his shoulder clumsily. 'George, George, I'm sorry. I know ...'

He burrowed into her lap and felt her arms clasp around him. He thought she might have been crying too. At last she kissed his forehead, then patted his shoulder as though looking for something else to say.

She didn't find it. He watched her stand up and step into the lighted living room, and then he tried to sleep.

Chapter 12

No bombs had fallen.

'They're calling it the Phoney War,' said Miss Randall, one of Aunt Miriam's friends, on a Sunday afternoon. She reached for a piece of toast. There weren't many cakes in the shops now that butter and sugar were rationed. Bacon and meat and cooking fat and tea were on the list too.

Even baked beans and canned fish had got hard to find, like so many supplies that had come from overseas. All food was precious now, especially anything that had to come by ship. German U-boats, which sailed under the water, had sunk many ships and were trying to sink others too — not just English ones, or those of British Dominions like Canada and Australia, but also ones from Sweden, a country that wasn't even in the war at all. They targeted any ships that were carrying food or other supplies to England.

Georg missed bananas most. It was funny — he had never known that he really liked them before. But now he missed peeling the skin in strips, like a monkey, and eating it from the top down.

Aunt Miriam's friends brought a teaspoon of tea from their own rations to add to the pot when they came to visit these days, and always some little gift: apples sent by a cousin or a pot of plum jam, made with almost no sugar 'so eat it fast before it goes mouldy'.

Bread wasn't rationed, though Georg had to stand in line for half an hour to get it. He'd made toast for Aunt Miriam's friends today, with no butter — there wasn't enough butter in their ration to share — and spread the plum jam thin. Aunt Miriam's friends seemed to like it. Everyone was always just a little hungry now.

Miss Randall swallowed her mouthful of toast politely before she spoke again. 'Have you seen how many children have been brought back to London? Stupidity, after all the work and upset getting them out.'

Aunt Miriam snorted. 'People only see what they want to see. They think that because today is safe tomorrow will be too.' Like Papa, thought Georg, from his seat on the stool. 'Don't they read the newspapers? I call it "aggressive ignorance". Some people work very hard to ignore what they don't like.'

'Denmark, Norway, Holland and Belgium.' Miss Randall counted the countries that had fallen to Germany on her fingers. 'I give France another week at the most.'

Georg glanced at Aunt Miriam, startled. The British army was fighting alongside the French army in France. They couldn't lose so soon! France was only twenty-five miles across the Channel. He hadn't realised that the Nazis were so close. Had he been guilty of 'aggressive ignorance' too, trying not to see the danger?

He imagined the German tanks rolling along London's streets, the soldiers giving their stiff-armed salute. *'Sieg heil! Sieg heil!'*

The crash at the door as the Brown Shirts grabbed him and Aunt Miriam and dragged them away.

There would be concentration camps in England.

'At least we have Churchill in charge now,' said Aunt Miriam tiredly. Mr Churchill had taken over the week before. Georg had listened to his gravelly voice on the wireless. He'd said: 'I have nothing to offer but blood, toil, tears and sweat.'

Another prime minister might have said, 'Don't worry. We are the best soldiers in the world. We'll win.' But somehow Mr Churchill's harsh words felt better. Mr Churchill was like Aunt Miriam, who knew things.

Miss Randall looked at the big clock. 'Time for the news.' Every news bulletin was important now. Aunt Miriam reached over and turned the wireless on.

'*... and, in news just to hand, the situation in France is grim. British troops are fighting a desperate rearguard action against the German troops that surround them. The Secretary of State has ordered immediate plans for evacuation.*'

Lost in France, thought Georg. The British army are lost and we are lost.

He looked over at Aunt Miriam. Her eyes were stone. 'We'll get them out,' she said. 'Somehow, we'll get the army out.'

The army came back. Most of it, at any rate. More than seven hundred little fishing boats, ferries, pleasure boats and yachts, even a paddle steamer, crewed by fishermen, by men from the navy, by ferry captains, sailed back and forth across the shallow waters of Dunkirk where the big navy transport ships couldn't follow, taking soldiers out to the waiting troopships.

More than three hundred thousand men were evacuated over nine days.

Once more Georg listened to Mr Churchill on the wireless, still grim but triumphant now too.

Already the voice was unmistakable. The gritty words blew like sand into the quiet flat as Mr Churchill spoke of how he had feared that the whole army had been lost; how Britain would keep fighting. '... *we shall fight on the seas and oceans ... we shall fight on beaches, landing grounds, in fields and in streets and on the hills. We shall never surrender ... even if England fell,*' said Mr Churchill, '*the empire would keep fighting.*'

Georg thought of the big pink splodges on the map, and of Aunt Miriam's words: Canada and its lakes and forests; India with its fierce but too few soldiers; Africa fighting its own war; and Australia with its deserts.

If England fell how could the pink splodges keep fighting too?

Chapter 13

And still the bombs didn't fall.

The vicar, Mr Holderson, opened a school in the church hall for the children who had come back to this part of London. It was only for four hours each morning and there weren't really lessons either. Mr Holderson just handed out textbooks and exercise books, then walked between the desks to check that each student was copying out chapter after chapter.

But Georg liked the familiarity of lessons, although he didn't try to make friends. These children wouldn't cry *'Jude! Jude!'* but he was afraid they might yell 'Hun!' instead. His English was good enough to be polite in, to answer questions too. But what if a game was so exciting he called out *'Macht schnell!'* instead of 'Come on! Hurry!'?

At first there were half a dozen children. Then, as the months went by and no bombs fell on London, more children came back, till there were twenty, then more than thirty — and not enough desks to hold them all.

One of the local schools reopened soon after that. Most of the children vanished again, either to the school or to play in gangs among the lanes and the rubbish bins where the adults wouldn't notice them.

Aunt Miriam didn't seem to know a proper school had opened again. Georg was glad. The other children seemed alien now. No adults seemed to notice as they grew older. They scrawled rude words about Hitler on brick walls or sang insulting songs.

Except for one.

The girl sat in the row in front of him at the church hall, where he could look at the shine of her plaits, as black as the ink in the little ceramic inkwell that they dipped their scratchy pens into. There was always ribbon on the plaits, sometimes blue and sometimes white. Her socks were brilliant white as well, with lacy tops. Some days she wore a Scottish kilt in red with black and yellow stripes, with a white blouse. Other days it was a skirt with a pink jumper patterned with tiny shells.

Her name was Elizabeth, like the princess in Buckingham Palace, where Aunt Miriam had taken him to see the Changing of the Guard with the soldiers in their red uniforms and big bearskin hats. This Elizabeth was younger than the royal princess: eleven like him.

He would have liked to talk to her; be friends perhaps, ask her why she kept going to the church school instead of the proper one she must have gone to before. Her voice was low and clear and somehow he knew he would remember to only speak English when he was with her. But she was brought to the school by a tall woman in the grey skirt and jacket of a governess and the governess was waiting for her when school finished at half-past twelve too. Georg didn't like to try talking to her when the governess was there.

Maybe Elizabeth has never gone to school before, he thought. Maybe she'd been sick, like he was supposed to have been, and had been taught by the governess instead. Or maybe she was so precious her parents didn't want her jostled by other kids. That sort of fit. Elizabeth's skin was so white and clear and her hands looked so soft, just like a princess's.

He followed them one day — the woman in grey and the girl with her shiny black plaits — to a tall thin house in the same street as the library, near the park. After that he followed her every day, though it wasn't really following because he had to go that way too, to share his sandwiches with Mrs Huntley.

Mrs Huntley had honey that her sister had sent up from Kent and Aunt Miriam had cans of corned beef someone at work had given her. Georg didn't like corned beef, especially with the sharp pickled walnuts that Aunt Miriam loved, so he swapped his corned beef sandwiches for Mrs Huntley's honey ones. Mrs Huntley loved corned beef and pickles.

After a few weeks, Elizabeth smiled at him every morning when they started school. She waved goodbye too, as she went in her gate and he climbed the steps to the library.

One day, thought Georg, I'll ask if she'd like to come to the library with me. Even the protective governess would let Elizabeth go to the library. Mrs Huntley would make a fruitcake, one of her new war recipes that used fresh plums instead of dried fruit. He'd show her his favourite books, and then maybe the next day the governess would ask if he'd like to come to Elizabeth's home for tea.

He wondered what they ate at Elizabeth's house for tea. Clean white things, he thought, like tiny sandwiches with crusts cut off and sponge cake eaten from white plates with tiny cake forks, like Aunt Miriam used with her friends.

It was funny to be dreaming again of good things that might happen, instead of just the good things that had gone. The stories had still vanished from his brain, but at least he had his dreams.

Chapter 14

The bombs came on a Saturday afternoon.

It was hot and stuffy even though it was autumn. Aunt Miriam had gone in to work; she had to work often on Saturdays now.

There was no school of course. Georg made his bed, then washed up and swept the kitchen floor. The maid had left the flats to work in a munitions factory, so he and Aunt Miriam had to clean their home themselves now. The flat was starting to look grubby.

Neither Aunt Miriam nor Georg had ever scrubbed a floor before. They'd worked out how to set a fire, though it left them coal-stained and red-faced at first, but when Georg tried to scrub the kitchen floor it was still wet when Aunt Miriam came home, and even the next morning.

Maybe he and Aunt Miriam would try it together tomorrow, and maybe work out what to scrub the bath with as well.

He made himself a sandwich with the last of the plum jam and the bread crust, then walked past the sandbag walls in the park. Above him a giant barrage balloon floated back and forth on its

96

cables. The balloons were supposed to make it harder for German planes to fly over London.

There were no new books at the library these days — paper was precious, and few of the books that the government approved for printing were for children. He picked out some of his favourites to read again and put them in the string bag.

'Going shopping?' asked Mrs Huntley, looking up from her knitting needles. Once she would have been knitting jumpers for her grandchildren in far-off Australia, but now it was a khaki sock. All over Britain women knitted for the army.

'Just to the baker's. Would you like me to get your bread too?' The line at the baker's was even longer now.

She shook her head. 'My hubby gets the groceries. It's good when he can feel useful. It's hard on him, so many men in uniform and him not able to join up. He's talking about being an air-raid warden but it's not the same. An air-raid warden doesn't do anything, do they, except wander round the streets yelling, "Put that light out."'

The line at the baker's shop was even worse today. Georg started to read one of his books, inching forwards every time someone was served. The books in the string bag grew heavier, and his gas mask too. No one was supposed to go anywhere without their gas mask.

'Two high tops, please,' he said to the girl at the counter. The second loaf would be a bit stale by the time they ate it, but no one bought a single loaf any more, not when it took an hour to buy. Suddenly he remembered Lotte putting the basket of hot rolls on the table. Soft white bread, all soaked with butter. Cherry jam, bitter and sweet at the same time, and hot rich chocolate …

'That'll be sixpence,' said the girl.

Loaves weren't even wrapped in paper these days. He put them in his string bag. He had just reached the park when the siren went. It sounded like a wolf in pain: a howl that went on and on.

He had heard the siren before, but that was make-believe, to get ready for when it was real.

Now the real was here.

Women in headscarves or hats looked up, clutching each other. An old man swore, 'B—— Huns,' then tipped his hat to the ladies nearby and apologised, before hurrying down the street.

Everyone ran now, like ants when the school bully stamped on their nest. Georg stood with his gas mask and string bag with the bread and books in it. He was supposed to shelter under the stairs when an air raid came, with the doorman and the other tenants. But Aunt Miriam's apartment block was still ten minutes' walk away. Five minutes if he ran.

'Come on, duckie! Run!' A woman grabbed his hand and began to haul him down the street. 'Can't you hear them?'

There was a grinding engine noise far above them. Aeroplanes, thought Georg, as she half dragged him along. He peered up, but there were no planes to see. They must be still behind the buildings, out of sight. 'Where are we going?'

'Railway station. That Hitler can't get us underground.' She caught a look at his face. 'Don't you worry, duckie. Your mum and dad will find shelter too.'

Will they? wondered Georg.

The noises sounded like a giant in the sky. 'Fee fi fo fum,' the giant had roared in the fairy story. 'I smell the blood of an Englishman. Be he alive or be he dead, I'll grind his bones to make my bread.'

He shivered. There were no giants. But still he gazed up, expecting enormous planes to soar across the sky.

And then he saw them. They looked tiny, not giant. Only two, though he could hear more, far off down the end of the street. They must be above the river ... Even as he thought it, the air ripped into noise around him, something too loud to be a crash or a bang. Seconds later the ground shuddered, and shuddered again.

How could such small planes make the whole world shiver?

'Hurry, ducks!' urged the woman.

But it was hard to hurry in the crush of people. High heels, workmen's boots, shop assistants' sensible shoes, his own school shoes. He had a sudden vision of someone falling under those feet. Would anyone notice, or stop?

Georg glanced behind. Smoke puffed in black bursts into the sky. A tongue of flame licked upwards like it was trying to taste the clouds.

The air tasted strange. He wanted to cough, but forced himself to keep breathing so he could keep running with the woman.

Sudden terror struck him. Had the enemy dropped poison gas? He glanced around, waiting for people to start choking, to drop to the ground, waited to cough up blood like the air-raid warden had said.

But the cough stayed a tickle. People around him panted, even screamed, but didn't choke.

How will we know when the poison gas drops? he wondered.

They had reached the railway station now. The crowd was even thicker here. People pressed down the stairs, bumbling and shoving each other. Someone screamed, and really did fall under the press of feet. Georg tried to see who it was, see if someone had helped them up, but the crowd was too thick, the adults tall around him. When he looked back the woman who had been shepherding him into the underground station had vanished into the crush.

It didn't matter. He let himself be swept down the stairs and out on the platform. There was more room here; the air was sooty from the long black tunnels on either side, but somehow fresher too. As they came down the stairs, the crowd began to disperse along the platform, settling themselves against grubby walls and cold tiles.

Georg found a piece of wall between a fat woman, wheezing like a vacuum cleaner and gripping a string bag just like his, and a smart-looking lady with a bird's wing on her hat. He looked around, hoping to see someone he knew. The vicar, maybe, or Elizabeth. But Elizabeth must have her own shelter in her backyard, just like Aunt Miriam had a basement shelter at work. They are safe at least, he thought.

The crowd was strangely silent. Listening, thought Georg. Waiting. But we are too far down to hear anything here ...

Boom! It was more than noise. The underground platform shook and the air seemed to shudder, then whoosh away, as though it wanted to suck your eyeballs out.

He blinked to make sure his were still there, then touched his ears automatically. They rang from the noise. Funny, how you could hear your ears ringing with so much more noise around.

Women screamed. A baby began to cry.

Boom! Boom! Crash! The sound was nearer now. The planes must be right above them. It was as though he could hear every stick of the buildings ripping apart. Giant booms that were the bombs, impact, then smaller ones and also great toppling thunders as he imagined buildings fall.

Another sound ripped through the air now. Guns. Ours or theirs? wondered Georg, and then realised that he was thinking like an English boy.

Our guns fighting the enemy. The enemy that is trying to kill us, kill me, kill the women on either side, Elizabeth, Mrs Huntley and Aunt Miriam. Mutti.

He hoped Aunt Miriam had made it down to the basement. What if she'd stopped to take one of her precious files? He hoped Mrs Huntley was safe too, that she had reached home and her Anderson shelter before the bombs began to fall. Hitler had tried to kill him before; he might already have killed Papa and Mutti too — he could admit it now, in this cold tunnel that smelled of trains, with the lights flickering on and off and the chorus of people's cries. Death was real for all of them.

But now, for the first time, he knew — knew with his stomach and his heart — that the planes up there were flown by the enemy: that Hitler was the enemy. For the first time he felt the taste of hate.

Boom! This one was even nearer. A child along the platform wailed. Someone began screaming, over and over …

'Quite enough o' that,' muttered the fat woman next to him. She began to sing, her wheezy voice only just audible over the shouts and crashes.

'*My old man said "Follow the van*
And don't dilly dally on the way …"'

Someone laughed. 'That's right, auntie. Our boys aren't going to dilly dally over Mr Hitler. They'll show him what for all right.'

Everyone around had joined in the song now. Suddenly the whole platform was singing, except Georg, who didn't know the words. He picked them up soon though.

The fat woman heaved herself up and went over to the clear spot near the railway lines. She lifted up her skirts, showing stockings rolled just above the knee. Her veins were a tracery of blue among the fat. She began to dance, a strange half-shuffle, half-tap dance. Her breath heaved like bellows.

'That's the stuff to give the troops, Ma!' yelled a young man by the stairs.

The fat lady kicked up one foot, and then the other, showing an acre of pink bloomers. She curtseyed. The crowd cheered, laughing, but admiring too. They aren't just cheering her, thought Georg. They are cheering themselves, cheering all of us, because we sing instead of sob.

The crowd swung into another song. The fat lady puffed her way back to Georg, and slid down the wall next to him again. She patted him on the leg. 'We 'aven't begun ter fight,' she told him. 'Keep yer pecker up, laddie. While we can sing there's life. All we can do is carry on.'

It was night when the wail of the all-clear echoed down the railway tunnel nearly two hours later. He had shared his bread with the people around him — as well as dealing with hunger it had passed the time. He made his way slowly through the straggling crowds up the stairs.

Would there be anything left outside? What if all of London was rubble — broken buildings and cratered streets like in the photos of Spain and Belgium in the newspaper? One photo had shown children desperately seeking food in the wreckage. What if the flats had gone? What if the shops had burned down?

He stepped onto the footpath and stared around.

The world was still there. For a few seconds he looked at what remained — the baker's shop, a café — and then he saw what had gone. Gaps like broken teeth spilled rubble onto the street.

It should have been dark, but instead the street was red, flame red, fire eating what had once been a butcher's shop; there was an explosion as it found a kerosene heater.

Strangely, it wasn't smoky. The flames fanned his face but the fire forced the air upwards in a strange hot wind, leaving the street clearer than he'd ever seen it, dappled in its black and red.

Far down the street a great spire of red sparkled against a pink sky. It was almost as though someone had built a great tower while he was underground. Of course this tower would last only until its fuel was gone.

He took a step, and then another. Suddenly he was afraid to see whether the flats were there. Glass shattered like broken biscuits under his feet. He looked again at the remaining shops and saw their windows were shattered, like broken eyes staring into the street.

He tried to avoid the glass at first then let it crunch under his shoes.

There were more screams now: different screams. They were screams of horror and of loss.

It *wasn't* the world he'd left that afternoon. He looked at the white faces of the people around him and knew it wasn't their world either. But, like the fat woman said, what could you do but carry on?

He turned the corner and stopped. A body lay in front of him. For a second he thought it was a person, then he saw it was a dog, one of those few whose owners had refused to put them down at the start of the war despite the official orders, feeding them bread and their own precious rations to keep their pets alive.

Until now. He wondered who had loved this dog. He wondered if they were alive to mourn its loss tonight. He bent down and touched its fur, to make sure it was dead, not just stunned and in need of help. If it was hurt he could look after it — surely the doorman would let him look after a dog hurt in the bombing.

But the dog was already cold, despite the flames and the pink sky. It didn't even seem injured. Somehow, that made it worse.

He stood up and began to walk again. The park was free of rubble, at least. Even the sandbags hadn't fallen in the blasts. He was halfway across the park when he saw the other side.

Elizabeth's house was crumpled rubble.

He hadn't noticed before because there were no fires there, just darkness where it and the houses either side had been. He ran across the park and down the street.

'Hey, laddie, where are you off to?' It was an air-raid warden, an old man in a blue uniform and white crash hat. He grabbed Georg's arm with hands like wrinkled grapes. 'Can't go any nearer, lad. It isn't safe.' He hesitated. 'You live there?'

'No. My friend does.' It was true. Even though they had never spoken Elizabeth was his friend.

'I'm sorry, lad.' The man nodded at the wreckage. 'Nothing could be alive in that.'

'They had a shelter in the backyard.' He didn't know that for certain. But surely people who dressed their daughter in such clean white socks, and a freshly ironed tartan skirt, would make sure there was a safe shelter in the garden.

He began to run. The warden hesitated, then followed.

The street had vanished under bricks and shards of glass and other things that were just ... things, their purpose lost. Georg scrambled over to what was still almost a bit of footpath. Elizabeth's front gate was intact, still a pristine green despite the ruin of the house. For the first time Georg opened it. 'Come on,' he called to the air-raid warden. 'We can get through here.'

The man followed.

Half of Elizabeth's house seemed to have been blown entirely away, leaving a space between the rubble of the two structures either side. Her paling fence was almost intact; he instinctively pressed himself against it as a beam crashed down in the wreckage next door, bringing a thunder of debris with it.

'Watch out, lad!' yelled the air-raid warden.

The thunder dimmed to a trickle, a *spat, spat, spat* of small bits of wood … or tiles … or toys. Georg hardly listened. What good would 'watch out' do? By the time you saw a beam fall it would be almost on you.

The red sky cast black shadows in a world lit by flame. It was as though a giant held a torch up so he could see. He stopped, staring at what had been a back garden. Now it was rubble.

It looked like a child's pile of blocks, crushed in a temper. A flash of myrtle flowers peered up out of a crush of shattered tiles and splintered wood. The air was thick with brick dust.

The air-raid warden touched his shoulder. 'Too late, lad. I'm sorry. Have you somewhere you can go?'

Georg nodded dumbly. He turned to follow the man back to the street.

And then he heard it. It was like a cat's cry, sharp and weak. He heard the word: 'Help.'

He turned back. 'Where are you?' he yelled.

'Help! Please, please help!' The voice was louder now. 'We're trapped down here.'

The air-raid warden was already blowing his whistle. 'Got a live one!' he yelled. 'One, maybe more!' He shook his head at Georg. 'Rescue party will be here soon, lad.'

Georg thought of Elizabeth, down in the darkness of the buried shelter. No air to breathe, no light. Like it had been in the suitcase — though at least in the suitcase he had known that the lid would open, if he only held on. At least he'd had holes to let in air. But down there …

The wreckage might fall further and crush her. Maybe she'd run out of air to breathe.

He ran forwards and grabbed a bit of wood, then cried out as it burned his hands: not badly, but enough to hurt. He ripped off his jumper, and used that to pad his hands as he pulled at the wood again.

'Lad, leave it till the men get here —'

'She might be dead by then!' He tugged, but the beam was too heavy.

The man looked back towards the street, then up at the flames dancing in the sky. He grabbed at the beam too with his thick gloves.

It moved.

'We're coming, lady!' yelled the air-raid warden. 'Just you hold on. How many are down there?'

'Two of us.'

It was a woman's voice, not Elizabeth's. But she must be down there too.

'Me and a little girl,' said the voice. 'She's hurt. You have to hurry. Please!'

'Hurrying all we can, lady,' said the air-raid warden. 'Ah, here come the troops now.'

Georg looked around in relief — but they weren't soldiers. These 'troops' were two more old men — one even had a walking stick — and a teenage boy with pimples. One of the old men carried a stretcher and the other a shovel. The teenager had a crowbar.

The shovel was no use against shattered brick and beams, but the crowbar was. The old men worked surprisingly fast, as though they could read each other's minds. One beam, another, and then the corrugated iron that had formed the roof of the shelter. It must have collapsed when the building fell on top of it, thought Georg. But the roof had still protected the people trapped inside.

'Nearly there, love!' yelled the air-raid warden.

'Hurry. Please, hurry.' The voice was a whisper now.

The two old men wrenched the last of the corrugated iron away.

The hole was dark. The pink sky cast shadows and no light here. The air-raid warden flicked on his torch.

At first Georg could only see dirt, dark dirt, then suddenly a flash of white. 'There she is!'

Something moved: something dark as the dirt, because it was dirt-covered too. No, not just dirt, but blood. The figure rose up, the soil falling away, then gave a cry as the air-raid warden picked her up and laid her carefully on the ground. 'Where are you hurt, love?'

'My head. Elizabeth! She's still in there! You have to get Elizabeth!' It was the governess. She struggled to get up, but Georg had already scrambled down into the trench. He began to dig like a dog where he thought Elizabeth's face would be, thrusting the dirt behind. Then suddenly there she was, pale in the torchlight, her eyes shut.

Elizabeth couldn't be dead! She couldn't. All at once her eyes opened. She blinked, and whispered, 'Cold.'

'Got a blanket here.' One of the old men dropped into the trench beside him. 'Soon warm you up, love. Now come on, let's get you out of here. You, boy, take her legs.'

Her shoes were gone, but it was easy to see the white socks. Georg grasped Elizabeth's feet firmly, lifted when the old man lifted, not far, just enough to get her free of dirt. The old man gathered her in his arms.

She seemed smaller than she had at school. Her head drooped onto the old man's shoulder.

Suddenly the old man swore. 'Bandages!' he snapped. 'Harry, look lively there.'

'What is it?' Georg tried to get closer. Strong hands pulled him away.

He gazed at Elizabeth, lying on the old man's lap. The old man's hands were black as they pressed against her neck. No, not black. Red. Even as he looked more blood dripped into the ground.

And then it stopped.

The old man gave a cry. He laid Elizabeth down on the dirt. He rubbed his hand against his eyes, leaving a smear of blood.

'You can't leave her there! She has to get to hospital.'

'Shh, son. Shh.' The air-raid warden put his arm around Georg's shoulders. 'Can't help her now.'

'But you have to!'

'Bit of the corrugated iron must have ripped into her neck,' said the old man dully.

'She's ... she's dead?'

'Aye, son. I'm sorry. If we'd got to her earlier we might have saved her. Put pressure on the artery to stop the bleeding till it could be stitched. It were too late even when we got here, I reckon.'

The governess crumpled into a puddle of filthy clothes. 'It was my fault.'

'No, love.' The old man's voice was gentle. 'You couldn't see she was hurt, not down there in the dark. No one's fault but Hitler and the Jerries. Not yours. Not anybody here's.'

'You wait.' The teenager spoke now. 'Tomorrow our planes will be over Germany. They flew to Berlin last week. We'll get the Jerries back for this, you'll see.'

Georg stumbled off into the blood-tinged shadows. Bombs on England. Bombs on Germany. Back and forth and back and forth, he thought, we hit you and you hit us and round and round again. It was like stubborn bullies in the playground.

He bit his lip to stop it trembling. He had to find Aunt Miriam. She was all he had now.

Chapter 15

Crashes shook the air — different crashes now, not the dull roar of bombs but long slow crumbles as buildings stopped trying to stay up.

People had already stretched tape across the worst bits, buildings that were likely to fall down or collapse further. He dodged the tape, tripping over bricks but somehow managing not to cut his hands on glass. His palms stung a bit from the burn, but not too much.

The streets looked almost like the hospital ward when he'd cut his foot, filled with people hurt, bleeding or sitting in shock: a strange hospital, with no walls and a red ceiling that pulsed fire. Bodies lay on stretchers. No, not bodies. These people moved, cried, screamed in pain. The real bodies were laid in groups: whole families, neighbours, friends lying together in death.

An old woman sat in a rocking chair, miraculously preserved even though the house it came from had crumbled, clutching a cage with a budgie in it. Incredibly the bird was chirruping. The woman smiled at Georg as he passed, as though all that mattered was her chair and her bird.

He turned another corner, then thrust his hand into his mouth. Another pile of rubble spilled across the street.

For a second he thought it was their block of flats, then he saw it was the block next door.

Bits of brick and lengths of wall; smashed tables; a chair standing upright as though someone had put it there; a bundle of rags he hoped were clothes or towels, not what remained of a human.

There was too much debris to get to the door of their own building. He watched as men with stretchers carried people away, more men shovelled rubble, and others dug, calling out to see if anyone was still alive. He wanted to help but these men seemed to know what they were doing. He would only get in the way.

His mouth was dry with brick dust. He could feel it clogging his nose as he breathed too.

'George! Thank goodness.' A shadow ran to him out of the red-flamed darkness. It was Aunt Miriam. She hugged him to her black work coat, then coughed, her throat rough from dust and smoke too. 'I couldn't get back before. Are you all right?' She stepped back. 'Is that blood? George!'

'It's not mine,' he said tiredly. He knew he should be afraid because their building had so nearly been destroyed. He knew he should be grateful that Aunt Miriam was safe, that he was safe too. But it was as though all feeling had seeped away with Elizabeth's blood.

Aunt Miriam held him close as they looked at the rubble. She didn't have to say, 'If that had been our building, if we had been inside, we would be dead.' Hiding under the stairs would not be enough.

'Where have you been?' she said at last.

'Railway station.' He didn't mention Elizabeth. Somehow he knew he would never speak of her, as long as he lived.

Aunt Miriam nodded. 'People aren't supposed to go there. Three of them were bombed tonight.'

'People were killed?'

'Yes.' She didn't say how many. Lots, he thought dully. People at his station would have been killed if a bomb had hit them too, despite being underground. The fat woman who had danced, the younger one who had led him to what she had thought was safety.

'It was stupid to go there then?'

'No,' she said wearily. 'Hardly anywhere is safe if you get a direct hit. The shelters only protect you from debris.'

He thought of the blood and dirt on the corrugated iron. Sometimes, he thought.

She didn't ask him any more questions. He was glad of that. She didn't tell him to be careful either. Aunt Miriam might not know much about children, but she knew what they were capable of. She respected him. She knew he would do what he had to.

'I'm sorry, I shared our bread with the people in the underground,' he said.

'Good,' said Aunt Miriam. She hugged him again.

The glass was broken in their windows. The clock's glass was broken too. They pulled the blackout curtains across, though there was so much flame that Georg thought the bombers would find their way back easily. The whole of London was a torch now to show the pilots the way. They swept the glass up, taking care not to be cut by the splinters. Georg ached with shock and weariness, but he knew the glass was too dangerous to leave. If he got up in the night, barefoot in the blackout, he might forget it was there.

At last the floors were clear. Miraculously there was still water in the taps — the pipes must not have been hit. They took it in turns to wash. He tried not to see the red water swirl down into the basin. He would never see Elizabeth again. Now even her blood was running down into the pipes ...

'Your hands!' said Aunt Miriam, as he came out of the bathroom in his pyjamas.

He looked at them vaguely. One was blistered, the other a bit red. 'I must have burned them,' he said.

Aunt Miriam glanced at him swiftly, but said nothing. She fetched the first-aid kit, and spread salve over his hands, and then a light bandage. It looked white against his skin. White, like Elizabeth's socks, like Papa's face, his blood, Elizabeth's blood, red on the grass. Death came from the sky, from a plane, or you flew to it through a window.

'Go to bed,' said Aunt Miriam softly. 'I'll bring you some cocoa.'

'I don't want any.' He didn't want to ever eat or drink again.

'I'll bring it anyway.' She sat with him while he drank it, sipping her own, though he suspected she was no more hungry than he was. He felt better when he'd drunk it though. Aunt Miriam looked better too, even with the shadows black under her eyes.

'Get some sleep,' she said. 'I have to be at work at seven.' She looked at her watch. 'In three hours' time.'

'They can't expect you to come in after this?'

'It's war,' she said simply. 'We do our jobs or they don't get done. If they don't get done we lose the war. But you sleep as late as you can. Good night, George.' She bent and kissed his forehead.

'Good night,' he said.

The bombers came the next night, guided up the river by the flames still burning bright from the day before. This time Aunt Miriam was with him as they struggled through the crowd down to the station, the refuge that wasn't safe at all, but 'better than nothing', carrying a bag with a change of clothes, a Thermos of tea and sandwiches, as well as blankets and a pillow. 'Just in case,' said Aunt Miriam.

The all-clear didn't go till early morning. He was asleep on the pillow by then, rousing blearily to follow Aunt Miriam out into the fire-lit night. It seemed almost normal now to step around bodies, to see women rocking back and forth, sobbing and covering their faces, old men wandering as though hoping somehow their bombed houses might appear miraculously untouched if they searched just a little longer.

'Have you seen a little girl? Yellow hair ribbons.' A woman clutched a rag doll, as though the child might sense its presence or it would call her to it.

'I'm sorry,' said Aunt Miriam.

'I'm sorry,' she said to a man and a woman who stood clinging to each other, their children holding their knees, staring at a shop and flat as they vanished in the flames.

'I'm sorry,' she said, as they stepped between stretchers of bodies laid out on the footpath waiting to be picked up. The dead didn't hear, but Georg said sorry too. It seemed wrong to ignore them so soon.

Their block of flats still stood there. It looked different now, blank-faced. Men had come and boarded up the windows to keep out the wind and the dust. I'll have to work out how to scrub the floor properly, thought Georg. There was dirt all through the flat now. Tomorrow, he thought. I'll think about it then.

Once again Aunt Miriam made cocoa. They sat on the sofa together and drank it. It was almost cosy, the blackout curtains drawn in case a chink of light seeped between the boards. You couldn't see the wood now, or the flames outside.

At last Aunt Miriam set her alarm for an hour's sleep before she had to go to work. 'Stay here tomorrow,' she said to Georg before he went to bed. 'I mean today. Don't leave the flat unless the siren goes.'

He nodded, too tired to ask why.

―⟊◎

She was gone when he woke up. He washed — they had filled bowls with water in case the taps stopped working, but it seemed the bombs still hadn't damaged the water pipes.

He made toast for breakfast, with jam but no butter, in the dimness of the boarded-up kitchen. The paper said that there'd be sugar rationing soon. He would have liked to have a glass of milk, but even though that wasn't rationed yet, of course the milkman hadn't come. He had a glass of water instead, and turned the wireless on, then off. He didn't want to listen to it now. He didn't want to hear of horrors far away. His brain could only deal with *here* and *today*.

He had just washed up the dishes when he heard the key in the lock. Aunt Miriam took off her hat and coat, then sank onto the sofa. 'George?' She patted the seat next to her. 'George, I'm sorry. I have some news you won't like.'

'Mutti?' His voice seemed hardly there.

She looked at him blankly. 'No, nothing from your mother. There's no way she can get a message to us now. No, this is something different.'

'What?'

'My office is being sent into the country. Tomorrow in fact. We've been given twenty-four hours to get our affairs in order.'

The country! No bombs. Chickens maybe. Cows. A dog, he thought. A cottage with roses and quiet nights.

'Where are we going?'

'I'm sorry,' she said again. 'I can't take you with me.'

'What?' He stared at her, unbelieving.

'We'll be living all together, the women in one room. I can't take a child.'

'I'll be here alone?' No, he thought. Not in the darkness of the blacked-out nights. He'd had a lifetime of darkness in the suitcase. He couldn't stand to be alone in the black now.

'Of course not. I'll make sure you're safe.'

'How ...?' Realisation came slowly. 'I'm to be evacuated?'

To a stranger, he thought. Up in Wales maybe. One of the boys who had briefly been at the church school had been sent to Wales. They spoke another language there, and it was cold. The boy knew another boy who had been beaten when he couldn't bring in the sheep, but one of the girls said her foster family had been nice, just strange.

'Not to the country. Not here, anyway.' Aunt Miriam tried

to find the words. 'I've managed to get you on a ship going to Australia.'

'Australia?' He stared. The pink splodge on the map at the bottom of the world! Where Mrs Huntley's daughter lived. Where there were butterflies and ... and what else? The English had sent convicts there long ago, and now they played cricket and some had black skins and boomerangs.

'But ... but why?'

'George, things are going to get worse in England. Much worse. Most people have no idea how bad things will be. This bombing is going to go on and on. The Germans could invade at any time. There are stories of what happens when they invade countries — what they do to Jews, even to children. Australia is far away. As far as you can go across the world.'

'I know,' he whispered.

She tried to find a smile. 'You'll be safe there. In England there are so many evacuees, it's hard for people to cope. But over in Australia there are lots of families who really want to help. One ship has taken children there already. All the reports say they are settling in well.' She hesitated. 'I have a new passport for you. I told the official your old one was damaged in the blast. It's only a little change — you are "George" now on your passport too.' Just one letter changed, he thought. An 'e' to make me English for the Australians.

'Australia,' he said again. It was hard to get to England from Germany. Impossible for Mutti or Papa to get to Australia in war-time. No way even to let Mutti know where he was.

'I can't look after you,' said Aunt Miriam quietly. 'Even though I'd like to.' He thought that almost was true. 'But my job is important. Every job is important if we are going to win this war.'

He was silent for a while. She let him think. Aunt Miriam wasn't good at some things but she was good at giving you time to think. At last he asked, 'When do I go?'

'The boat train leaves at two o'clock this afternoon. I don't know when the ship sails — things like that aren't public any more in case a spy tells the enemy. But I think it will be tomorrow or the day after.'

She stood up. 'You'd better pack your suitcase — all your clothes and your passport. There'll be other papers to fill in that you'll need to keep to give to your foster family too. Toothbrush, soap. A book.'

'Only one?'

She tried to smile. 'The list said only one. I don't think they'll notice if you take more. Just one suitcase though.'

He had hoped he would never have to touch the suitcase with its tiny holes again. Now once again it would be his companion on another uncertain journey.

It had seemed so far from Germany to England. He thought of the vast stretches of blue on the map between England and Australia. How many submarines crept stalking beneath those waves? Storms, whales … The ocean was frightening. But he knew that those who stayed here faced worse dangers.

'Can we say goodbye to Mrs Huntley?'

'Of course,' said Aunt Miriam, still trying very hard to smile. 'Of course.'

—❦—

Already it seemed strange to be going to a train station when there wasn't a raid to shelter from. They walked across the park to the library first, Aunt Miriam carrying his suitcase. They had reached the pond when Aunt Miriam stopped.

The library was gone.

In its place was a heap of rubble, just like any other heap of rubble. A few pages fluttered about, but apart from that you'd never have known it had been a library, and not a house or shop.

'It must have been hit last night,' said Aunt Miriam tightly. 'Mrs Huntley would have been at home.'

In her shelter in her backyard, thought Georg, with her husband and the photos of her children and grandchildren. But not with her dog.

He hoped that the shelter had kept her safe, but there was no way to find out, not this afternoon.

There had only been two nights of raids so far. What would London be like if the raids went on for weeks, or months? No Aunt Miriam at the flat. Now no library either. Mutti, Papa, home, even Elizabeth. Would everything he ever loved vanish?

'I'm sure Mrs Huntley is safe,' said Aunt Miriam, in the too-firm tone that adults — even Aunt Miriam — used when they knew you'd never know if what they said was true or not. There was no time now to even try to find Mrs Huntley. What could he say if he did, except goodbye?

They turned back towards the station.

Chapter 16

They stood like a tiny army, almost a hundred boys and girls, some as young as four or five. He was one of the oldest; he was twelve now, though his two birthdays had gone unnoticed by Aunt Miriam.

There were no parents. Goodbyes had been said back at the station. Instead they stood silently, each in a coat, a hat, a scarf, with papers in one hand, a single suitcase in the other. Some of the little ones sobbed, but most stared dry-eyed and defiant, as though they dared Hitler to make them cry.

Around them soldiers bustled, sentries with rifles and bayonets to guard the port; and even more sailors in blue uniforms saluting, marching, purposeful. The few adults not in uniform had clipboards and showed their passes every few minutes as they marshalled the children towards the ship. There were grey-painted guns everywhere — giant ones, pointed at the sea and sky.

Georg glanced down at the strips of sea visible between the big grey ships. It looked oily, black and cold, like the darkness of the suitcase. He forced himself to look at their ship instead.

It was a big ship. Georg was glad. They were going to face a big ocean, with German U-boats below as well as bombers above. In front of their ship was the long grey destroyer that would accompany them beyond England, into the safety of the oceans beyond the usual shipping lanes where, the adults hoped, the circling U-boats and bombers wouldn't find them.

The escorts lined them up in two rows. Two of the escorts were nurses, in white veils and blue dresses under white aprons. Two others were chaplains, in clergymen's collars. The others were women in ordinary clothes. He supposed men couldn't be spared these days to take children across the world. The women were neither young nor old. They looked a bit like Aunt Miriam, not in appearance, but in the way they dressed — sensible heels and thick skirts and leather gloves — and the calm competency with which they moved.

'Come on, step lively,' called the shortest of the chaplains. 'Left right, left right. Let's show the navy how British children can march.'

Georg thought the sailors had better things to think about than how well kids marched. None of them even glanced down as the escorts marched them aboard and then down the stairs, into a large room. Their names were called out, they were put in groups of five or six and then each group marched to a cabin.

There were six bunks in his cabin. He stared at the other boys. They stared back at him, and at each other. They'd been flung together by the mysterious workings of adults.

'Now, I'm sure all of you will soon be friends,' said their escort a bit too brightly. Her name was Miss Glossop, and Georg had the feeling she might be in charge of the whole shipment of children. She looked at her list, then back at them. 'Now this is

Harris. Harris is five.' Harris had a sticky nose and swollen eyes. He knuckled away his tears.

'This is Joe Pondley. You're seven, aren't you, Joe?'

'Yes, miss,' whispered Joe.

'And Joe McIntyre, he's eight. And George and Jamie, you're both twelve, so that means you're in charge of the younger ones.'

Jamie and Georg glanced at each other in hope and suspicion. We're stuck with each other, thought Georg. At least Jamie didn't look unfriendly.

'Keep an ear out for the whistle,' said Miss Glossop. 'One sharp burst means get into bed, or lights out if you're already in bed, or time to get up. Two long whistles means you have five minutes to make sure you're dressed properly and come and stand in the corridor.'

'What do we do then?' asked Jamie.

'Wait,' said Miss Glossop crisply, 'till someone tells you what to do. Three whistles means put on your warmest clothes and sturdy shoes and coat and grab your life belt,' she gestured to the life belts on the wall, 'then stand in the corridor.'

'What happens then?' asked Jamie again.

We sink into the cold dark sea, thought Georg.

'Someone will take you to your lifeboat. But it'll be just a practice,' said Miss Glossop brightly. 'We've the big ship to look after us, and then, well, it's a big ocean. The enemy will never find us there.'

Then why do we have to practise with life belts? thought Georg. He wondered how long a life belt would keep you floating. What if you drifted off, in the sea, and no one ever found you? What if the torpedo blew up half the ship and there was no one to tell them to go to the lifeboats? Would the children stand outside their cabins, like the guards outside the Palace, not moving as they sank under the waves?

'What does being in charge mean?' Jamie gestured at the two Joes and little Harris. Georg was glad Jamie asked the questions, not him.

'Make sure they brush their teeth and go to bed when they are told and especially don't try to climb the mast or up on the rails,' said Miss Glossop. Georg had the feeling she was used to boys. She handed him and Jamie a typed sheet. It was the weekly timetable with clearly marked meal times and physical training and games times and lessons.

'Any more questions?' asked Miss Glossop.

'When's dinner?'

'When the whistle blows twice you —'

'I know. We stand out in the corridor and wait.'

Miss Glossop looked like she was going to correct Jamie for interrupting. But she didn't.

'You'll like the food.' Miss Glossop sounded resolutely cheery. 'There's bangers and mash tonight.' She bent down and whispered, 'And red jelly.'

'I feel sick,' said little Harris.

'There's a basin under the bottom bunks,' said Miss Glossop. 'Bathroom is down the corridor and down the stairs — they're called a companionway on a ship, so I suppose we should also start saying that, just like real sailors. What do you think?'

'I feel really sick,' said little Harris.

'It's going to be a wonderful voyage,' said Miss Glossop, smiling grimly. 'Now I'll see you all later.' She shut the door.

The boys stared at each other. 'Can I be sick now?' asked Harris.

But he wasn't. Instead he curled up like a hedgehog in winter on one of the bottom beds — the older boys decided they'd have the top ones and the youngest the bottom, and put their coats on the empty bunk in the middle.

Georg lay on his bunk and pretended to read. So did Jamie. He thought the two Joes were crying, but he knew they wouldn't want him to look.

It was dusk when Georg felt the rumble of the ship's engines.

'We're moving,' said Jamie. He sat up. His eyes looked red, but they stared fiercely at Georg, daring him to even think that he'd been crying too.

Suddenly the whistle blew — once, twice.

'Well, at least we're not sinking yet,' said Jamie. 'That were a joke,' he added, as the smaller boys stared at him.

'Out into the corridor,' said Georg.

They lined up against the wall, as one by one the other children came out of their cabins too. The escorts moved among them, lining them up, then two by two they marched along the corridor. The escorts called out 'left right, left right' as the children marched up the companionway and out onto the deck. Sailors strode here and there, doing whatever it was that sailors did.

The air tasted of salt and oil. The wind stung Georg's cheeks. He ran with the others to the rail. There in front of them a chubby little tug pulled the ship away from the dock and into the main channel of the Thames.

They were under way.

He was vaguely aware of Jamie beside him, of Harris and the Joes on the other side. They were strangers, but they only had each other now.

The ship crept down the river to the sea, the big grey destroyer leading the way. At last the whistle blew. They lined up again, and marched down to their cabin.

Georg looked back, but his last sight of England was lost in the dark.

—※◎

Harris wasn't seasick. But the two Joes vomited for two days into bowls that Georg and Jamie took turns to empty down the 'head'. Then suddenly they were well again, able to eat the slices of toast and jam and the porridge at breakfast and stew at night, and join in ball games on deck or sit with their age group for their lessons.

They weren't hard lessons, not to a boy who already knew the textbooks off by heart. A lot of the time was spent rehearsing songs and dances for the ship's concert. A few of the older girls said they could play the piano; and after that there was always a group singing around it.

They had exercises called physical jerks up on deck — they had to touch their toes a hundred times and then do running on the spot. There was life-belt drill and lifeboat drill, and cabin inspections by the captain, who said that their cabin was 'acceptable' (which Miss Glossop said was the highest praise he ever gave).

They marched everywhere, obeyed the blasts of the whistle, ate breakfast at exactly the same time every day, and lunch and tea and supper too.

In a strange way, despite the threat of torpedoes, of shipwreck and the cold, dark sea, and being responsible for the younger boys, the beginning of the voyage was almost peaceful. It was the first time in almost a year and a half that he had no decisions to make, no need to plan his day. Even his companions had been chosen by others. That was good too: almost like a family with younger brothers. They played tag and 'sheep, sheep come home' and 'kitten in the corner' up on deck, using chalk marks for places. At night there was his narrow bunk, and the reassuring breathing of four others.

Only Harris still cried each night, curled like a puppy around his pillow. He wet the bed too. Jamie and Georg took it in turns to get fresh sheets and rinse out the little boy's pyjamas.

Even Jamie didn't yell at Harris after the first time. The kid was scared. They were all scared and, in some deep part of them, all lost as well. You had to do your best with what you had.

Georg was making his bunk when the whistle blew. It was hard to 'make the bed' on a top bunk. He had to stand on Harris's bunk to get the seams straight, and that meant Harris's blanket got wrinkled so he had to straighten it for him again. But it was worth it for the tiny privacy the top bunk afforded.

One whistle, two whistles, three …

Three whistles! He froze.

'Just a practice,' said Jamie uncertainly. He reached for his coat, then handed Harris his too.

Georg listened to the engine's beat. It sounded different. Faster. He had the faint sense that the ship was turning too.

'Come on,' he said. 'Outside. Hurry.'

The other children muttered in the corridor. Some of them had also guessed that this wasn't just a drill. But we can't have been hit by a torpedo, thought Georg. There'd have been an explosion. We'd have felt it, heard it.

Was there an enemy plane above them? He supposed planes bombed ships as well as cities.

Miss Glossop strode down the corridor. 'Right, everybody line up. You all have your coats?'

There was a chorus of 'Yes, Miss Glossop'.

'March to the boat station then. I will explain when we get there.'

The other escorts made their way through the children to walk behind them. Will they really tell us what's happening? wondered Georg. Or will they pretend everything is all right in case we cry or panic?

The children's boat station was the First Class lounge, where the richer passengers had gathered before the war. Georg supposed there had been fancier furniture then. Not the battered wooden chairs and tables the children used.

Miss Glossop clapped her hands for silence. She looked at them for a moment, as though considering.

'I'm not going to pretend this is a practice,' she said at last. 'You are British boys and girls so I know there'll be no screams or panicking. A torpedo was seen a few minutes ago. It just missed our escort. We think the enemy submarine left before our escort could retaliate, but it may come back, so we are all to sleep here till we're sure it's safe. Now could the oldest in each cabin go down and bring up a pillow and blanket for each of their cabin-mates.'

That's me, thought Georg. He stood. He was older than Jamie by two months. He made his way with the others out of the lounge and down the companionway. Already it felt funny to be walking normally, not marching.

He tried to feel the rhythm of the sea in the sway of the boat about him. But you couldn't sense a torpedo before it hit you, could you?

He gathered the bedding quickly. He'd have liked to take a book too, but it was going to be hard enough to carry all the bedding.

What would happen if a torpedo struck when he was down here, alone? Bad enough to sink with others around you, horrible to be alone, like in the suitcase, just the dark and him.

He grabbed the last pillow and hurried out, up to the boat station. He handed out the bedding to the others. It was good to be together again. Somehow fear didn't seem as bad when it was shared with friends. At least whatever happened now would happen to them all.

~❦~

They slept in the boat station that night, a broken restless sleep. They were woken too often by kids crying out with nightmares. The lights were left on, Georg supposed so that they could get out quickly if the ship was hit.

He and Jamie checked Harris's bottom sheet the next morning. It was wet again. Harris looked scared — more scared of the other kids finding out he'd wet his sheet than of the lurking submarine.

Jamie winked at him. 'We'll roll it up and put it over here, see? No one will know. You can sleep with one sheet tonight.'

Harris nodded. 'I wish my mummy was here,' he whispered.

I wish mine was too, thought Georg. Whatever danger they

were in now, he knew that his mother — and Harris's — might be in even more.

Miss Glossop clapped her hands again. She looked like she hadn't slept at all. 'All bedding pushed to the walls,' she said wearily. 'Then I want you sitting cross-legged on the floor. Breakfast will be served here today. Just bread and cheese, I'm afraid, and cocoa.' She gave a determined smile. 'Nothing's too bad if there's cocoa, is it?'

Some of the kids smiled back.

Miss Glossop played the piano after breakfast while they sang songs instead of doing their lessons. Georg didn't know the words, but he opened and shut his mouth anyway, and followed the others when they sang the songs with gestures.

'*Under the spreading chestnut tree …*' He touched his hips for 'spread', his chest for 'chest', his head for 'nut'. 'There I sat' (a touch on the bottom) 'with you' (pointing to Jamie) 'and me' (touching his chest again).

It was a bit like singing in the railway station while the planes snickered overhead and the city turned into stones and fire. But here there was only silence outside, the rumble of the ship's engines, the sway of waves.

Lunch was more bread and cheese. Dinner was bread and corned beef. Georg ate his because that was the ship's rule: you ate everything, even your crusts. Jamie nibbled his own sandwiches next to him. No one had much appetite tonight, both from fear and because their bodies had been cramped in this single room all day.

'What happens if we have to get into the lifeboats?' he whispered to Georg.

'What do you mean?'

Jamie gestured at the walls around them. 'Takes a big ship to cross an ocean, don't it?'

Georg nodded.

'Then how can we get back to England in lifeboats?'

'Another ship will pick us up.'

'Mebbe. But who says it'll be an English ship? There's more German ships than ours, ain't there?'

'Yes,' said Georg slowly.

'So what if a Jerry picks us up?'

'I don't know.' Did they put children in concentration camps? They probably did. The children in this ship were enemies too. And he was a Jewish enemy.

Australia and safety seemed a long way away.

They slept in the boat station the next night too. We'll have to give Harris one of our sheets if we stay here much longer, thought Georg, as he tried to make himself comfortable under his blankets. But after another restless sleep, they had only just gathered up the bedding — and Harris's wet sheet — when Miss Glossop appeared again. Her face looked almost blue-white from tiredness today. Georg imagined her sitting with shark eyes, waiting for the crash that meant she had minutes, if they were lucky, to get her charges to the lifeboats and a chance to survive.

There was no need to clap her hands for silence. The children stared at her, quiet with fear.

'It's all right,' said Miss Glossop. 'The captain of the destroyer says the submarine has gone. Back to your cabins now. No lessons this morning, so you can have a nap if you want, then there'll be physical jerks out in the fresh air.' She tried a smile. 'A game of deck cricket too. Won't that be good?'

The children didn't smile. A few nodded. Most looked blank-faced. The last two nights' fear, on top of leaving their homes and the terror of falling bombs, had been more than most of them knew how to deal with.

Georg and Jamie got the two Joes and Harris lined up.

Harris tugged Georg's hand. 'Is it really gone?'

Georg nodded. 'Yes.'

'Will it be back?'

'No.' I'm lying, he thought. I'm lying so he won't cry, just like adults lie to us.

For the submarine could come back. Perhaps it was waiting till the destroyer left. Waiting till their ship was alone on the great ocean, with no one to see them when they sank. Who knew what lurked under the ocean? How could anyone see an enemy below?

—❧—

The ship sailed along, a grey ship on a grey ocean, with grey skies above.

What colour are submarines? wondered Georg. Grey like the sea, he supposed. Or black, like the ocean depths, like thunderclouds that split the world with lightning.

He tried to look down over the rail after physical jerks on deck, to see into the water. Was that a submarine shimmering in the depths? But when he blinked the image was gone.

In any case, a submarine wouldn't be close enough to see. That was why they had torpedoes that could zip unseen through the cold, dark water till they exploded, turning a ship into a sun of flames and wreckage.

Destroyers could fire torpedoes too. That was why the enemy sub had left, when their torpedo had missed before. But how long will the destroyer stay with us? he wondered. How long can it be spared to guide children across the sea?

Every day now the destroyer was the first thing he looked for, as soon as they came on deck, its reassuring bulk, the white waves in its wake, the seagulls that screamed above it, hoping the cooks would throw out scraps.

Then one morning it was gone. Overnight their destroyer had slipped back into the grey of sky and ocean to escort another ship away from England and the enemy who circled her. Now the children's ship was on its own.

'Think the sub is going to torpedo us tonight?' Jamie, like all the children, knew the destroyer had left them. He spoke in a whisper over their bread and cocoa supper at the long wooden tables.

Georg considered, then shook his head. 'Germany doesn't have enough submarines, not to guard every part of the ocean. They'd be after more important targets than us.'

'Do you really think so?'

Georg nodded.

He hoped that it was true.

It was midnight, perhaps, when Georg heard the scream. He tensed, listening for the three whistles that meant that they were in danger, but they didn't come. He sat up in his bunk and put the light on.

The portholes were all closed, with blackout curtains across them, so no enemy ship or plane would see their lights. Below him the two Joes yawned. On the other side of the cabin Jamie leaped out of bed, and stood with his fists out in front of him, trembling. 'What was that?'

'Harris,' said Georg. He swung his legs out of bed and kneeled by the younger boy's bunk. 'Harris, wake up. It's just a nightmare. Wake up.'

Harris blinked, and looked like he was going to scream again. Georg put his fingers lightly over the boy's mouth. 'Shhh. You'll wake the children in the other cabins. It's all right. Go back to sleep.'

'Want to go home,' said Harris.

'Well, you can't,' said Jamie flatly.

'Want to go home!' Harris's voice rose in a wail.

'Blimey, he's going to wake the whole ship,' said one of the Joes.

'Harris, you're going to a new home. There's lots of sunlight and ... and butterflies.' Georg searched for the little he knew about Australia.

Harris shook his head stubbornly. 'Going to be blown up,' he whispered. 'The submarine is going to get us. Going to drown in the ocean, just like Uncle Herbert. Drowned men turn blue and then the fishes eat them.'

'Shut up, will you?' hissed Jamie. He looked at the two Joes, staring wide-eyed and white-faced from their bunks.

Georg felt the boy tremble against his arm. 'How about I tell you a story?' he said.

He hadn't known he was going to say it till it came out. Once he had made up so many stories, but since he had left Germany it seemed the tales had fled.

'What sort of story?' asked Harris suspiciously.

'A good story. A ... a story about a dragon.'

'A dragon?' The other boys were listening now.

Georg thought quickly. 'A fierce hungry dragon. It was grey, with metal scales, and fire came from its mouth. It was old, so

133

old, hundreds of years old. But no one believed in dragons any more. No one was scared.

'So the dragon decided to change into the scariest thing of all. A submarine!

'It was long and grey, just like the dragon had been. It shot fire from its mouth, called torpedoes.'

The cabin was silent as they listened to his words. Heard how the dragon hunted its prey all over the grey ocean. No one could stop it, until a grey knight appeared: a British destroyer with smoke pouring from its smokestacks.

Silent through the battle, the two Joes sat side by side on an upper bunk. Harris was hardly breathing, intent on Georg's words; and Jamie wore a half-smile as he watched what was happening.

The hate Georg felt towards the enemy trickled into him as he spoke, giving him the story. Their hatred for the dragon/U-boat was drawing them together: a nation of five boys in a cabin waiting for their enemy to be destroyed.

... and then the end, as the grey dragon sank down, down to the bottom of the sea, never to roar again, leaving ships to sail safely and happily to a land of sunlight and butterflies and bananas.

'Is that true?' whispered Harris at the end. 'Has the destroyer killed the dragon?'

'Maybe,' said Georg. And it was true, perhaps. A tiny chance, but possible, that their destroyer or one like it, or a British plane, had already sunk the submarine that had tried to kill them. Perhaps now there was no enemy at all between them and safety.

Perhaps.

The two Joes were asleep minutes after the story ended; Harris slept too, with the first smile Georg had ever seen on his face.

Hating had helped.

Hating things together gave you comfort when you were scared. For the first time Georg felt a whisper of understanding how hating the Jews could help a nation desperate with war debts, its children starving, its grown-ups humiliated by the French soldiers marching along their footpaths.

He felt drained and strange and somehow more alive than he had for a long time. He and Jamie sat on Georg's bunk and shared a bar of chocolate.

'I've been saving it for something special,' said Jamie. 'Mum gave it to me. She'd been saving it too. I suppose this is as good as any. Be lots of chocolate when we get to Australia. And bananas.' He glanced at Georg. 'Why did you put in the bananas?'

Georg shrugged. He didn't know where the rest of the story had come from, much less the bananas. The chocolate was good.

'You know anyone who's ever been to Australia?'

'No,' said Georg. 'I knew a lady whose daughter and son-in-law and grandchildren live there. But she didn't know much about it.'

'I knew a kid who was sent to a farm up near Scotland,' said Jamie. 'They made him get up at four in the morning to milk the cows, and whipped him when he got it wrong. He said he had scars all down his back, under his shirt, where they'd whipped him.'

They were silent a moment. 'Do you think that's true?' asked Georg.

'Don't know. Don't think so.' Jamie swallowed the last of his chocolate. 'He never took his shirt off so we could see the scars. My dad's a farmer. Chickens. I've got to collect the eggs before I go to school. Used to anyhow. Got up at six o'clock. I want to go to a family in a town. One with a picture theatre.' His voice grew eager. 'And where I don't have to get up till seven or even eight.'

'I'd like to be on a farm.' It was the first time Georg had allowed himself to think of what the family he was going to might be like. 'With a dog and hens and ... and rabbits. Do you think they'll let us choose?'

Jamie snorted. 'Grown-ups never let boys choose. I bet I'm stuck with a chicken farmer who wants me because I know how to mix up laying mash.'

'I could ask Miss Glossop.'

Jamie considered. 'She might know.' He crossed over to his own bed. Georg stretched out the length of his bunk. He was drifting off to sleep when he heard Jamie's voice again. 'I'm glad you're here. In this cabin, I mean.'

'You too,' said Georg.

He wondered if Jamie would have said that if he knew he shared his cabin with a German boy.

In the morning Harris's sheets were dry.

───✦───

Georg found Miss Glossop unoccupied on the night of the children's concert, waiting for the girls to finish dressing up in costumes they'd made from each other's clothes. 'Miss Glossop?'

'Yes, George?'

'Do you know which foster people we're going to? I mean, each one of us?'

'Not yet. I don't think it's been decided, though the volunteer families have been selected. Why?'

'I wondered ... Jamie wants to go to a town, even though he comes from a farm, and I want to go to a farm.'

Miss Glossop gave a hint of a smile. 'I think that could be arranged.'

'Or could we — could we be together? Me and Jamie? I'd rather stay with Jamie than go to a farm.'

He wanted to ask if the Joes and Harris could stay with them too, but that might be too much for any family. And already Miss Glossop was shaking her head. 'Only one child per family. So many want to help the British Children's Appeal, you know. It wouldn't be fair to give one family two and have another family miss out completely.'

As though we are parcels, thought Georg, thank-you presents for a colony that sends its army to help the English war. What about that is fair to us? But he didn't say anything. If Miss Glossop said there was nothing she could do, there was no point.

Chapter 17

AUSTRALIA, OCTOBER 1940

Australia crept up at them, out of the grey ocean. One afternoon there was nothing but white-capped sea and a sky swept clean by the wind and as blue as a balloon. The next morning when they marched along the corridor and climbed the companionway to physical jerks there it was: a stretch of dull khaki in the distance, like the land had been painted with camouflage colours too.

The air smelled of warmth and soil, not just the tinny tang of sea.

None of the children and few of the adults on board knew which route the ship was taking, or when they would land, or even what part of Australia this was. 'Loose lips sink ships' the posters stated. What you didn't know a German spy couldn't find out. Were they looking at the pointy bit at the top, or one of the big curved sides? It wouldn't be the big flat bit in the middle of the bottom edge called the Nullarbor Plain, thought Georg, as the encyclopaedia had said that was desert.

Now, at least, the portholes could be opened. Fresh air gusted into stale cabins. At night, thin beads of light could shine onto the blackness of the sea — they were so far from Europe that there was no longer any need to hide from enemy bombers or U-boats.

Day after day they waited for the ship to head in to port. Green land turned to yellow, red and then far-off cliffs glimpsed only once through Miss Glossop's binoculars. Georg was pretty sure that was the Nullarbor Plain because it didn't have any trees on it, and the encyclopaedia had said Nullarbor meant 'no trees', but he didn't tell anyone, in case he was wrong, or in case he was right too, and was giving secrets away.

The land turned green again.

The six weeks of surging across the ocean hadn't seemed as long as the next three days. But at last, at the children's dinner at midday, one of the chaplains made the announcement.

'We'll land in Port Melbourne at quarter past nine tomorrow, or thereabouts.' He grinned as the noise rose, and for once didn't call for silence. As the chatter died down he continued. 'Half of you will be going to families there; the rest will go on to Sydney. But you'll all have a chance to see Melbourne. There'll be a bus tour up to the mountains in the morning and then a special afternoon tea. After that the following children will meet their foster parents.'

He picked up a clipboard. The children seemed suddenly to turn into small statues as they waited to hear what would happen to them. The chaplain began to call out the names. They were in alphabetical order: 'Adams, Estelle; Bateson, Samuel; Carrington, John ...'

A few kids clapped their hands when they heard their names, glad that at least now they had a solid destination; they hadn't been forgotten in the confusions of war. Others smiled at friends. But most were quiet. Grown-ups had put them on this ship and they had accepted that. Now they accepted this without a murmur too.

Jamie's name was called. Georg gave Jamie a nudge with his elbow. It didn't mean good or bad: just an acknowledgement that he had heard.

Harris's face lit up when he heard his name. Georg wondered if the boy thought his mum might be already here in Melbourne, or his gran, whether he even understood he would find only a family of strangers. But there was no point frightening Harris any more than he had been already.

The chaplain had got to 'Norland, Donald' when Georg realised that 'Marks' would not be called. He was in the group that was sailing on to Sydney. He listened as the rest of the names were called out.

One Joe's name had already been called, and then the other was too. Georg tried not to let his feelings show on his face.

All the others in his cabin were bound for Melbourne. Once again he'd be alone.

He hadn't thought that he'd have to face his foster family without any of his new friends. Yet part of him was glad that he still had a few days of the orderly ship world, especially now that the danger of torpedoes or bombs had vanished down here at the end of the world.

Another part of him wanted to get it over with. He had hoped for the faint chance that even if he couldn't go to the same family as Jamie, they might be placed in homes nearby. Even being near the Joes or Harris would be something familiar.

But packages couldn't choose where they were sent.

None of them slept well that night. The ocean with its threat of waiting submarines had been terrifying. This was safety, yet somehow the next days of waiting until they would be claimed by strange Australians were even more frightening than the sea.

They took turns looking out the porthole as the ship sailed into Port Phillip Bay. The port looked like the one they had left, just fewer ships and not as smoky and the sun still too high up in the sky.

Georg marched up to the deck with the others; and stood in a line to shake hands with the captain and the first mate. He sat next to Jamie on the bus while their ship-mates sang English songs, trying to be what the adults expected them to be: happy at being safe on dry land, instead of scared of a land of strangers. They drove through the Melbourne streets lined with houses and gardens that looked strangely home-like, his own German home, not Aunt Miriam's, as though Mutti could come out of one of those doors in her flowered dress and walk down the path.

'Wish you were coming here too,' said Jamie for the tenth time since their names had been called out.

'Me too,' said Georg, for the tenth time too.

The city centre looked like it could be part of London, except here there was clear, untaped glass in all the windows, there were no piles of sandbags, nor fires nor rubble. The faces on the street were white and there was no one wearing suits with convict arrows on them or carrying boomerangs, or even playing cricket.

It was only as they headed up into the hills that the land grew strange, the trees the wrong shape and the wrong colour, the spaces too wide with no hedges or stone walls neatly dividing them. He liked the hills better — even if the trees were wrong, the mist and the cold were familiar.

But they only stayed long enough to be marched to the toilet, and to eat the sandwiches that Miss Glossop and the others handed out. Some strange sickle-shaped leaves lay on the ground. Georg picked one up, thinking that he would dry it and send it to Aunt Miriam.

The bus journey back was more silent, no singing this time, each of them wondering what the afternoon would bring, new families or, at the very least, separation from friends.

The tea party was in a hall, with 'Welcome' on a big banner over the doorway. Trestles covered with different coloured cloths held sandwiches and small cakes with pink or white icing and pikelets with jam and bowl after bowl of sweets, though the Australian women called them lollies, which was confusing at first.

There were cream cakes too: small ones with their tops cut out and filled with whipped cream, then the tops replaced, standing up like wings. *Küchen mit Schlagsahne.*

Georg felt his throat burn. He'd be sick if he ate a cake with cream.

Then he saw the bananas. They sat at the end of one of the trestles, in a great long bunch. Georg had never seen so many before. He hadn't known they grew in bunches either.

He ate seven, one after another, peeling the skin down like a monkey, and nibbling till each one was gone. He was eating the seventh when Miss Glossop called for those who were to stay in Melbourne to report to the other room.

So he wasn't even going to see the people his cabin-mates were going to. He hoped they'd at least be kind. Georg looked around for the others to say goodbye, but the two Joes and Harris must have been near the doorway when the call came. They had already vanished. There was only Jamie. They looked at each other awkwardly across the trestles.

'See you sometime,' said Jamie at last.

Would they really ever see each other sometime? Or were they just like bits of driftwood, coming together then floating off across the sea of war? Would Jamie have still been his friend if he had known that Georg was German? He doubted it.

They had shared so much, even if some of it was built on lies. There was too much to say: things that couldn't be said even if he'd had the words. He wished, suddenly, desperately, that there was just one person he could tell his secrets to. 'I … I hope your family is nice. I hope they are kind to you,' he managed at last.

'Yours too.'

It would have been good to hug, but you didn't hug another boy. Instead he waved as Jamie marched back, his head high, a small soldier doing his part in the war.

Georg was the only one in the cabin now. He liked having a room to himself again, though he missed the others more. Everyone I like vanishes, he thought. Or maybe it's me that keeps on vanishing. Even the refuge in Australia was only till the war was over. Or maybe not for that long, if they didn't like him, or changed their minds, or found out that he wasn't an English boy called George at all.

He didn't bother trying to talk to any of the others at breakfast, or in their free time after dinner. Most of the children his age who were heading to Sydney were girls; and they had already formed their own small groups. Besides, why make a new friend now, when in a few days you'd be wrenched apart?

The coast drifted by, the same anonymous green, with blue hills or maybe mountains in the distance.

It only took a day and a night to sail to Sydney. Georg felt the ship change course and ran to the porthole.

Cliffs! Tall craggy brown ones, streaked with seagull droppings, with more of the gumtrees on top.

He wished he could go up on deck. You could see only glimpses of the world from a porthole. Even as he thought it the whistle went twice.

He dashed for the door — no need for a coat here — but some of the girls had made it out of their cabins before him. They grinned at him, not because they were first but in companionship. Seconds later Miss Glossop appeared. She was smiling too.

'Forward march!' she called.

It was the fastest march they'd ever made. Miss Glossop didn't make them keep time today. Up the companionway, into early-morning sunlight that seemed brighter than he'd ever known it. He ran onto the deck with the others and gazed around.

The ship wallowed as it changed direction between two giant cliffs, ragged and rocky and brown and topped with green. Behind them the sea was green and choppy. And in front of them …

Sydney Harbour gleamed. It was blue, not green, as though it was a sister to the sky. Every wave looked like it was tipped with the sun. Houses sprawled down between trees to the harbour edged with smooth brown rock, but there were coves too, as though this harbour was a mighty hand with a hundred fingers, each with tiny beaches at the end, and fishing boats tied up and bobbing on the water.

It looked like a city. It looked like forest and beach too. A ferry bobbed by, so close the passengers waved and cheered as they steamed by. Georg reckoned that any ship that made its way to port these days was a triumph against the enemy.

There were ships everywhere. Not just the tiny ferries with green trim and big funnels that criss-crossed the harbour as though they owned it, but pale grey ships — small ones, big ones — though none as big as the destroyer that had accompanied them for a while from England. One ship passed them only a hundred yards away. The sailors waved to the children on the deck too.

Georg thought of the grim and silent sailors on the day they had left England. These sailors looked like they still knew how to laugh, had spare minutes to wave to children.

It seemed to take forever for the ship to sail to the wharf, but not long enough either. He could have stared out of the harbour forever, grasping the rail, smelling the scents that were almost familiar from Melbourne — the smells of strange trees — and a special scent that seemed to be the harbour's own.

But they weren't allowed to see the ship being tied up. The whistle blew again. They lined up obediently and went below.

Georg sat on his top bunk, his legs dangling. He'd packed last night. Even his pyjamas were folded in the suitcase. He almost felt affection for it. It was his last link to Mutti, to home and England and Aunt Miriam. He had now even grown out of the clothes he had worn from Germany.

He'd read his books a hundred times. So he just waited, staring out of the porthole, which wasn't interesting as all he could see was the side of a big grey ship, with not even a porthole near enough to see into. The cabin was stuffy after the sunlight outside. He almost wished there were lessons or physical jerks today. He supposed the escorts wanted their charges to look as neat as possible when they arrived.

At last the whistle sounded for breakfast. He waited in the corridor, marched up to the dining room and sat at a table of girls — they had been allowed to sit where they liked after Melbourne, not only with their cabin-mates. Even though he hadn't made friends with any of the girls he didn't want to sit at a table by himself.

'No tour today then,' said the oldest girl, spooning up her porridge. Her name was Elizabeth, but Georg never used it. It would hurt to say that name now.

'How do you know?'

She shrugged and went on eating. 'No time. If we was going to have a tour they'd have let us get off this morning.'

At last the whistle came to 'fall out'. He gathered up his suitcase and his coat — it wouldn't fit in his suitcase and it was too hot to wear it — then joined the others as they stood at attention outside their cabins. Even the littlies knew how to stand at attention now.

They marched two by two down the gangplank. Soldiers and sailors bustled about them, too busy to stare. Men in overalls carried toolboxes or manoeuvred bits of wood or metal. Some of them grinned as the children passed, and gave a strange two-fingered salute.

The wharf looked old. Somehow Georg had expected it to be new. Australia was a new country, wasn't it? They marched across it into a bare room and showed their passports to men in uniforms, who stamped them quickly with a grin and a brief welcome to Australia. Each passport had to be stamped, and their evacuation papers too.

Some of the kids grinned back. Two of the littlest girls were crying again, hiding their faces in the big girls' skirts. They got into line again and marched down the footpath.

It was a grey footpath, like London's. The warehouses on either side looked like England's too. Only the harbour looked different from any stretch of water he'd seen before, glittering like someone had scattered it with jewels; and that too high, too blue sky was new as well. A tiny cloud was creeping into it now, looking timid against all that blue.

At last they came to a big stone building. They marched into the foyer, their shoes sounding hollow on the marble, and then into a room beyond.

It was a big room, with an arched ceiling, but Georg could only see the people sitting on the plain wooden chairs: couples mostly, but more women than men. They were old, young and in between. They looked eager and nervous and sort of hungry, and curious too, as they tried to work out which child was going home with them.

He gazed back, embarrassed, and as nervous and curious as they were. He'd have to spend months with these people. Years … He shut his mind to that. The last war had gone on for over four years. Impossible to think he might be in exile, in double exile, for another three whole years.

Which family was his? That woman with three chins and a smile? It would be good to go with her. Or that couple who both had big brown eyes like spaniels and an anxious look, like they wanted to be liked by their new charge too. Or the severe man with the red face, or the lady with a string of pearls and a black velvet hat with a veil?

Miss Glossop handed a list to the chaplain. He began to read the names, one by one.

They were doing it by age this time, he realised, not by the alphabet, the littlies first — he supposed so there'd be less chance of them crying, even refusing to go.

'Frances Mayland.' That was the name of the little girl clutching not-Elizabeth. She grabbed not-Elizabeth's skirt in both fists, till not-Elizabeth gently unhooked her fingers and whispered something in her ear.

Whatever she said, it worked. The girl took three steps towards the crowd, but by then the woman with three chins had rushed forwards and folded her in her arms. It must have been like being folded in a washing basket, as when she was released the little girl was almost smiling.

More names. The red-faced man and his wife got a seven-year-old boy from two cabins down, who had twice tried to climb the mast, and suddenly the man's face didn't look severe at all, but happy, as he and his wife each took one of the boy's hands.

They were down to six children now, then five, then four. Georg stared at the dwindling cluster of adults in dismay. Were there enough people left for all of them? What if there wasn't anyone for him? Would they send him back? There was nowhere to go back to. Aunt Miriam would have left London weeks before. She wasn't even allowed to tell anyone where her office was now, so no one could ever find her. Maybe he'd have to stay in this bare marble room till the organisers hunted for another Australian who'd take a strange boy from England.

Another name and another.

At last it was just him and not-Elizabeth. And there was only one couple sitting on the chairs. They looked kind, but Miss Glossop had said that no family would take two children.

He and not-Elizabeth exchanged a look as the next name was read out.

'George Marks.'

He was almost used to George now.

He stepped forwards.

It wasn't the couple sitting down. They must be not-

Elizabeth's, he thought with relief, glad that she wouldn't have to sit here alone, unclaimed.

He hadn't seen this couple in the crowd. They had been over by the door, out of sight behind the officials from the ship.

They were older than he expected. This man was big, not just tall: not fat, but with big-boned hands and face. He wore a good grey suit and held a grey hat, and his hair was grey too. His wife's hair was white, drawn up in curls around her ears under a tiny hat with cherries on it. She wore a dark blue dress, black belt, black shoes and gloves. Despite the gloves her fingers *click-clicked* nimbly at four thin knitting needles, with a rim of khaki cloth.

Not farmers then. Georg had seen farmers in Germany and they didn't look like these. He had never known any old people — both his grandfathers had died in the Great War. Papa's mother had died soon after he was born, and Mutti's mother when Georg was only small.

Miss Glossop came over to them. 'Mr and Mrs Peaslake, I'd like you to meet George Marks. George, this is Mr and Mrs Peaslake.'

She smiled at Georg. 'I wasn't able to find you a farm, I'm afraid, but the Peaslakes live in the country, at least.'

'Bellagong,' boomed Mr Peaslake, holding out his hand. The hand had calluses, and brown age spots on the back. For a moment Georg thought he was speaking another language. 'Mother here comes from Bellagong. We went back to her family place when I retired.' His voice was embarrassingly loud.

Georg shook Mr Peaslake's hand. 'Good morning,' he said stiffly.

'What's that?' boomed Mr Peaslake.

'He said "Good morning", Father. You'll have to speak up a bit,' explained Mrs Peaslake, still knitting even though she was standing up. Her voice was high and clear. 'Father's a bit deaf

149

from the shelling in the last war. Bellagong's just a little place, down on the south coast.' Georg realised Bellagong was a town. 'Our home is next to my brother's farm. And we have chooks,' she offered hopefully.

'Hens,' explained Miss Glossop.

Georg realised that the Peaslakes were as nervous as he was.

'Do you have a dog?' He tried to speak loudly enough for Mr Peaslake to hear.

'You like dogs?' Mr Peaslake's voice echoed in the nearly empty room. Georg wished he'd speak more quietly. People were looking at them.

Georg nodded.

Mrs Peaslake's face relaxed. Her hands kept knitting as though she had forgotten they were moving. 'Father, keep your voice down. You're not calling the cows home now. Do we have dogs? Only two of the most stupid animals in New South Wales.'

'Nonsense,' said Mr Peaslake, a bit more quietly. 'They're very well trained.' He picked up Georg's suitcase, and his coat too, before Georg quite knew what was happening.

'Yes, they've trained us to let them out as soon as they say "woof" and let them hog the sofa,' said Mrs Peaslake. She hesitated, then stopped knitting to give Georg a quick, efficient hug. Her hands seemed even stronger than her husband's. She had stepped away before he could work out if he should hug her back. 'You'll need to keep your bedroom door shut or Samson will be on your bed.'

'I don't mind,' said Georg.

'He snores,' said Mrs Peaslake.

'Do you have children?'

A cloud brushed Mrs Peaslake's face. 'Just our Alan. He's a lieutenant in the army. He's overseas now. Don't know where.'

'Loose lips sink ships,' said Georg, quoting the poster that warned everyone not to talk about army things.

'We really don't know where he is,' said Mrs Peaslake, her voice carefully matter of fact. 'But he'll be thinking of us, when he can, just like we think of him. And there'll be you now.'

They shook Miss Glossop's hand.

'Good luck,' she said to Georg. She leaned down and whispered, 'I think you'll be fine.'

Georg nodded. He felt scared, but it was a different sort of scared now. Not a *frightened* scared, but one that was almost hope.

Chapter 18

NEW SOUTH WALES

They took a taxi to the train, Georg in the front seat by the driver 'so you can see out', looking at the buildings and the people, all a bit like London or, at least, how it had been before the bombs. Different too — wider, steeper streets and too much light and the people strode in a way that hardly anyone did in Europe, even the women in high heels and hats, somehow brighter and brisker than the women in London.

The train station was like the train stations he was used to, echoing and big. But here no air-raid siren would bring a stampede of terrified people.

The train was just a train too, chuffing and chugging and blowing steam and cinders that floated into the carriage when they went through the tunnels till Mrs Peaslake shut the window. *Click, click* went her knitting needles. The rim of cloth was turning into a khaki sock.

Georg felt somehow comforted by the familiar click, even if the way she held the needles was different from the way Mutti did.

Mr Peaslake looked at him, as though he wasn't sure what to

say to a boy from so far away. 'Have a look at this,' he offered at last. Suddenly his teeth popped out of his lips, clacking together, then back in again.

False teeth, thought Georg. He smiled, because that seemed to be what Mr Peaslake wanted him to do.

Mrs Peaslake put her hand on her husband's arm. 'Just you leave the lad for a while, Father,' she said close to his ear. 'He'll need time to take things in.'

Georg nodded gratefully. He didn't want to talk. Talking might mean explaining where he'd come from or where Aunt Miriam was now or what was his mother's fictitious illness.

The train chuffed above its rails, stopping at each station. A soldier got on, shoving his big khaki kit bag onto the shelf above the seat. He grinned at Mr Peaslake, as though he wanted to talk, even to an old man he didn't know. 'Goin' home on leave. This your son?'

'Eh, what was that?' boomed Mr Peaslake.

'Foster son,' said Mrs Peaslake quietly.

It sounded strange. He was a son already, and not the Peaslakes'.

The soldier winked at Georg. 'Look at this, laddie.'

He crouched down on the floor of the carriage, rummaged in his pocket and drew out a handful of pennies, big and brown like the pennies back in London. His hands moved like magic. Suddenly all the pennies stood up on their edges, side by side, despite the jolting of the train.

The soldier grinned. 'Come on, laddie, knock 'em down.'

Georg bent and touched the nearest penny. Suddenly they all fell into a long shining coppery snake on the floor.

The soldier sat up. 'Me younger brother loves that trick. No matter how many times I set them up he always wants to knock 'em down.'

Georg tried another polite smile. He thought of Harris on the ship. Harris would have liked the fall of pennies. He'd have liked the clicking false teeth too.

He wondered where Harris was now.

The soldier got off at a station with a long flower garden and pots even on the platform. As the train slid away Georg saw a family run towards him, steps and stairs of children, a cluster of grown-ups, mother and father and aunts and uncles maybe ...

... and then they were gone.

The train kept clacking, but the silence grew, despite that noise. Georg glanced at the Peaslakes. Mrs Peaslake was casting off her sock now. At least she had something to do.

He looked out the window again, though it was still just more of the straggly green trees.

Suddenly a voice thundered beside him.

'*There was a wild colonial boy,*

Jack Doolan was his name,' roared Mr Peaslake. His face was expressionless, his hands at his side, his voice echoing in the emptiness of the carriage.

> '*Of poor but honest parents,*
> *He was born in Castlemaine.*
> *He was his father's only hope,*
> *His mother's pride and joy,*
> *And dearly did his parents love*
> *The wild colonial boy.*'

'Don't mind Father,' whispered Mrs Peaslake. 'He does like his poetry. He wouldn't do it if there was anyone else in the carriage. He likes to recite to the beat of the train.' *And he's trying to entertain you too, but doesn't know how.* The words could almost have been spoken. Georg and Mrs Peaslake looked at each other with understanding.

'I ... I don't mind,' said Georg.

And he didn't. The poem's words were about someone else, but somehow they seemed to be about him too, about Mutti and Papa and things that were lost and might never be found again.

> *'Come away me hearties,*
> *We'll roam the mountains high,*
> *Together we will plunder,*
> *And together we will die.*
> *We'll scour along valleys,*
> *And gallop o'er the plains,*
> *And scorn to live in slavery,*
> *Bound down by iron chains,'*

recited Mr Peaslake, a gleam of triumph now as he watched the interest on Georg's face.

That's Aunt Miriam, thought Georg. And the air-raid warden and ... and Jamie and the Joes and even Harris. That's why they fight this war. They scorn to live in slavery, bound down with iron chains.

> *'At the age of sixteen years*
> *He left his native home ...'*

That's me, thought Georg. I was only ten. Twelve when I left Aunt Miriam. How could a poem be so different from you, but make you feel the right things too? Was this what Papa felt about his Schiller and Goethe?

> 'And through Australia's sunny climes
> A bushranger did roam.
> He robbed those wealthy squatters,
> Their stock he did destroy,
> And a terror to Australia
> Was the wild colonial boy.'

Georg stared. This poem was about a THIEF!

> 'In sixty-one this daring youth
> Commenced his wild career,
> With a heart that knew no danger,
> No foeman did he fear.
> He stuck up the Beechworth mail coach,
> And robbed Judge MacEvoy,
> Who trembled and gave up his gold
> To the wild colonial boy.

> 'He bade the judge "Good morning",
> And told him to beware,
> That he'd never rob a hearty chap
> That acted on the square,
> But never to rob a mother,
> Of her son and only joy,
> Or else he may turn outlaw,
> Like the wild colonial boy.

'One day as he was riding
The mountain-side along,
A-listening to the little birds,
Their pleasant laughing song,
Three mounted troopers rode along
Kelly, Davis, and Fitzroy —
They thought that they would capture him,
The wild colonial boy.

'"Surrender now, Jack Doolan,
You see there's three to one.
Surrender now, Jack Doolan,
You daring highwayman."
Jack drew a pistol from his belt,
And fired the wicked toy.
"I'll fight, but not surrender,"
Said the wild colonial boy.

'Now he fired at Trooper Kelly
And brought him to the ground,
And in return from Davis
He received a mortal wound.
All shattered through the jaw he lay
Still firing at Fitzroy,
And that's the way they captured him —
The wild colonial boy.'

The carriage was silent again, except for the clack of the rails.

'Well, what did you think of that, lad?' demanded Mr Peaslake loudly.

Georg tried to think what to say. Who were these people who made a poem that glorified a thief? But this thief had been brave; and had only robbed bad people. At last he said: 'I ... I liked it.'

'Good, isn't it? Dinky-di too. Australian,' Mr Peaslake added when he saw Georg didn't understand. 'One of Australia's earliest poems.'

'I reckon Father knows every poem in Australia,' said Mrs Peaslake, casting on the stitches for another sock. 'Recites them even in the bath. He'd tell them at dinnertime too if I didn't stop him.'

'You like poetry?' Mr Peaslake looked at Georg eagerly.

'Yes,' said Georg. It was the right thing to say. Mr Peaslake's face relaxed into pleasure. That poem hadn't been the kind of poetry Papa had liked — the kind you had to think about or that made you shiver inside, not the story kind like this. But Georg liked it. Even — he thrust away a whisper of disloyalty — even more than Papa's kind. 'My father used to tell me poems. Every night before I went to sleep and other times too.'

'Your dad's dead, isn't he?' said Mrs Peaslake sympathetically. 'And your poor mum is sick too?'

Was that what Aunt Miriam had told the officials? He nodded, even though he wanted to yell 'No!' He hoped they wouldn't ask how his father was supposed to have died or when, or what was supposed to be wrong with Mutti.

'I'm sorry, lad. Well, I'll tell you a poem every night too. How about that?'

'Now you've started it,' said Mrs Peaslake resignedly.

'No, I really do like poetry,' said Georg.

'What did you say?' Mr Peaslake held his hand up to his ear.

'I do like poems!' yelled Georg.

'Tell me one of your dad's then,' said Mr Peaslake. He sat back, as though waiting for a treat.

Georg stared at him. He knew lots of poems. But they were all in German. He had never bothered to learn an English poem, not by heart, although he'd read some.

'Let the boy be,' said Mrs Peaslake. 'No need to go telling poems if you don't want to, George.' Her face clouded. 'Sometimes remembering hurts.'

Suddenly he remembered the last poem Papa had ever told him. It was short, so short he could remember too the translation. He began to speak, tentatively at first; then it seemed like the poem knew its own way from his mouth. It felt funny to have to say a poem about peace so loudly.

> *'Quiet touches the treetops,*
> *The breeze hardly breathes*
> *Through the leaves;*
> *The tiny birds are silent in the forest.*
> *Wait ...*
> *Soon you'll be at rest too.'*

'I ... I'm sorry it doesn't rhyme.' He hoped the Peaslakes didn't ask him who had written it. They'd be shocked to know it had been written by a German. Might even — he bit his lip — suspect there was something strange about him. Maybe he shouldn't have said it at all.

'Poems don't have to rhyme. It's a good poem,' said Mr Peaslake. 'Poems have to make you feel in here.' He banged his fist against the tweed jacket above his heart. 'That's what matters, not the rhymes. "The tiny birds are silent" — yes, that's a good line.'

Mr Peaslake looked out the window. The trees had changed to fields while they'd been talking. He stood up and grabbed Georg's suitcase. 'Next stop's ours.'

This station was even smaller than the others. It had flowers too, in boxes and baskets and in long beds on either side of the yellow-painted ticket office and waiting room.

They climbed a set of tall metal stairs that led over the tracks and waited at a bus stop, where they ate lamb and pickle sandwiches and slabs of fruitcake, sweet and buttery, that Mrs Peaslake produced from her handbag. Georg wondered if it had a small universe in it, as well as food and balls of wool and the handkerchief she'd used to wipe the soot smuts off his face and Mr Peaslake's. The bus finally muttered along under more of the strange hanging trees.

The bus was half full. Old or middle-aged men lifted their hats — old hats with hair-oil stains or worn fingerprints at the edges where they lifted it; and women in comfortable floral dresses and straw hats murmured greetings. They stared at Georg with curiosity and friendliness as the Peaslakes got on, Mr Peaslake still holding Georg's suitcase and coat. They found two seats at the back — one for Mrs Peaslake and Georg and the other for Mr Peaslake.

Georg gazed out more intently now. This was the country where he had to live: strange untidy country, its fields too big, not rectangular enough. The cows stood a long way away beside ponds that looked ragged and unkempt too. Even the trees didn't have enough leaves. Their bark looked torn and tatty.

Georg got the feeling that this was a land that didn't care about people. The grass was brown and the green of the trees was faded. Every colour looked slightly wrong — even the too-rich blue of the sky.

He glanced at Mr Peaslake, hoping he wouldn't break into poetry again. It would be embarrassing with others in the bus.

But he didn't.

The bus rounded the corner and suddenly he could see the sea, vivid and sparkling, the waves white-capped as they rose and fell onto a slip of beach.

It was the first truly beautiful thing he had seen since Sydney Harbour. The bus trundled past a headland and they lost sight of it, then there was the ocean again, a glimpse, then gone. He craned his head to catch a final look.

Mrs Peaslake touched his hand gently, then withdrew it when he jumped. 'Like the beach, do you?'

He'd never been to the beach. Never seen it except for the day the ship left Southampton. But an English boy would be expected to have gone to the beach, so he nodded. The memories of playing in the water at the lake's edge shone through the dimness of the last year and a half.

'Good swimmer?'

'No. I can't swim.'

'Soon teach you. The beach is only ten minutes' drive from our place, though we have to walk it now with petrol so scarce. Get the sea breeze at our place too. You'll need a jumper if there's a southerly.'

Georg didn't know what a southerly was, but he nodded anyway as the bus drew to a stop.

He saw a dozen houses, brick or wooden bungalows with verandahs and not much garden, a small stone church, a single shop and two of the long untidy fields before a tiny wooden building painted dull yellow. It had a sign that said 'Bellagong Public School'.

Georg stared at it. It was so small! How could a real school be as little as that? His classroom back in Germany could have sat on it and hidden it completely.

No proper playground, with swings or a slippery dip, just ground worn to dirt by many feet. There was a big tree — a normal tree, not an Australian tree — in the corner and three ponies peering over a wire fence.

They didn't ride horses at Australian schools, did they? He'd fall off!

'School on Monday,' said Mrs Peaslake, as the other passengers filed off the bus. The Peaslakes made no move to join them. 'You've got the weekend to settle in.'

Georg realised that he had no idea what day of the week it was. The only day that had been different on the ship was Sunday, when there were no lessons and a longer prayer service. He asked, cautiously.

'It's Friday,' said Mrs Peaslake. She looked at the watch on a chain around her neck. 'Four thirty. You'll be perishing for your tea, I expect.'

The bus jerked forwards again, around a corner past the houses, around two more corners and along barbed-wire fences, more brown and white cows looking up curiously as they passed. They pulled over, although there was no sign of a bus stop.

Mr Peaslake lifted Georg's suitcase and coat, then let Mrs Peaslake and Georg precede him down the aisle and out onto the roadside. 'Thanks, Harry,' he said to the driver.

The bus pulled away, and turned back to what Georg supposed was big enough to call a town.

He looked at what was going to be his home, for a while anyhow.

He had hoped, somehow, that it might be like home — his real home — with its attic bedroom, its neat hedges, the quiet library of Papa's books.

This was big and messy.

At first all he could see was garden: shaggy green bushes in a hedge along the front; a red-painted gate that opened to a path with garden beds on either side; and tangled yellow and red flowers.

And then the house, two steps up to a wide verandah, with a sagging old sofa on it and a sprawl of windows on either side.

He supposed the house was a bungalow, but even though it was only one storey it looked too rambling to be called that. It seemed to have grown, rather than been built. It didn't fit into any category of 'house' he knew. Poor people lived in cottages or dirty rooms in tenements. Kings lived in castles. People like his family lived in neat two-storey houses or proper flats like Aunt Miriam. But this was much too big to be a peasant's cottage.

He had only just taken it in when there was a flurry of woofing. Two dogs bounded off the sofa down to the gate, jumping and grinning, their tails wagging in delight. They were big, brown and shaggy with long black noses.

Georg stepped back warily. The dogs he had known before were small ones who trotted neatly beside their owners. These looked like wolves. Australia had wild dogs, didn't it?

'Are ... are they dingoes?'

Mrs Peaslake laughed. 'Bless the boy, no. Down, Samson! Delilah, behave yourself. I said down, girl! Down! This is George. George, put your hand out, so they can sniff it. That's right. You can pat them if you like.'

'Down!' roared Mr Peaslake. The two dogs reluctantly lowered their tails onto the path. Georg offered a hand cautiously.

The dogs stood to sniff his hand, quieter now, though their tails still wagged like they were practising semaphore. They weren't quite as big as he had thought. Their bouncing had made them seem larger.

He reached out carefully and patted one on the top of its head. Its fur felt like Tante Gudrun's velvet cushions. The dog sat again, staring up at him adoringly.

'Now if you give her a biscuit she'll be your friend for life. Come on. Both of you,' said Mrs Peaslake. 'You must be starving for your tea.'

Chapter 19

BELLAGONG

The front door opened to a wide corridor with a floor of wooden boards and a carpet runner. There were doors off either side. The house was at least as big as his back home, but curiously unfinished: no carved woodwork, no paintings on the walls.

The dogs galloped past them, ears flying, into a room beyond.

'Lounge room's in there.' Georg caught a glimpse of a room overstuffed with floral-covered chairs, flowered wallpaper and a fat sofa, with crocheted antimacassars on the back of every chair in every colour possible, and a tall, battered-looking piano, its top covered in framed photographs.

'There's the dining room, but we'll eat in the kitchen tonight. That's Mother's sewing room. Don't mind the mess. Kitchen here.' Georg peered into a cramped room with a wooden table, most of its paint scrubbed off the top, a dresser with plates and cups, and a giant black stove, lace curtains and framed photos on the walls.

The two dogs flung themselves down on a braided mat by the stove. Mr Peaslake led Georg down the corridor past a bookcase full of books with faded covers and opened a door.

'This is your room. The bathroom's the last room down the hall. Put it in just before the war. Got a bath and everything. Dunny's down the backyard.'

'Dunny?'

'Toilet,' boomed Mr Peaslake. He put the suitcase down as Georg followed him in.

Georg bit his lip. Poor people had outside toilets. He had never used one.

But this didn't look like a poor person's bedroom. It was big, with wooden blinds closed against the growing darkness, and a wood floor. There was a battered wardrobe and chest of drawers, a small desk with a chair, a bed with a woollen patchwork comforter and, on top of that, a kite, the biggest Georg had ever seen.

'Is … is this your son's room?' He wondered if he'd be allowed to fly the kite.

'No, Alan's is opposite. Just as he left it,' Mr Peaslake added, a bit too firmly. As though while the room remained safe Alan Peaslake would be safe too. 'No, this is yours.'

'The kite too?' asked Georg cautiously. He'd seen kids playing with kites, but never tried flying them himself.

'Made it for you myself when we heard you'd be coming. Don't suppose you like kites?' The loud voice was hopeful again.

'I've never flown one. I've always wanted to though.'

Mr Peaslake's wrinkles danced as he grinned. 'Used to fly kites every Saturday afternoon with Alan, up on the cliffs in the sea wind. I made him a Chinese dragon kite for his birthday once. Got box kites in the shed as well as regular. We had a club when I worked up in Sydney. Used to make all kinds …'

His voice trailed off. Perhaps he realised that Georg needed time alone.

'You unpack,' he said. 'Tea'll be ready when you are.'

Georg tried to work out what the phrase meant. Was 'ready when you are' Australian, or an English term he hadn't learned? At least here the Australians might think any mistakes he made came from being English.

He opened the wardrobe and put his clothes away tidily, leaving his pyjamas out on the bed, then went down the corridor, following the sound of the voices to the kitchen.

'... funny little thing,' he heard the too-loud voice say. 'Looks too scared to say boo to a goose.'

'Terrible time for a child in London now,' said Mrs Peaslake. 'Good thing he's out of it, at least.' She looked up as Georg came in. 'Here, have the seat by the stove.'

The room smelled of cake and what he supposed was dog and of course of wood smoke too.

Only servants ate in kitchens, but this kitchen looked like it was the most lived-in room in the house. Somehow it had changed with Mrs Peaslake in it. A white cloth with flowers embroidered at each edge covered the table. The silverware gleamed. Willow pattern plates stood on the bench by the stove. There were pots already steaming on the stove even though they'd only just arrived, and a black-topped loaf of bread was already cut. Mrs Peaslake put a cream jar filled with pink flowers on the table in front of him as he sat down, then turned back to the stove and bench.

Her hands flew, swift and efficient, mashing, stirring, ladling food out onto plates. Georg wouldn't have been surprised to see her knitting as well as cooking. But the wool and needles lay beside what he supposed was her place at the table.

It was warmer now, he supposed from the wood stove. Mrs Peaslake must have damped it down when they went up to

Sydney to collect him, then added more wood to the firebox as soon as they'd come in. The smell of a burning wood stove was the first thing that had reminded him of home.

He looked up at the photos on the dresser. There was one of a man in an army uniform: their son. 'Is that Alan?' he ventured.

'Took that just before he joined up,' said Mrs Peaslake. 'Enlisted the day he left school. Didn't even tell us he was going to, just came back proud as punch. He's a full lieutenant now.'

'You told me.' He glanced at Mrs Peaslake. There was more than pride in her voice, her face. Is my face like that when I think of Mutti and Papa? he wondered. Is there always a hint of fear behind my eyes?

Mrs Peaslake put a plate in front of Georg. 'I hope you like chops. We get our lamb straight from next door.'

Georg had a vision of tiny lambs marching up to the Peaslakes' back steps. The thought made him feel slightly sick. He thrust the image away and looked at his plate. Three chops, a pile of peas, mashed potatoes all buttery, boiled carrots.

The hunger returned: hunger he hadn't even known he'd lost.

Samson and Delilah leaped to their feet as the food was put on the table, tails wagging, slight slobber on their lips. Delilah nudged Georg's leg with her nose.

'Down!' roared Mr Peaslake.

The dogs took no notice. Georg tried to imagine dogs at the table in any of the neat homes he'd known in Germany, or Aunt Miriam's flat. He couldn't.

'There's apple crumble for pudding,' said Mrs Peaslake.

'You like apple crumble, don't you, George?' asked Mr Peaslake.

He looked so eager that even though Georg had never eaten

apple crumble (although he thought he might have seen it on menus in London cafés), he said yes.

He ate what he could. It was all good, with sort of bright flavours — the food on the ship had all tasted the same — but he was too tired to eat the giant portions on the plate. Samson and Delilah stared at him, their expressions saying, 'We are good dogs and so we won't grab the chops from your plate but when you are finished we'll gobble what's left.'

'Look at the lad. He's half asleep. Come on, George, I'll run you a bath while you finish up your crumble.'

The bath was big and deep. The only baths on the ship had been tin tubs filled with salt water that left your skin dry and itchy. There had been no time for baths during the air raids and hot water had been in too-short supply to have a deep bath anyway the last year.

He lay in the hot water till it cooled, then listened to it gurgle down the plughole. He hesitated.

He needed the toilet, the — what had Mr Peaslake called it? — the dunny. But it was in the backyard. It looked dark and strange out the window and he had no idea if a dunny was like the toilets he had known.

At last he urinated down the plughole, running the water over and over and hoping the Peaslakes wouldn't guess what he had done, then wrapped himself in the towel. Mrs Peaslake passed his pyjamas to him as he padded past the kitchen door. 'Just stuck them in the oven for a minute. That's the beauty of a wood stove.'

They felt wonderfully warm. He slipped between the thin cotton sheets and then discovered a hot water bottle in a woollen cover in his bed.

Mr Peaslake stuck his head in the door, the dogs at his heels.

'Ready for your poem?' The booming voice didn't sound as loud here as it had in Sydney, as though the fields outside absorbed it.

He wasn't sure anything else would fit in his brain today. But he nodded.

Mr Peaslake sat on the bed, his weight making the mattress sink. 'This one's called *The Man from Snowy River*, by a bloke called Paterson. It's a good 'un. Alan always loved it.'

> '*There was movement at the station, for the*
> *word had passed around*
> *That the colt from Old Regret had got*
> *away ...*'

It *was* a good poem, and a long one, about an Australian boy who managed to round up wild horses when the adults failed. A poem that told a story, just like the last one.

Somehow the poem made him feel better. It wasn't like Papa telling him good night. But it was as though his brain had been given a signal: you can rest. In a funny way the poem had made him feel he really was in Australia too.

'Good night, laddie.'

'Good night, Mr Peaslake.' He tried to speak loudly but without shouting. 'Thank you.'

'My pleasure,' boomed Mr Peaslake. 'We've all got to do our bit against the enemy.' He grinned. 'You're one of the best bits.'

Mrs Peaslake appeared behind him, a book in her hand. 'Thought you might like to read this before you drop off. It's about a kookaburra called Jackie. You'll hear them laughing in the morning.'

'Kookaburra?' He stumbled over the word.

'They're birds. Laughing Jackasses they're called too. You'll know them when you hear them.' She hesitated, then dropped a kiss on his forehead. 'We're so glad you're here, George. Turn the lamp off when you're ready to sleep.'

'And don't you worry, lad,' said Mr Peaslake. 'You're safe here. And we'll have the Jerries on the run soon. You'll see.'

Mrs Peaslake turned off the overhead light and shut the door as she went out. He heard the dogs' toenails click along the hall behind them.

He picked up the book and looked at it. Not too young for him and just the type of book he wanted to read too. A book about an Australian bird.

He lay back on the pillow. It was all a boy called George could ever want: the kind people, the big dogs.

But it was all for an English boy. Not a German boy called Georg.

Chapter 20

He slept deeply and dreamlessly, then found himself awake, wondering why the ship was still, why his bed didn't roll. It took him a moment to realise where he was.

It was still dark. The room smelled of old wood and books and ironed sheets. He found that he was crying for the first time in months: crying for Mutti, who was far across an ocean, who he couldn't even name or talk about; and for Papa.

Papa who was dead. Somehow, being so far away made it easier to accept that now.

He suddenly realised that if Aunt Miriam died, if the bombs got her, then Mutti might never find him again, nor he her. How did you find a boy who'd sailed across the world? Who had changed his name and country?

At last he slept again.

꧁ꕥ꧂

It was still early when he woke. The light was different here: hard bright light, like it had been on the ship the last few weeks, but softened by the green of grass and trees. But this was early-morning light.

The house was still.

He dressed quietly and tiptoed out to the kitchen. The wood stove still gave out its warmth. Next to it on the bench was a big enamel dish covered with a damp tea towel. He lifted it up and saw it was bread dough, all puffy.

The dogs looked up from the mat by the stove. One of them — Samson? — thumped his tail before he put his head down again when Georg made no move towards the pantry and food; Delilah got to her feet, stretched, yawned and padded after him.

Through a scullery, with big sinks for washing vegetables, and shelves with cans and bottled fruit, and an enamelled food safe as well as a strange tall box thing that smelled of kerosene; then through a laundry with a bare concrete floor, out the back door past a pot of mint and two funny steel tanks up on wooden platforms. He could see a big barn, open at one side, and a paling fence that turned out to surround a giant vegetable garden when he peered over it — rows of cauliflowers and cabbages and other plants he didn't recognise, but suspected were vegetables too.

He looked around. Hens clucked in a wire run with a corrugated-iron shed. There was row after row of trees, proper trees, for when he got closer he could see small fruit on the branches among the leaves, too tiny yet to tell what kind they were. The trees were all thick-trunked, and higher than the house.

And that must be the dunny. It looked like a sentry box, with a strange tangled vine over it. He opened the door cautiously.

It smelled funny. There was no porcelain cistern, but a sort of wooden box with a lid that he lifted tentatively. A spider ran off, down the side. He looked down the hole, but it was too dark to see much. His nose told him what was down there though.

He sat cautiously, hoping the spider didn't come back, then looked for the toilet paper. There wasn't any, just sheets of torn newspaper jabbed onto a bit of wire. Was that what he was supposed to use?

He was just about to put the lid down when he noticed the bucket of sawdust with a battered tin cup in it. So that explained part of the smell down the hole, and why it didn't stink more too. He put a couple of cupfuls down the hole, then washed his hands at the garden tap.

Delilah dropped a stick at his feet. He picked it up and threw it. She bounded off and grabbed it as soon as it had fallen, then trotted back, but not to him. She stopped at one of the biggest fruit trees, and looked up, wagging her tail slowly.

Georg looked up too.

A face peered down at him — a girl's face, slightly grubby, brown hair falling out of two pigtails. She wore what looked like a boy's old shirt and shorts. Her feet were bare, black and calloused on the soles. He remembered Elizabeth — the first one, not the one on the ship — with her soft skin like a white peach, her neat black hair. This girl couldn't have been more different.

Was her family too poor to afford shoes and proper clothes for her?

'Hello,' he ventured, slightly embarrassed that she must have seen him go to the dunny. 'What are you doing up there?'

'Waiting for you.'

'You knew I was going to be here?'

'Course. Everyone knows you've come. Your name is George like the King and you're escaping the Nazi menace.' It sounded like she was quoting someone else's words. 'And we have to be nice to you 'cause you've been bombed and we can't ask you lots of questions in case you're homesick or a spy hears about your ship. I'm Mud.'

For a second he thought she was talking about the smudge on her face. 'Mud?'

'Well, it used to be Maud. But on my first day at school I tried to write my name and left out the A. The big girls called me Mud. They meant to be nasty but I liked it. I like mud. It grows things. We wouldn't have things to eat if it wasn't for mud.' She held out a hand. Her fingernails were torn and dirty. 'Come on up.'

He glanced back at the house. 'The Peaslakes may not let me climb trees.'

'What?' She peered down at him as though he had grown donkey ears. 'Of course they'll let you climb trees. What are trees for?'

For fruit and shade and wood, he thought, but didn't say. Instead he clambered up, careful not to tear his shorts, and sat on the branch beside her. Delilah lay down, resigned, below them.

'The girls at school — are they all nasty?'

'Nah,' Mud said scornfully. 'Not once you know how to handle them. Those ones've gone now anyhow. Amy is working at a factory in Wollongong and Morna married one of the Stoker boys. You and me are the oldest in the school now. There're only nine of us,' she added.

'In the whole school?'

Mud nodded. 'And they're all younger so you and me have to be friends because there's no one else. I asked Uncle Ron for a girl,' she added. 'But they came back with you. Maybe all the girls were taken.'

'Uncle Ron?' He felt strangely flattened that they'd wanted a girl. Or maybe they hadn't. Maybe they'd chosen a boy, chosen him, but not told Mud.

'Mr Peaslake. Mrs Peaslake is my Auntie Thelma. She's Dad's older sister. We live over there.' She pointed in the direction of a hill, past another mob of slowly chewing cows.

'Do you like the Peaslakes?' He suddenly wished they'd asked him to call them Aunt and Uncle too.

She looked surprised. 'Course. Uncle Ron's grand. He used to be a bank manager up in Sydney. Auntie Thelma was *really* old when she had Alan. When Uncle Ron retired they came down here. Do you know he makes kites? He takes me kite-flying on Saturday afternoons unless we've got to help Dad with the fencing.'

He felt a pang of jealousy. Mr Peaslake hadn't mentioned Mud, or that there might be someone else sharing their kite-flying excursions.

'Auntie Thelma's the best gardener in the world. She wins first prize every year for her pumpkins. She even cooks better than Mum. Well,' she allowed generously, 'maybe Mum is better but she's busy with the farm now the boys are away. My brothers,' she added, at his look. 'Ken and Len are in the army in Malaya; Kenny's a corporal. It's just Mum and Dad and me at home now.'

'It must be hard with them all away,' Georg offered tentatively.

'I can do anything they can do! Uncle Ron helps,' she added. 'You can help now too.'

'What sort of farm do you have?'

'Cattle. Herefords. Eight hundred head. Twenty-three sheep too, but they're mostly for meat for us.'

'You milk *eight hundred* cows?' He thought of Jamie's story of early-morning milkings and beatings if you got it wrong. How long did it take to milk eight hundred cows? Though if they had land for eight hundred cows then they couldn't be all that poor, could they?

She laughed. 'We don't *milk* them. Well, only two of them; and just Daisy now — she's Mum's pet. I brought the milk over this morning. Herefords are *beef* cattle.'

'To eat?'

'Of *course*.' She looked at him curiously. 'Have you ever been on a farm before?'

'No.'

'Never mind,' she said comfortingly. 'You're here now. I'll show you the beach later. Maybe Auntie Thelma will make a picnic. You want to watch me climb this tree to the top?'

'How can you climb right up there?'

'Easy. I can do *anything*.'

'Anything?'

'I bet I can. If I try.'

'You couldn't fly.'

Mud considered. 'Yes, I could. It'd just take me a while to learn how to work a plane.' She stood up, her bare toes slightly curling around the branch. 'This tree is simple.' As Georg looked she tucked her legs around the trunk, pushed, then reached up for the next branch, and then the next and then another —

Delilah barked and stood up.

'George? Breakfast's ready.' Mrs Peaslake wore an apron and her hands were still clicking her knitting needles. 'Mud? I might have known. Do you want some breakfast or have you already eaten?'

'That was *hours* ago.' Mud peered down from almost the very top of the tree. It swayed alarmingly, but Mrs Peaslake didn't seem worried.

'It'll be ready when you are,' she said. Georg had worked out what that meant now. Delilah pranced at Mrs Peaslake's heels as she went back in.

~♒☙

Mrs Peaslake's hands again seemed to flash all over the kitchen. The knitting lay on the table, ready to be picked up in any spare moment. The dough from the enamel bowl went into long tins then into the oven. *Crack*, *crack* and eggs from the bowl on the bench went into a saucepan, one hand stirring while another added butter — not butter from a neat rectangle but from a deep yellow dish that had been taken from the strange box in the laundry which was called a refrigerator. It kept things cold.

Snip went her hands as she added chopped green stuff, moving smoothly over to the metal bucket with a lip to pour out milk into two big glasses. The milk frothed as it filled the glasses. Mrs Peaslake handed one glass over to him with a smile.

He looked at it cautiously. This milk had been inside a cow this morning. Inside a *cow* …

He sipped, then drank some more. It was cool and somehow thicker and sweeter than any other milk he'd ever tasted.

Mrs Peaslake put plates of scrambled egg on the table, one, two, three, four. Her hands hovered over the fifth place, by an empty chair.

Alan sits there, realised Georg.

Mrs Peaslake sat too, and began to eat, casting glances behind at the big-ridged plate on the top of the wood stove, where the toast was browning. She seemed to know instinctively when to flick it off and put on another slice.

'Plum jam, honey or Vegemite?' she asked. '*Down*, Delilah. You've had your breakfast.'

'What's Vegemite?'

'They call it Marmite where you've come from,' rumbled Mr Peaslake, busy with his scrambled eggs. 'Delilah, *down*!' The dog subsided briefly onto the rug by the stove, drooling slightly at the smell of eggs and toast.

Georg didn't like to say he'd never tasted Marmite either. He watched Mud slather the home-made butter on her toast, then spread black stuff from a jar on it. It looked a bit like grease: not like jam at all.

He placed a bit on the corner of his toast, then bit it. It tasted like grease too, but salty. He could feel the flavour run down his throat. He wondered if he could spit it out. Suddenly Delilah's head appeared on his lap. He spat the toast quickly into his hand, then passed it down to her. She swallowed it in one great gulp, then licked his fingers.

Georg reached for the plum jam instead. Mud grinned at him.

'I like him,' she said to the Peaslakes.

'That's good,' said Mrs Peaslake calmly, spreading butter and honey on Mr Peaslake's toast.

'Why?' asked Georg. The question surprised him. He had been quiet for so long, asking questions only when he had to.

Mud reached for her fifth piece of toast. 'Because you didn't say I couldn't do anything I want to do; you just wanted to know how. And because Delilah likes you. Dogs always know. You talk funny though.'

Georg froze. But Mrs Peaslake was smiling. 'It's an English accent.'

Mud nodded. 'Like on the wireless.' She looked at Georg sympathetically. 'You can't help speaking posh. But don't worry. If anyone laughs at you I'll use my secret weapon on them.'

'What secret weapon?'

'It's a secret.' She looked back at the Peaslakes. 'Can George and me have a picnic?'

'After chores, this afternoon. And no going down to the beach unless we come too. George can't swim yet.'

'Can't *swim*?' Mud made it sound like he didn't know how to breathe.

'Nowhere to swim in London,' said Mrs Peaslake. 'And it's too cold most of the time.'

There had been the river, but Georg had never seen anyone swim in the Thames.

'He'll learn soon enough.'

'And tomorrow I'll show you how to milk Daisy — George thought we milked *all* the cows — and then, after church, you can help us bring the cattle in. I don't suppose you can ride a horse either,' said Mud. 'And the next day we can go to the bushranger's cave — you have to climb around the cliff to get to it.'

'Next day's school.' Mrs Peaslake was smiling.

'Well, next Saturday after chores then. You can come to the bushranger's cave too if you like,' she added to the Peaslakes generously.

School. It sounded ...

Normal. Day after day of school, and no bombs, and other children: smaller ones, not nasty ones.

He looked at Mud, happily eating her sixth piece of toast, and slipping the crusts to Samson under the table. Despite the wrong colours and the strangeness, it sounded good.

And suddenly it seemed he had found a friend — or she had found him. He grinned: a friend called Mud.

Chapter 21

The first chore, it seemed, was feeding the hens. Mud grabbed the bucket of scraps that stood on the bench out of Delilah's reach, then looked at Georg's feet. 'Why are you wearing shoes?'

Georg stared at her. 'I don't understand.'

'*Shoes*,' she said, as though repeating it would make him understand. 'It's not like we're going to church or a party or anything.'

He looked down at her bare feet. 'I always wear shoes.'

'It's cold in England,' said Mrs Peaslake comfortably. Mr Peaslake had already gone out. 'All the children wear bare feet here. You don't want to wear out your good clothes either. I've put some old ones of Alan's on your bed.'

They *wanted* him to go without shoes? And wear old clothes? And their dunny was in the backyard ...

But the Peaslakes didn't seem poor, even though they didn't have a maid or gardener. Mr Peaslake had mentioned a car — even the Rektor of the University hadn't been able to afford a car — and the wireless on the dresser looked new.

'Come *on*,' said Mud.

He was leaving his old life behind with his shoes. The bare floorboards felt funny under his toes. He walked out carefully as Mud shoved the back door open. She led the way down to the hens, who saw them coming and clucked excitedly behind the wire.

'Chooks don't like orange peel,' said Mud. 'So don't put any in the scrap bucket. Or lemon peel.' She opened the gate and threw the scraps in. The hens fussed happily around the pile, then settled down to eat.

Georg tried not to look disgusted. 'They eat in the dirt?'

'Chooks like dirt. Dirt is good. I told you. They bathe in it too.'

Was she teasing him? 'You can't bathe in dirt.'

'You can if you're a chook. They fluff up and the dust cleans their feathers. They comb it out with their beaks.'

'But they'd be dirty!'

'Do they *look* dirty?' asked Mud patiently. 'It doesn't stick to them. Not unless it's wet. It takes away mites and fleas and things.'

'Hens have fleas?'

She looked at him curiously. 'You don't know anything, do you?'

He thought a boy from London wouldn't know about 'chooks' either. Or Vegemite.

'I know lots of things.'

'Like what?'

He tried to think of all the things in the encyclopaedia, back in Mrs Huntley's library. It still hurt, to think of the books fluttering in the rubble. 'Capybaras are the biggest guinea pigs in the world. They're much bigger than,' he framed the word carefully, 'chooks. They are as big as pigs actually and live in swamps.'

'Are they really?' Mud considered. 'That *is* interesting.'

She's serious, Georg realised. He relaxed a bit. It was good to find someone who liked knowing about things like he did. 'Why do you call them chooks?' he ventured.

'That's the sound they make. *Took, took, took.* You can call them and they come too. *Chook, chook, chook.*'

The chooks ignored them, scrabbling and pecking at the chop bones. 'Well, they come if you call and you've got the scrap bucket.' Mud didn't sound put out. 'Come on, we've got to get the eggs.' She led the way into the chook house. It was dark and dusty and smelled of feathers. 'You need to watch out for snakes.'

'Snakes!' He thought of the giant boa constrictor in *The Adventure Book for Boys*.

'Browns. They like eating eggs. They're *this* long.' To his relief she only held out an arm's length.

'Are they poisonous?'

'Of *course*. They're snakes.'

'Oh,' he said.

'Don't worry. The dogs keep them away. Mostly. If you're bitten you have to keep still and yell for help.'

'I will,' he said sincerely. He reached down and picked up an egg, then nearly dropped it when it felt warm. That egg had been inside a hen — a chook — just like the milk had been inside a cow. And the honey Mr Peaslake had eaten had been inside a bee. He'd never eat honey again. Or a scrambled egg …

But that was silly. He'd eaten eggs and milk and honey all his life. They weren't any different because now he could see where they came from. But it did *feel* different, just like the grass under his bare feet.

Mrs Peaslake was taking the loaves of bread out of the oven as they brought the eggs back in. She hacked off the crusts at both ends as soon as they were out of the oven and handed them to him and Mud.

Georg copied Mud as she slathered on butter, watched it melt into the bread, then bit into the soft sweet crust. It was perhaps the best thing he'd ever eaten.

They dug up potatoes and carrots for lunch after that — more dirt, thought Georg, looking at his filthy fingernails — and picked baby runner beans from the big trellis at the edge of the garden.

Mr Peaslake put his head out of the shed as they passed. He held up the kite that had been on Georg's bed. 'Just adding more rags to the tail.'

'Can we fly it after lunch?' demanded Mud.

'Too right,' boomed Mr Peaslake.

They walked up the lane to the headland, past Mud's house, Mud and Georg and Mrs Peaslake carrying kites, Mr Peaslake carrying the picnic basket — in case we feel faint from not enough food, thought Georg, slightly stuffed from breakfast and an enormous 'baked dinner' of mutton and vegetables for lunch. Mud had stayed for lunch too. He was already getting used to the feel of the dirt under his feet, though he made sure to avoid any stones. The dogs bounded at their sides, or pretended to find rabbits in the tussocks.

Mud's house was much like the Peaslakes', but with even more rooms straggling from both ends of the main building. Perhaps a new room had been added as each child came along.

Georg examined it. It didn't look like the house of a poor person either, although it could have done with repainting, and the garden was just shrubs and rough grass. But there was a new-looking truck in the shed, and it seemed that Mud's family owned all the land between here and the beach too. He thought only kings owned as much land as that.

They trudged through a gate and over lumpy land dappled with cow droppings. ('You've never seen a *cow* dropping?' said Mud incredulously. She picked one up, all dried and flat, and sent it skimming over the grass for the dogs to chase.) The hill rose in front of them so they were nearly at the cliff edge when Georg saw the sea. It almost hurt with its beauty, the blue like the stone in Mutti's ring, the froth like white lace on the waves. The water washed back and forth on bright white sand, and licked the rocks at either side of the bay.

The wind lashed their backs and the spray spat at their faces. The rocks were black and shiny where the sea had washed them.

Georg looked at the kite in his hand. It was supposed to go up, but how?

'Like this,' began Mr Peaslake. His roar sounded right up here in the wind from the sea.

'Let me show him!'

Mr Peaslake looked at Mud, and smiled. Mud handed her own kite to Mrs Peaslake. 'Hold the string of yours,' she commanded Georg. 'I mean, not the string, the wood it's wound around so the string can roll out.'

'I don't understand.'

She grinned. 'You will.' She took his kite and began to run, into the wind. Suddenly the wind tore the kite from her hand. In seconds it had leaped up into the air. Georg nearly dropped the winder in surprise as the string began to unfurl. The kite climbed higher, and higher still.

It was impossible. It was wonderful. It was like somehow earth and sky were one thing, not two. He pulled the string experimentally and the kite soared even higher.

Mud had her own kite up now, and Mr Peaslake his.

'Don't let them get tangled,' he yelled. 'If it droops, start running into the wind till it rises again.'

'Like this!' shouted Mud against the wind. She began to run, the dogs bounding with her. The kite shadows flickered across the ground.

Georg ran too. He stubbed his toe, but it didn't matter. Just for a moment he felt like the wind himself.

Suddenly there was a fourth shadow. Georg looked up.

It was a bird, brown and white. It balanced on the wind, just hanging in the blue sky. The kites flew, but this bird owned the air.

'Sea eagle.' Mr Peaslake's kite string grew slack while he stared at it. 'Alan …' He hesitated as he said his son's name, then went on. 'Alan says that one day he's going to fly a kite as high as the eagle.'

'Do you think he can?' shouted Georg, so the old man could hear above the wind. It seemed that nothing, not bits of string and bamboo and paper, could ever challenge that bird up there. But bits of wood and paper shouldn't be able to fight the wind at all.

'I reckon he might,' shouted Mr Peaslake. 'After the war is over.'

Mrs Peaslake opened the picnic basket and put out a Thermos of milk and another of tea, more of the fruitcake and big swollen oranges from the trees out the back of the house.

Georg remembered the last picnic basket he had watched being unpacked. It had all seemed so neat, so tame and safe that day — the quiet lake, the smooth green grass, Papa's playful teasing and Mutti's blushes — so different from this howling headland and its waves.

But it had not been safe. Neat grass had hidden hatred and secrets too.

'Who'd like a scone?' asked Mrs Peaslake. 'There's plain and there's date or pumpkin.' She picked up her knitting again.

Chapter 22

Bellagong
New South Wales, Australia
30 November 1940

Dear Aunt Miriam,

I hope you are well. Thank you for the money order. I bought a book and a box of chocolates for Mrs Peaslake and some sweets that I shared with Mud. Mud's name is Maud but she does not spell it right. Or say it right either. Her last name is Mutton which is funny because they have a farm for beef, not mutton, but Mud did not laugh when I told her. She said they do get mutton from their sheep.

I did not need to buy clothes with the money order as Mrs Peaslake has made me shorts and shirts and knitted me a jumper and three pairs of combinations. I wear old clothes from Alan Peaslake and Mud's brothers when I am on the farm because we get dirty, but do not worry, there is a big bath so I am clean each night.

It is a big farm with lots of cattle. We have to move them from paddock to paddock. I thought they would run over me but then Mud said 'Yah!' and they all walked away and through the gate.

Mr Peaslake and Mud and Mud's dad, Mr Mutton, ride horses. Mud said she would teach me but her dad said maybe next year. You have to be a good rider to chase cattle on a horse so I only help with the cattle when we can walk. Did you know that it is not true that bulls run at red things? Mud has a red hat but they do not chase her. They do what she tells them to do.

It is good here. There are oranges growing right in the garden! They have puffy skins, not like the oranges in shops, but they taste the same.

I have learned to prop a fence post. I have not been bitten by a snake yet. Mr Peaslake says not to worry, it has been years since anyone was bitten by a snake, but I am careful when I collect the eggs. Snakes like eggs.

I am top of the class this week but that does not really count because there is only Mud who is my age too. Mud was top last week but Mrs Rose says we are both precocious which means we are very clever and do our work well. Mud likes books too but only when it is dark and she cannot do things outside or if it is raining. She is all right.

If anyone asks could you say I am very happy here and remember to say where I am, in case anyone does not know where I have gone?

Your loving nephew,
George

PS Here is a gumleaf I dried for you. Mud can play a tune with two gumleaves but it is not much of a tune. The gumtrees look funny and the leaves smell strange but you get used to it.

Georg stared at little Sally and Susie and Mary-Anne skipping in a corner of the rutted school yard. They chanted as they skipped.

> 'Underneath the water six feet deep
> Old man Hitler fell asleep
> All the little fishes ate his feet
> Underneath the water six feet deep.'

It was hard, even now, to accept that the Führer he had believed in two years before was the same man as the Hitler the kids chanted about now.

'Hey, George, want to play Spitfires?' Big Billy picked his nose, then inspected his finger before he ate what was on it. Big Billy was taller than him and Mud, even though he was six months younger and still hadn't learned how to read or even write his name. These days he mostly just picked up firewood outside for the school's potbelly stove.

Big Billy didn't mind. He was happier at school than working on his uncle's farm, and he got to play with the other kids at lunchtime, and they shared their lunches with him too, because Big Billy's uncle never packed him lunch.

'You can be the Spitfire,' added Big Billy generously. 'And I'll be the Stuka and you can shoot me down. *Clakka, clakka, clakka, clakka* ...'

A friend of Mr Peaslake's had shown a newsreel at the town hall the weekend before, so now all the children had seen Spitfires and Stukas fighting above the city during the London Blitz. It had been strange seeing the London he'd once known in black and white, flickering on the hall wall.

'George wants to play cricket,' said Mud.

Big Billy shrugged agreeably. Georg nodded. He didn't want

to be a Spitfire, or a Stuka either, and he'd learned the basics of cricket on the ship. They'd had to make up new rules to make sure the ball didn't go over the rail, so no one noticed he'd never played cricket before. He knew enough about the game to be able to play a school-yard game now, with a fruit box for stumps and Mud's brother's old bat.

Georg liked Bellagong Public School, even if it was nothing like school back home, with its deep bell to tell you when lessons had ended, and neat uniforms and proper marching, and all boys too.

Here the girls sat down one side of the room and the boys on the other, except for him and Mud who shared a desk because they had to share their textbooks. No one wore a uniform, or even shoes, except the teacher, Mrs Rose.

It was more like the school in the church hall back in London, just noisier and with more flies and a water tank that a possum had drowned in last year 'but it's all right to drink the water now,' Mud had assured him. 'Because when it started to stink Dad and Uncle Ron drained the water out and cleaned it.'

Instead of proper lessons he and Mud were given their textbooks to learn from, checking each other's answers on the tests at the end of each chapter, while Mrs Rose taught the littlies how to read and do their sums on their slates. Mrs Rose had been a teacher before she got married. Now the real teacher was in the navy so Mrs Rose had come back again, till the war was over.

Sometimes he and Mud helped teach the littlies the five times tables or got them playing 'sheep, sheep come home' or 'defence' in the playground. Helping the littlies with Mud and playing with children of all different ages felt a bit like being on the ship. It didn't even matter now that Mud was a girl.

On Saturday mornings he helped Mrs Peaslake put the wet, clean washing through the mangle, squeezing out most of the washing water, then hanging it all out on the big lines propped up by wooden poles in the backyard. Mrs Peaslake didn't have a servant, just Mrs Purdon who came three mornings a week to 'do the rough'. They'd had someone who came every day, before the war, but now you were only allowed to employ people over forty-five years old to help with your house or garden.

Georg learned how to sweep a floor properly, even the corners; how to black lead the stove to make it shine; how to swirl sand in the glass vases to scrub away the flower stains, and why flower stems had to be cut under water before you arranged them to make them last.

He learned to tell a carrot from a weed, and how to know when the beetroot were big enough to pull up, and how much mint to pick for the sweet-sour sauce Mrs Peaslake made to go with roast mutton, which was weird but good.

Now and then when he came into a room Mrs Peaslake was there, just sitting, looking at nothing, only her hands moving as they made another sock, a jumper, a pair of 'combinations' to keep him warm in winter.

She always jumped up when he came in and bustled off to stir up the stove, or put the dinner on. She never said what she'd been doing, but Georg knew, because he did it too.

She had been remembering. She remembered Alan and he remembered Mutti and Papa, Aunt Miriam and Elizabeth. There was so much they didn't talk about but only remembered now.

Sometimes it was as though Alan Peaslake was only off down the shop to buy a pound of sugar. His picture stood on the mantel in the kitchen and the living room, on the sideboard and on top of the piano.

Even at the table his place was always vacant, in case he should appear. No one sat in his chair in the lounge room either, or the dining room. Mud knew not to sit there, and Georg learned not to as well, even though Mrs Peaslake never said anything about it.

They had their big lunch in the dining room on Saturdays and Sundays, with roast lamb or beef, slightly blackened roast pumpkin, parsnips, carrots and potatoes, and boiled beans and, over it all, gravy speckled with the bits of roast vegetables left in the pan, followed by apple crumble, because that was Mr Peaslake's favourite and their Alan's too.

There were always leftovers, partly so there'd be cold meat to eat with salad at what the Australians called 'tea' but the English called 'dinner', and so the cold roast potatoes could be fried up with eggs and cabbage for bubble and squeak for breakfast the next morning, or the lamb sliced for sandwiches during the week. But mostly, Georg thought, it was in case Alan suddenly appeared. Alan might be across the sea but there always had to be a plateful more, a tin full of cake or biscuits, in case he magically arrived.

Alan Peaslake was with them too when he and Mud and Mr Peaslake flew kites up on the headland. Mrs Peaslake usually came as well, sitting on the tussocky grass, not flying kites but knitting yet another sock or balaclava, the kites bobbing and laughing down at them, the dogs bounding at the shadows that flickered over the ground.

Each week Mr Peaslake took the Muttons' horse and cart (there wasn't enough petrol these days to use the truck except for emergencies) to gather firewood for the fireplaces in each room and the wood stove in the kitchen.

The straggle-branched gumtrees were careless with their branches, dropping them whenever they felt like it, so there was lots of wood. It burned with a strange sweet-smelling smoke that wasn't at all like the stuffy smell from the coal in London, or from the wood Lotte had burned in the kitchen at home. Samson and Delilah ran beside the cart, snuffling in the horse and cattle droppings and bringing sticks to throw.

Sometimes Mud challenged Georg to see who could gather the most wood; so they'd race for the long wiggly branches that looked like snakes. Of course, the snakes here were shiny black with red bellies, like someone had painted them to shout a warning — Careful! Poisonous snakes!

Mud always won, whether she was racing him to the cliff or seeing who could play 'Chopsticks' the fastest on the piano. It annoyed him a bit: that she always had to be the best. But he didn't mind too much.

Sometimes it even felt like he was happy in his new life at the end of the earth.

Chapter 23

Bellagong
New South Wales, Australia
2 December 1940

Dear Aunt Miriam,

I hope you are well. It is hot here. Big insects called Christmas beetles fly into the roof and roll down. They make a lot of noise. Delilah, who is one of the dogs, tried to eat one and was sick. Mrs Peaslake says she tries every year and never learns.

It is funny to have Christmas coming and be hot.

Mrs Peaslake is worried that my mother has not sent a letter, but I explained how sick she is and that you will write and tell me how she is.

Mr Peaslake has taught me two poems. They are Australian poems. One is about black swans. Swans are black in Australia, not white. The other is called How McDougal Topped the Score *and is about how a dog won a cricket match but it was not a proper orderly cricket match. It was a funny poem just the same.*

I hope you are safe and that you have a good Christmas dinner. I hope you like this Christmas card. I made it myself at school. I hope you like the chocolates and the cake. I bought the chocolates. Mrs Peaslake gives me pocket money for doing the chores. Mrs Peaslake made the cake. It has a pound of butter in it and eight eggs.

I collected the eggs but I did not make the butter. Mud made it. Mud traps rabbits for their fur. She made twenty-six pounds this year. She said she will show me how to do it but I do not want to but I might next year, as Mud says the rabbits eat all the grass and then the soil washes away and the rabbit skins are useful to make men's hats and coats for women and I can put the money into War Bonds which will help win the war. So even if I do not want to hurt rabbits I think maybe I should do it too.

I do not know if your friends are where you are now. I hope they are. I know you won't get this before Christmas, but I hope you have a merry one.

Your loving nephew,
George

—⁂

'*Twas the night before Christmas*,' chanted Mr Peaslake, peeling potatoes at the kitchen sink.

> '*When all through the house*
> *Not a creature was stirring, not even a mouse;*
> *The stockings were hung by the chimney with*
>   *care,*
> *In hopes that St Nicholas soon would be there.*'

'George? There you are. Come and put up the decorations with me,' said Mrs Peaslake. 'You too, Father. Just leave the spuds to soak till dinner. We need you to put the angel on top of the tree.'

Georg followed them into the lounge room. It looked even more crowded with the big gumtree branch propped up in a bucket in a corner. He stared at it. How could a bit of gumtree be a proper Christmas tree?

Mrs Peaslake handed him a red crepe streamer from a cardboard box on the floor. Georg stared at it uncertainly, then began to drape it around the tree, in and out of the leaves and twigs, just as he had draped tinsel on a proper pine tree with Mrs Huntley in the library the year before; and all those other years with Mutti and Papa.

Mrs Peaslake nestled a ball of cotton wool among the leaves and then another. She is pretending it's snow, he realised.

He draped another streamer while the Peaslakes added more 'snow'. Then Mrs Peaslake opened a small papier-mâché box. She took out a rounded cardboard angel, badly coloured in. She touched it reverently. 'Alan made that,' she said softly.

Georg stared at it. Alan wasn't very good at colouring in then, though he didn't like to say it.

Mrs Peaslake saw his look and smiled. 'He was only five. First Christmas at school. It's been on top of the tree every year since.' She looked into the distance. 'I hope the Christmas cake gets to him in time. And the pudding.'

And the socks and bunch of gumleaves, and the card signed by them all, thought Georg. But all he said was, 'I bet they make a special effort to get the mail to the troops in time for Christmas. Wherever he is.'

'Probably rather have a beer,' boomed Mr Peaslake. He reached up and fixed the angel to the highest twig of the tree; it lurched a bit to one side. 'Mother, have you got the rag bag? I want to make some ties for the new kite.'

'Can't send beer through the post,' said Mrs Peaslake, in the loud clear voice she always used for her husband. 'The rag bag's in the linen cupboard, where it always is. Men can never find things. *In the linen cupboard!* No, I'll get it.'

Mr Peaslake watched her go. 'Glad you're here,' he said suddenly. 'House has been too empty. Bad for her: an empty house.'

Georg looked at the over-filled room. Delilah had arrived too and was sniffing the tree with interest. Empty? But he knew what Mr Peaslake meant. 'But you're here with her.'

'Not the same. You miss the snow?'

The hairs on Georg's arms rose in his alarm. Snow? It had never snowed in London at Christmas, but it had at home. Papa had shown him how to fall on his back with his arms out to make a snow angel.

Mr Peaslake was staring at him. 'What's wrong? Look, I'm sorry, lad. I didn't mean to make you homesick talking about snow.'

'No, I'm all right. It doesn't snow in London at Christmas. Not often,' he added, in case it sometimes did.

'George!' It was Mud at the back door.

'Knock politely,' called Mrs Peaslake from the linen cupboard. 'You weren't brought up in a tent.'

'I did knock. You didn't hear.' Mud burst in from the kitchen. 'What are you doing? Come on,' she added to Georg before they could answer. 'We've got to practise for carol singing.'

'Carols?' His heart lurched. He knew lots of carols; he'd sung them every Christmas at church and at home too. But all the carols that he knew were German.

He followed her automatically onto the road, then down the tussocked footpath towards the school. His feet had toughened so he didn't even think about stones under his bare feet now.

Carols? How was he going to get out of this?

His heart began to pound. Even the shop had a poster: 'Beware the horror in our midst.' Would something as simple as carols be the thing that betrayed him as a German?

'We sing carols at every house in town every year: every kid in the district. Not just kids either — Ken and Len and Alan, and all the girls. You love carol singing in England, don't you?' To his relief she didn't wait for a reply. 'But there's only us at school to sing this year. It's got to be really good so that everyone puts lots of money in the hat. The money we raise is going to buy rope to make camouflage nets.' She flung the school gate open.

The other children were already there, playing jacksies on the school-room floor, even Big Billy. Mrs Rose looked through music on the old piano.

'Right,' she called. 'Everyone over here, please.'

'I'll conduct.' Mud began to wave her hands in the air as the music began. 'One, two, three ...'

The smallest kids began to sing.

'*Silent night, holy night,*
All is calm, all is bright ...'

Their voices trailed off one by one, as though they didn't know the words. Big Billy had stopped after the 'Silent night'. Georg found them all staring at him.

'Why aren't you singing?' demanded Mud.

He knew the tune.

He knew the words to it too.

German words.

'I ... why aren't you?'

Mud flushed. 'I can't sing.'

'Everyone can sing.'

'I can't.'

199

Big Billy laughed. 'You show him, Mud.'

Mud's flush grew deeper. 'No.'

'Go on!'

'No!'

'Mud's a scaredy cat! Mud's a scaredy cat!'

'Billy ...' Mrs Rose said.

'I'm not scared of *anything*!' Mud clenched her fists. She opened her mouth. A noise emerged. It was like the bullfrogs in the lake back home.

'*Silent night, holy night,*

All is calm —' Mud glared at them all. 'There. Is that enough?'

Georg stared. Mud was good at everything! How could she not be able to sing?

'I can't sing either,' he said, inspired.

'What? Both of you?' Mrs Rose threw her hands up. 'Well, you can't go carol singing now.'

'But we always have carol singing!' Mud's voice was anguished.

'Not this year.' Mrs Rose sounded tired. She sounded tired often these days. She stood up and began to gather the music. 'The littlies won't remember the words without at least one of you singing along. Billy can't read them either.'

'Nope,' said Billy cheerfully. He began to pick his nose.

'But we *have* to!'

'There's no have to about it,' said Mrs Rose.

Suddenly Mud ran from the room.

'What's got into the girl?' Mrs Rose snapped the music into her case. 'Sometimes I think —'

Georg didn't wait to hear what Mrs Rose thought. He ran out the door, then gazed around. But Mud had vanished.

He hesitated, then jogged back home, up the front path then around the house, into the orchard. He stood under the pear tree and looked up into the leaves.

'Go away.' Mud's voice sounded strange.

'No.'

'I said go away. This is my tree.'

'No, it isn't. I live here too.'

'Well, I'm using it now. Go and find your own tree.'

'I'm coming up,' said Georg. He wasn't sure why. Mud didn't want him. He was glad there wouldn't be carols too. But something in Mud's voice reminded him of something, someone ...

Of himself, he realised. Of times when everything was too much, when he knew he could take no more, but had to keep on going.

Mud was a small angry ball, curled up by the trunk on the second branch. 'What do you want?'

'To help,' said Georg simply.

'You can help by learning to sing.'

'I'll try to learn for next year.' He would too.

'Too late next year.'

'Why does it matter so much?'

'Because it does! Don't you understand? If we don't sing Hitler has won! We have to do it, just like it's always been done. Just like everyone does it every year, all together. Except now there's only us.'

And this year her brothers aren't here to sing too, Georg thought. And Alan Peaslake. Just us, to do all they used to do. Me, to make the rooms less empty. Mud, to take the place of her brothers.

No wonder she has to be best, he thought suddenly. I only have to take the place of Alan Peaslake. She has the emptiness left by two absent brothers to fill. Mr Peaslake might be able to take over fencing duties, but nothing could really fill the spaces left by those you loved.

Was that why Mr Peaslake recited his poems so loudly? Not just because he was deaf, but to fill the emptiness too?

Suddenly he had an idea. 'Mud ... we don't have to sing.'

'We do!'

'I mean, not *sing*. Mr Peaslake has a Christmas poem.'

'So what?'

'So we can recite it! You and I can learn it. We can write it out for the littlies to read. And ... and we can make reindeer antlers for them. It's all about Santa and reindeer, six of them. We'll make a sort of play of it. The littlies can be the six reindeer so it doesn't matter if they lose their places and forget their words in the poem.'

Mud gazed at him. 'Big Billy can be Santa. We can stick on cotton wool for a beard and he can wear my red beanie and Dad's red jumper with a pillow underneath. We can use sticks for the antlers — cover them in brown paper.'

'And at every house we'll recite the poem.' He looked at her anxiously. 'Not the same, but better.'

'We'll make heaps.' To his relief Mud was grinning through her tears. 'It's a long poem,' she added. 'I've heard Uncle Ron reciting it. Bet I can learn it by heart before you.'

'Bet you can't,' he said, but he knew she could. And even if she couldn't this time he'd let her win. For now he knew why winning — all the time — was important to Mud.

He was doing his maths homework at the kitchen table when he heard the clucking from the hen yard. He ran to the door in time to see Mrs Peaslake emerge, one hand holding two young roosters upside down by their legs. The birds squawked and fluttered their wings indignantly.

Mrs Peaslake walked over to the tree stump by the shed and picked up the axe in her other hand. In an instant she had laid the roosters' necks on the stump and given them two short sharp blows.

The heads rolled onto the grass.

Red blood. Green grass. Georg felt sick. He was going to be sick …

He ran to the bathroom and retched, but nothing came out. He tried again, then drank a handful of water.

'You all right in there?' called Mrs Peaslake.

'Yes.' Georg padded down the hall and looked into the kitchen. Mrs Peaslake was at the laundry tubs, pulling out black feathers; the dogs were at her feet looking hopefully at a pile of — Georg's stomach lurched again — what must be rooster guts on an old newspaper on the bench.

'Not for you,' she said to the dogs. She smiled at Georg. 'Christmas dinner.' She nodded at the roosters. One was half naked now, it's pimply skin very white.

He stared at her. This woman who warmed his pyjamas every night for him could kill roosters without thinking about it.

She looked at him with understanding. 'I felt sick first time I saw my gran kill a chook. Meat comes from somewhere, George. We're just closer to it than in the city. And if we keep all the roosters they'll peck the hens to death.'

Georg thought about the scrubbed kitchen back in Alfhausen: Lotte in her white frilled apron; meat on an enamelled tray brought by the butcher's boy wrapped in white paper. Neat sausages and the legs of pork no longer bleeding. But there had been blood in that land all the same.

Chapter 24

He felt funny when he woke on Christmas Day. It was a day to be happy, but he was not — although he had been mostly happy in Bellagong. Happy, except when he remembered Mutti in the dark.

A kookaburra yelled to say that it was morning. He was glad. Today felt the emptiest of all. Even a kookaburra was good to fill the silence up. He had bought handkerchiefs for everyone for Christmas — Mud too. He hoped they were the right sort of gifts for Australia. Mrs Peters who ran the shop had said they were.

He sat up, then stared.

A pillowcase hung on the doorknob. Somehow he knew it was a Santa present, even though there had been no Santa Claus at Aunt Miriam's. It was almost, but not quite, like the Christkindl gifts at home. He padded across the floor and took the sack back to his bed.

A set of coloured pencils, a pen knife, a Violet Crumble bar — he'd never eaten one till he came here, but they were good — a faded tin that when opened was full of home-made toffees in little paper cases. And a football.

He rolled it over in his fingers. He just knew that Mud would be good at football. Somehow he guessed that Big Billy would like it too.

He padded out to the dunny, then back to the bathroom. He washed, then wandered into the kitchen, still feeling as though he was really somewhere else.

'Merry Christmas!' Mrs Peaslake smiled at him from the stove, the frying pan in her hand and a pile of pancakes on the warming plate. Her eyes and nose were red. He wasn't the only one who felt an emptiness this Christmas. 'Father's out the back giving the chooks their Christmas breakfast. Extra corn for them this morning. There're letters for you on the table.'

You never knew how long it would take for a letter to reach you these days. Ships were sunk or delayed. Mrs Peaslake must have kept these letters hidden for him to have today.

He sat down at his place. Delilah transferred her head to his feet, hoping for toast, as he picked up the first letter.

(Address unknown)
England

Dearest George,

Merry Christmas! I am afraid I didn't know what to get you, so I hope you will buy yourself something with the money order enclosed.

It was good to get your wire saying you had arrived safely. I hope a ship carrying a letter from you arrives soon. I am so very glad you are happy with the Peaslakes. They seem such good people. Mrs Peaslake has sent a wire to me too, telling me about your progress at school. Please thank her so much for the

Christmas cake for me and your mother that she says is on the way. It will be a treat for all of us here. It was so very kind of her, and is so appreciated. A butter ration these days isn't enough to make a Christmas cake. I am so glad that you are with such kind and thoughtful people and I am very proud of your bravery. Please tell Mrs Peaslake that sadly there has been no change in your mother's condition, but I know that she will be pleased that her son is with such a loving and happy family.

I am well here and enjoying the countryside. You will be glad to know that the flat is still undamaged. Mail is still forwarded down here. I managed a weekend in London recently and stayed there. Even the windows have been replaced with a new material that does not break.

The most surprising thing of all is that Mrs Huntley has opened the library again. The library now shares the space in the tea-shop next to where it used to be. Somehow she managed to rescue most of the books. She and her husband must have been days there sorting through the rubble. She has mended many of them most beautifully and, as she said, even if there are a few pages missing readers should still be able to work out the story.

She sends you her regards and asks if she could write to you. I have given her your address so you may receive a letter.

All my best wishes, dear boy.

Your loving aunt,
Aunt Miriam

'Your auntie well?' asked Mrs Peaslake.

'Yes, thank you,' said Georg. *And* she had managed to let him know that if a message came from Mutti she would get it. 'And ... Mummy ...' He hesitated on the word, hatred of the lie seeping through him. It was almost denying Mutti's existence to call her Mummy. 'Mummy's just the same.'

Mrs Peaslake touched his shoulder comfortingly. 'You know what the best thing you can do for your mum is?'

Georg shook his head.

'You be happy. That's what any mum wants most for her kiddies. Now you open your other letters.'

The second letter came with a package. Georg recognised the writing from his hours in the library.

> *Kensington*
> *London*

Dear George,

I hope this finds you as well as it leaves me. I was so very glad to know that you are safe and in Australia too! I hoped that perhaps you were in Brisbane where Elsie and John are but I am sure New South Wales is nice too. You will get very brown!

Your auntie may have told you that I have opened the library again. Some of the books were sadly damaged but we managed to rescue most of them, although the Encyclopaedia Britannica now lacks Vol 15 (Italy to Kyshtym) and Vol 28 (Vetch to Zymotic Diseases). As few readers want to read about zymotic diseases, especially in these days, I do not think they will be missed much.

It is very pleasant sharing the tea-rooms. Not only is there tea (!) but Miss Elrington and I share some of our duties. She minds the desk while I make scones, for she kindly says that my scones are much lighter than hers, even in these days when there is no sugar to sweeten them. It is very convenient for the customers too, as they can borrow a book to read while they drink their tea. I think anything that helps to brighten these days has to be good.

I am enclosing a book that I think you will like. It is not from the library of course. I bought it at the church jumble sale last weekend. We raised enough money to buy a whole wing of a Spitfire! The book is not quite new, of course, but has been well looked after.

My Ernest is an air-raid warden now. It was hard for him at first, not being able to join up, but as he says, we are all in this together and every hand helps.

With all the very best wishes for your stay in Australia. Until we meet again,

Mrs Eleanora Huntley

It was funny to think of Mrs Huntley as an Eleanora. Georg was glad she was in the tea-rooms with her books, and happy.

He looked at the book: *Greenmantle* by John Buchan. He had loved John Buchan's *The Thirty-Nine Steps* back in the library and read it over and over. Had Mrs Huntley remembered?

Of course she had. Mrs Huntley would never forget a book.

It was wonderful to get another one. The Peaslakes had two bookcases of books and Mud's family had books too, but he'd read them all now and school only had yellowed old textbooks. Mrs Peaslake had asked at the Red Cross meeting if anyone could lend George things to read. Boxes had arrived all the week after, from everyone in town — some of the books decades old — *Boy's Own Annual*s and books of hymns and a set of encyclopaedias from 1892. He'd read them all, and then read them again.

He picked up the third letter. He had never seen the writing before. Mrs Peaslake turned away, carefully looking at the pancake she was cooking.

He opened the letter.

Dear George,

Merry Christmas! I know it must seem strange to get a letter from a chap you've never met, but I just wanted to say 'welcome'. I know Mum and Dad are chuffed about having you, and I am glad for their sakes. I always wanted a younger brother too. I know it's just till the war ends and we have Jerry on the hop, but I hope we can meet then and, you never know, I might be posted somewhere I can get home leave too. You might even decide you want to stay in Australia and bring your auntie and mum out too! Tell them the Aussie sun would be good for them.

By the way, there's a box under my bed. I'd like you to use what's in it. Some things don't deserve to be hidden away in the dark. Have fun with it.

I hope you and the old folks have the best of Christmases.

All the very best,
Your 'older brother',
Alan

Georg glanced up at Mrs Peaslake. The pancake was cooked but she still said nothing.

'It's ... it's from Alan.'

'I know,' she said.

All at once he knew she was desperate for him to read it aloud, even though she was respecting that the letter was his, and might be private. Mutti would feel the same if she knew someone had a letter from him.

But he was safe here, and Alan Peaslake was far away, facing the enemy. For the first time the son of the house seemed real:

not just an empty place in the Peaslakes' home and hearts. For the first time too he knew that he liked Alan Peaslake. The man who wrote this letter was a good one.

'Will I read it to you?' he asked, as Mr Peaslake's shape darkened the kitchen doorway.

'Yes, please,' said Mrs Peaslake softly.

He read the words, there in the quiet kitchen, the dogs snuffling around under the stove for drips of pancake batter.

No one said anything at the end. Finally Mr Peaslake said, 'Thank you, lad. Pancakes ready, Mother?'

'Yes,' said Mrs Peaslake, a scrap of batter dropping from her spatula; Delilah leaped eagerly to grab it. Mrs Peaslake took a pancake and divided it between the dogs. 'Merry Christmas,' she added quietly.

And, somehow, despite the empty places at the table, it was.

They went into Alan's bedroom after breakfast. The dogs snored on the kitchen mat, but with their ears alert in case anyone tried to steal the Christmas dinner they could smell in the food safe, the refrigerator and the oven.

Alan's dragon kite gleamed on the bedroom wall. The dragon face smiled to itself, as though dreaming of the wind.

Georg crawled under the bed. He'd expected it to be dusty — he'd never seen Mrs Peaslake clean this room. But it wasn't: she must clean it when the house was empty and when she could be alone in here with memories of her son.

The box was big. He tugged and pulled; and at last he got it out. He looked up at the Peaslakes. 'You know what's in it?'

Mr Peaslake smiled, though there was pain there too. 'I know.'

'Alan's right,' said Mrs Peaslake. She still carried her knitting, the tips of her fingers flicking while the rest of her hands were almost still. Georg knew enough about the things she knitted now to see it was turning into a balaclava. 'Things need to be out in the light.'

Georg opened the box. It was a train set: tracks, some long, some rounded; a tiny engine, painted green and black; train carriages — six passenger carriages and one that looked like a cart and, under that, tiny animals to put in it; and train signals, little houses and a train station, signal boxes and model hills, one with a train tunnel through the middle.

'Electric,' said Mr Peaslake, staring at it. 'I gave it to Alan on his twelfth birthday.' He glanced at his wife. She nodded, as though she knew the question he hadn't spoken. 'Better put it together in your room so no one treads on the pieces.'

'Will you help me?' He could put it together by himself. Part of him would rather have done it that way: spend hours just working out what bit went where. But he knew that this was what Alan Peaslake wanted.

'We both will,' said Mrs Peaslake, so quietly her husband could not have heard. But he nodded, knowing exactly what she would have said.

Chapter 25

They opened presents after church. The Peaslakes gave him a giant kite with a sea eagle's face and fierce sea eagle eyes. Even the rags on its tail were brown and white, like sea eagle feathers. There was a tin of home-made honeycomb and a wooden pencil case made of different coloured woods.

'Every sort of tree that grows around here,' boomed Mr Peaslake, anxious but proud at the same time, so Georg realised he must have made the pencil case as well as the kite.

'I love it,' he said honestly.

They gave him a bicycle too: an old one but painted to look like new. It must have taken ages to paint the bike, to make the kite, the honeycomb, the pencil box. He loved them all. But somehow the gifts were almost too much. He thought of Mr Peaslake in his shed, painting the bicycle, working for hours on the kite just for him, Mrs Peaslake making the honeycomb in her kitchen. They're trying to fill up Alan's space, he thought.

Would Mutti be able to celebrate Weihnachten this year?

It was good to have the presents, he realised. Not just because they were *things* and belonged to him but because for the first time his room would look like a normal boy's room now, with the football, the new kite.

He looked at the Peaslakes' faces. Some of the strain that he had always seen on them, the strain they'd never explained or discussed, had gone. Instead they looked happy. Christmas happy.

Their happiness in his pleasure at the presents had done that. His own happiness grew — a sort of giddy wind so he could almost see it curl out the door and wiggle into other people to make them feel 'Merry Christmas' too.

He raced the bicycle against Mud and her horse when she and her parents came over after church. Mud won.

He didn't mind.

Mud still wore her best dress, even though there'd been time to change and she'd taken off her good shoes and frilly socks. She'd curled her hair too. It was funny seeing Mud with curls.

Mr and Mrs Mutton gave Georg a pair of riding boots — Mrs Peaslake must have shown them the right size — and a stockwhip Mr Mutton had plaited himself. Mud looked at the whip jealously. 'Why can't I have a whip?'

'Because you'd use it,' said Mrs Mutton. She was long and thin with brown curls that never moved, even in the wind. 'You're too much of a tomboy as it is.'

'I am not a tomboy!'

Georg snorted, but swallowed his laugh. Mud stared at him, then grinned. 'I'll borrow yours.'

'No, you won't,' he said. But he knew she would.

He gave everyone their hankies. He'd got Mud a big one — not a tiny girlie one with lace — and she grinned at him again. She had knitted him a jumper. One sleeve flopped over his wrist and there were so many holes it looked like the moths had been in it already.

'Thank you,' he said politely, a bit embarrassed because her present to him was bigger than the one he'd given her. 'It's very nice.'

Mud's grin got wider. 'Mum says it wasn't good enough to send to the refugees.'

'Mud!' said her mother.

'Well, you did. But it'll keep you warm and no one will see it when you're helping with the cattle.'

'Except you,' said Georg.

'I don't mind,' said Mud generously.

Mud and Mrs Mutton had silver bracelets Mud's brothers had sent from Singapore in Malaya. Mud stared at the bangle, then slipped it on her arm, her finger stroking its pattern. He had never realised Mud liked pretty things as well as things like stockwhips. Mud's brothers must understand Mud well, thought Georg, to know she did. Perhaps he should have given her a pretty hanky instead of a big man's one.

They ate Christmas dinner in the dining room. Georg and Mrs Peaslake had decorated it with more of the red streamers. Mr Peaslake had hung mistletoe over the door, though this mistletoe looked like gumtree leaves, not like the mistletoe from home.

Mr Peaslake kissed Mrs Peaslake under it, and Mr and Mrs Mutton kissed each other too. Mud's dad was as long and thin as his wife, though he was bald instead of curly-headed.

Georg wondered warily if he was supposed to kiss Mud, but she went through the door so quickly he didn't have a chance.

Mud's mum had brought over trifle to add to the Christmas feast: the two roast roosters filled with thyme and lemon stuffing (they didn't look like birds any more, just meat); giblet gravy, roast potatoes, parsnips, carrots and pumpkin (it still seemed funny to eat roast cattle food but Australians ate lots of it and he had to admit it tasted good); boiled beetroot and beans from the garden and cauliflower cheese; then the Christmas pudding with threepences in it and the trifle with fruit and yellow custard and red jelly; and finally mince pies and nuts and dried grapes called muscatels.

Mud's mum played the piano later and the grown-ups sang carols while he and Mud played fiddlesticks.

Mud had just won for the fourth time when Mr Peaslake cleared his throat.

'Now we're for it,' whispered Mud. But Georg had the feeling that she'd pinch anyone else who made fun of Mr Peaslake's poems. Mud's pinches hurt.

Georg waited for Mr Peaslake to recite the Christmas poem again, so that he and Mud could join in. But this poem was new to him.

> *'Our Andy's gone with cattle now,*
> *Our hearts are out of order —*
> *With drought he's gone to battle now*
> *Across the Queensland border.*
>
> *'He's left us in dejection now,*
> *Our thoughts with him are roving;*
> *It's dull on this selection now,*
> *Since Andy went a-droving.'*

The adults were quiet. Mrs Peaslake's hands were still in her lap, her knitting forgotten. Tears glistened on her cheeks.

The poem isn't for Andy, whoever he had been, thought Georg. It was for their sons, for all the men and women facing the enemy.

> '*Oh may the showers in torrents fall,*
> *And all the tanks run over,*
> *And may the grass grow green and tall,*
> *In pathways of the drover.*
>
> '*And may good angels send the rain,*
> *On desert stretches sandy,*
> *And when the summer comes again,*
> *God grant it brings us Andy.*'

Later, in bed, listening to the big wireless play softly from the lounge room, he sent a silent 'Fraulich Weihnachten' to Mutti, and 'Merry Christmas' to Alan Peaslake too.

He had the strangest feeling that his words whispered above the gumtrees, across the ocean; and that somehow, wherever they were, Mutti and Alan Peaslake heard them, and whispered back.

'Merry Christmas,' came the whispers. 'Fraulich Weihnachten to you too.'

Chapter 26

MARCH TO OCTOBER 1941

Dear Mum and Dad and George,

So much has happened since my last letter to you that it's hard to know how to bring you up to date. Best news of all — mail finally caught up with us and I got four of your letters, and one from Auntie Edie.

I'm finally settled in camp now, in a barren sandy desert, but I'd better not tell you where or the censor will start chopping up this letter. The tents are placed far apart to minimise the damage if we're bombed. No beds or stretchers, and sand makes a poor mattress. But we found an Italian rubbish dump with wood, canvas, camouflage netting and the like. Good old Australian ingenuity got to work and, with the help of a lot of string, we now all have beds, camp stools, boxes as chests of drawers, a rush carpet and a Milano hurricane lamp.

There are nine of us in the tent, all the old mates from before. At the moment a sandstorm is blowing, and I'm blowing too to get the grit off this letter. It seeps into everything. No landmarks outside — just sand.

Funny thing happened yesterday — we'd just come out of the mess hut after a breakfast of sausages and sand and there was this straggle of dusty, unshaven men, mostly hatless, some without rifles, but somehow you could tell just by looking at them that they were Aussies.

Turns out they'd been caught and had to fight hand to hand with the enemy. But they made it through.

Hope old Eileen is still sleeping in front of the wood stove. Give Auntie Edie and Uncle Don and Mud my love. Hope Ken and Len are going all right. Give my love to the old place too, and love to all of you,

Alan

Mrs Peaslake's voice cracked as she said her son's name. She put the letter down.

'He's safe and well, love,' said Mr Peaslake, his hand on hers. 'At least we know he's in Egypt now.'

She nodded.

Safe when he wrote that letter, thought Georg. But how long did it take to get here? 'How do you know where he is?'

Mr Peaslake smiled. 'Worked out a code before he left. "Hope old Eileen is still sleeping in front of the wood stove." Eileen means Egypt, Enid means England, Furry means France, Gertie means Greece. Some chaps have so much cut out by the censor you can only make out a sentence or two. But not our Alan.'

Everyone in Bellagong watched old Mr Finnigan the postman as he cycled from house to house now. Every family had someone in the army or navy or air force or nursing overseas. Letters were longed for, with a small private sigh each time Mr Finnigan passed a letter box without dropping anything in.

But most days there was at least one letter in the Peaslakes' letter box. Alan wrote every week, though sometimes there'd be weeks with no letter then two or three would come at once. Mrs Peaslake seemed to knit even faster those weeks, her smile visibly bright.

Every Friday night Georg and Mrs Peaslake sat at the dining-room table, the nibs of their pens scratching at the paper, writing their letters too.

Bellagong
30 March 1941

Dear Aunt Miriam,

I hope that you are well and that your work is going well too.

The School Inspector came today. He gave us tests and Mud and I did so well that he says we are two years above our age. I have a certificate now. Mr Peaslake is making a frame for it to hang above my bed.

The Inspector is really old. He was retired like Mr Peaslake but has come back to work because of the war. He has a moustache like Hitler, but his is grey, and he said he won't shave his off because he had his moustache before Hitler grew his.

The Inspector also said that Big Billy has to stay at school till he is fourteen, even though there is a war on, and not work on his uncle's farm all the time like his uncle wants him to. Big Billy is going to join the merchant navy when he is fourteen. He says he does not want to ever see a cow again and there are no cows at sea.

I like having cattle around though. They make all sorts of sounds, not just moo like in books. There are happy sounds; and sad sounds that the cows make when Mr Mutton and Mr Peaslake take the weaners off to the cattle sale up at Yerralong.

Mr Mutton has bought a new bull. Mud said that they should call him George but Mr Mutton grinned and said 'no way'. I said we could call him The King, because the King's name is George, and everyone laughed and said yes.

The King is in the paddock next to the house because he cost a lot of money and so we have to make sure he does not fight the other bulls. I asked Mr Mutton why they fought, and he said, 'Just because they are bulls, mate.' Mr Mutton knows everything about cattle. He can ride without even holding onto the reins and just sort of nudges his horse to tell it where to go.

I can stay on a horse now but Mud says that isn't riding, that is just staying on.

I had better go and set the table for tea. It is rabbit pie tonight. I wish I could send you some. Mrs Peaslake has packed up a cake and a tin of dripping for you though. She says she has boiled the dripping so it won't go off and flavoured it with rosemary.

Your loving nephew,
George

Letters mattered now. Telegrams would tell you if someone you loved died; letters could tell you if they were well, or happy, or just … doing all right. He thought that in a funny way both Alan's and Aunt Miriam's letters sounded happy. Whatever the hardships they were experiencing, they felt that what they were doing was good.

Every month he was allowed to exchange a cable message with Aunt Miriam at the post office. The post office was the end of the counter at the shop, next to the cheese. He told Aunt Miriam about the new calves and learning algebra and how he had helped pack hampers for the troops in Egypt and in Singapore.

Georg didn't say how ships had been sunk by mines in Bass Strait, where the ship that he had been on had passed on its way to Melbourne. Neither he nor Aunt Miriam mentioned to each other that there were no more evacuations of children to the Dominions now, after two ships laden with children had been torpedoed on their way to Canada.

There was a lot that no one mentioned these days, not just things that spies might pass on to the enemy but things that might hurt if said aloud. No one in Bellagong ever spoke about the pictures in the newspaper of London ablaze in front of Georg, how London endured night after night of bombing: a city consumed by flames and rubble but fighting on.

Perhaps the Peaslakes thought that Georg didn't read the papers, because he waited till there was no one around before he leafed through them, looking for news not just of London but Germany too. Or maybe they knew he read the papers, but guessed it would hurt him to have to talk of the bombings of what they thought of as his home.

Sometimes Georg felt there was so much unsaid inside him that he'd bust, not just his German life, the loss of Papa and the worry for Mutti, but things he too had to pretend not to see, even in Bellagong. Mrs Peaslake's tears as she sat in the kitchen reading and rereading Alan's letters; the way Mr Peaslake sometimes stared at the photo of Alan on the piano too; like Georg himself looked away from Mud's face when it seemed as though he might beat her in the school spelling bee.

He made a deliberate mistake then, so she won the round, and smiled at him in triumph. When you were the only child left at home and your brothers were in danger, you had to be the best.

But there were things everyone did talk about: good things, sometimes, like how the Australians had taken Tobruk from the

Italians in Libya (the British had been there too, somewhere) and then Benghazi; and how more Australian soldiers were sent to Malaya to the north, to make sure the fortress of Singapore was secure in case this war ever came to South-East Asia.

But most of the war news wasn't good at all. Every evening at seven o'clock they sat in the lounge room together by the wireless to listen to the news, the Peaslakes on the sofa and Georg sitting on the carpet, stroking the dogs' soft ears. It was easier to listen to bad news when you were together.

Yugoslavia fell to the Nazis; and Greece; then Crete too. City after city after city in Britain became the focus of the Blitz — the German for lightning — where German bombers rained down bombs night after night, trying to break the spirit of the ordinary people. How long could Britain and its Dominions hold on?

It was a strange year for Georg. The urgencies of the news from Europe seemed to matter less than the crows who attacked a sick lamb, or how he could finally stay on a horse well enough to ride to the bushranger's cave with Mud. The war was worse, was ever-present, but it was also far away.

He was George, who the other kids looked up to because he had seen bombs fall, and had sailed across the ocean. He was George, who loved apple pancakes so much that Mrs Peaslake made them for him and Mud nearly every afternoon after school. He was George, learning to throw dried cow pats like discuses with Mud or reading borrowed books by the fire at night, while Mr Peaslake nodded off as he listened to the wireless and Mrs Peaslake knitted khaki socks and balaclavas.

But it was Georg who looked out his window one morning to see a mob of roos bounding through the winter dew, impossible animals with tails that beat the ground. It was Georg who laid in bed at night and tried to think of stories: stories where Mutti arrived on the bus tomorrow, in her green coat and flowered dress.

It was Georg too who knew why this story never worked. The story wouldn't happen in his mind because it could not come true. Not till the war was over.

The war was far away, but still the background to their lives.

—⁂

8th Division AIF Headquarters
Malaya
5 July 1941

Dear Mum and Dad and Muddy Girl,

I've just got back to camp from leave. Three whole days in Singapore with soap that lathers. Had a good time with good mates but it was funny, driving back to camp in the back of the truck, all of us singing, and we passed into a part that was all people's houses, the lights on so we could see into their windows. I think every one of us in that truck thought of our homes and families just then.

Anyway, enough of all that tripe. How are things at home? What price did you get for the last lot of steers? Sorry old Brindle passed away. He was a good horse.

Wish we were doing a real job of work here, instead of just guarding a patch of rubber and jungle.

Len is well and is writing to you too. He didn't get leave. Sucks boo. Love to you all, and Auntie Thelma and Uncle Ron too,

Ken

PS Muddy Girl is NOT to use my new skinning knife. Tell her that I'll know if she's touched it and I'll give her three times

223

around the shed if she has.

⌘

The new crop of oranges ripened in the winter frost, turning soft and sweet. Frost grew white whiskers on the cattle droppings in the paddocks, and Mud brought in one of her brother's well-darned old jumpers for Big Billy at school. Mrs Peaslake sent Georg to school with a Thermos of soup to share with Mud. They shared with Big Billy too.

Mr Menzies, the Prime Minister, called on women to take over men's jobs, so more men could join the army. People were supposed to grow their own vegetables and keep hens for eggs too. But everyone around Bellagong did this anyway, except for Mud's family, who shared the bounty next door and in return supplied them with butter, cream, milk and meat.

To Georg's surprise he enjoyed gardening with Mrs Peaslake. Even weeding was all right when you could ask Mrs Peaslake questions, like why is the sky blue and are zebras striped all exactly the same. It was hard to find the answers to questions like that in the encyclopaedia, but mostly Mrs Peaslake knew where to find them.

Picking was best of all: pulling at the green tops of carrots, never knowing if you were going to haul up a whopper or a skinny 'un, all forked and twisted; filling buckets with peas and eating almost as many as he picked with a trick Mud taught him, pulling the pea pods through your teeth so the green peas popped out into your mouth.

He liked the hens, their clucking song, the eggs warm in his hand each morning, the chooks pecking around the scrap bucket. They liked old bread best and cheese rinds or lumps of sodden porridge. The dogs looked on, envious yet contemptuous, knowing that the best scraps were kept for them.

Winter stretched endlessly that year of the war, a high blue sky and gold sun that seemed to have hidden its warmth behind the blue. People were cold in Melbourne, said the newspaper, as there wasn't enough firewood this year — with few men to cut it and not enough petrol to cart it into the city — and gas supplies ran short. But here at Bellagong an afternoon with the cross-cut saw gave wood for weeks. Mr Peaslake and Mr Mutton sliced through fallen trees while Georg and Mud threw the hunks of wood into the cart.

Clothes weren't rationed like in England, but shops could only sell three-quarters each day of what they'd sold the same day the year before. Once they'd sold that they had to shut their doors. But, as Mrs Peaslake said, that amount was more nuisance than disaster, and she liked getting her shopping done early anyhow. She'd bought a big bolt of grey flannel before the war, and could 'run him up' new shorts or trousers when he wore through the knees or outgrew the ones he had.

The Germans had invaded Russia and were nearing Moscow now, said the newspapers and the man on the wireless who announced the news with an English accent even though he was Australian. Mrs Peaslake made sixty-three pots of lemon and melon marmalade, some for them and Mud's family but most to sell at the Comforts for Soldiers stall outside the general store, where the lists of the latest casualties were pinned up in the window so that everyone could see them even if the store was closed.

Mr Curtin was elected as the new Australian Prime Minister, which made Mr Peaslake glad, though he didn't exactly explain why, except to boom that 'the old man was a good 'un'.

━❦❧◯━

Dear George,

Mrs Martin says I have to write to you to improve my spelling but I want to write to you anyway. It is bonzer here. That is a new Australian word I have learned. We live on a street with lots of houses and no cows! I do not have to get up till eight o'clock to go to school, it is just down the road. We go to the beach every weekend. There is no barbed wire like at home. At school they called me out the front and said I was brave and everyone gave three cheers for England and sang 'God Save the King'. I won three marbles off Trevor Wilkes.

Guess what? Harris lives in the next street. He is called Harry now.

I hope your family is good like mine is.

Your friend,
Jamie Mallory

Georg was glad Jamie was happy. He thought he was happy too, mostly — except for those whispers in the night.

Sometimes the pain got bigger, like when Mr Justin the vicar gave a sermon on how Hitler had blotted out the good in all the German people and made their children loathsome.

He woke up sweating that night, seeing the loving faces of the Peaslakes turn accusing, staring down at him, Mud spitting at him: loathsome German boy, they hissed. Did you think you could fool us forever? Loathsome. Loathsome.

It took him long minutes to make himself accept that he was safe, in bed; that no one accused him; that no one was even likely to guess, so far away from anyone who had ever known that he was German.

He was safe, with the dogs sleeping by the fire in a house where the inhabitants were so secure they never even locked the doors, even when they were out. 'What if some poor soul needed to get out of the rain?' said Mrs Peaslake comfortably. 'They might get pneumonia without even a chance to make a cup of tea.'

Georg's world had narrowed now: school and Mud and flying kites. It was only in the cold well of the night that whispers came to him of enemies and hatred far away.

He was safe here. They were all safe. A small safe town with hatred (mostly) far away.

And then it changed.

Chapter 27

Bellagong
2 December 1941

My darling son,

It was so good to get your last letter. I'm glad all the socks have arrived safely. I know you've only got two feet and can only wear two socks at once, but I am sure your friends will like the socks you don't need.

All is good at home. Samson is getting fat — he doesn't follow Dad out into the paddocks like he followed you, but sits here by the stove. Sometimes I think he plans to sit here till you get back, except for kite-flying of course. He never misses that. But Delilah follows George and Mud everywhere.

It is a great comfort to have George here. I was worried about Mud, when Len and Ken went overseas. She was getting too serious for a girl of her age, and there was no need for her to work so hard, not with your dad and old Mr Hillman to help your auntie and uncle. It looks like they might get a couple of land girls too.

Now George is here Mud plays like a normal girl again. Well, she is always a tomboy so she plays cricket and that terrible game 'defence' — I have to darn George's shorts every time they play it at school — but you know what I mean. Your auntie is relieved and so am I.

There's not much other news. There's a bumper crop of peas this year and roses, but you don't want to hear about my roses! I made thirty-four jars of loquat jam for the Red Cross stall. I didn't put 'loquat jam' on the label, just 'home-made jam', so that people who haven't eaten loquat jam before will buy it thinking it is plum jam and, really, it is just as good or better, and it is for a good cause.

We miss you and are proud of you, always.

Your loving mother,
Mum

Mud and Georg had been picking cherries after school that Monday out in the orchard, bucket after bucketful, trying to get them in before the storm clouds on the horizon brought the rain. They had to push them through the cherry pitter out in the shed because the cherries spat red juice and Mrs Peaslake didn't want her kitchen spattered.

There were so many pitted cherries that Georg and Mud could scoop up handfuls to eat, staining their mouths and their clothes. They were the old clothes they wore for doing jobs around the farm, so a few more stains didn't matter.

The rain began to pelt, each drop heavy on the shed's tin roof. It was getting dark when they raced back to the kitchen with the cherries for Mrs Peaslake to make into jam and bottle. She turned the wireless on and then began to fill the big jam kettle with water and sugar and fruit.

'... *And we now repeat, Japan has declared war on the United States.*' Georg listened stunned as the almost-English wireless voice told how on early Sunday morning Japanese planes had destroyed the United States ships at Hawaii, without warning, without even declaring war on the United States first.

Japanese planes had attacked Malaya, Guam, Singapore, Ocean Island, Noumea ...

He looked across at Mud, her lips still stained with cherry juice, at Mrs Peaslake, her hands still, at the stunned face of Mr Peaslake.

What did it mean for all of them?

The Allies had won the last war when the United States joined in — but now most of the United States ships had been destroyed.

Noumea was near Australia, wasn't it? He tried to remember the pink splodges on the map.

The announcer's voice vanished.

Mr Curtin's dry tones filled the kitchen instead: '*This is our darkest hour, for the nation itself is imperilled.*'

The kitchen was silent, except for the Prime Minister's voice on the wireless. Even the dogs lay still before the stove. Georg sat back in his chair.

'... *We shall hold this country and keep it as a citadel for the British-speaking race and as a place where civilisation will persist.*'

Georg looked at the shock on the Peaslakes' faces, at their dawning anger too. Mud clenched and unclenched her fists. The Japanese had bombed Malaya, where her brothers were. England and its empire were already battered by the German and Italian forces. Now England — all Australia and the empire too — were at war with Japan as well.

'The treacherous Japanese swine,' boomed Mr Peaslake. 'Attacking without warning. Well, we'll show them what's what. Won't we, Mother?'

Mrs Peaslake looked down at her knitting. She didn't answer. The enemy was coming here.

Chapter 28

Malaya
14 December 1941

Dear Family,

I am writing this in the darkness of my tent. The blackout is the blackest ever and everything is quiet except when a plane roars overhead. After the bombing of Singapore on Monday everyone stops and listens when we hear a plane.

We are all waiting but we don't know yet what we are waiting for. We get four hours off in thirty-six. I should be trying to sleep now but am too keyed up to even lie down; and anyway, the mosquitoes are droning loud as aircraft and will have at me as soon as I shut my eyes. Don't worry, Mum, am drinking my quinine like a good boy so no malaria here.

Bad day today. Could hear gunfire across the sea. Thousands of refugees, Chinese, Tamils, with everything they own on bicycles, in trucks, on foot.

Suddenly I think maybe I do need that sleep. Just to say, don't worry. Len and I are still in the land of the living. We have clean clothes, dinner in our tummies, and a tent to sleep in. But when

this war is over neither of us ever want to see another swamp or
rubber plantation in our lives.

Love to all,
Ken

—✣—

Georg looked at himself in the mirror. George looked back at him.

George wore too-big shorts, discarded by one of Mud's brothers. His skin was brown; his hair was streaked gold by the sun. His feet were tough, so tough that even bindi-eyes didn't stick into them these days. His knees were scabbed from playing 'defence' in the rutted playground — he'd held the ball yesterday so Mud had dragged him and it over to the fence that was their 'goalpost'.

He didn't look like Georg now, but he wasn't George either.

He headed to the kitchen and took the writing paper out of the dresser drawer, and a bottle of ink, blotting paper and a pen.

Bellagong
15 December 1941

Dear Alan,

Thank you for saying I can call you Alan, not Lieutenant Peaslake. I hope that you are well. Everything is good here but everyone is angry at the Japanese treachery. We are not going to let them beat us.

The hens are moulting so we don't have so many eggs. Mud and I collected the feathers. Your mum baked the feathers in the oven to kill the mites and has made a new patchwork quilt with them. They are going to raffle it for the Red Cross. Mud and I have made patches too from two of Mud's old dresses, so it will have to be a quilt for a girl as it has flowers on it.

We flew kites yesterday. I think the sea eagle laughs at us. We are stuck on the ground and can only lift sticks and paper into the sky. But Mud says people can put planes into the sky so we are better than eagles.

I hope it is not too hot and you do not get sand in your sausages. We had a picnic down on the beach and I ate sand-wiches. (That is a joke.)

I hope it is a good Christmas where you are. I will wish the dogs Merry Christmas for you and make sure they get a big bone each for Christmas dinner.

Yours very sincerely,
Your foster brother,
George

He was folding the letter into its envelope when Mrs Peaslake hurried in through the laundry. Her face looked strange.

'George, can you help?'

He nodded. 'What do you want me to do?'

'Mud's up in the pear tree.'

'What's wrong?' he asked slowly.

'It's … it's her dad. He enlisted this morning.' Mrs Peaslake's face looked tight as though she wasn't letting any emotion show; as though, perhaps, she wasn't yet even sure what she did feel. Mr Mutton is her brother, thought Georg, as well as Mud's dad. 'Didn't even tell the family: just took the early train to Wollongong and announced it to everyone at lunch.'

'But farmers aren't allowed to fight.' Many men who wanted to join up weren't allowed to if they were in 'reserved occupations' — ones that were needed to keep the country going and fed during the war.

'He convinced the board that the place will be all right without him. He's arranged for a couple of land girls to help too.' Mrs Peaslake looked helpless. 'I've called for her to come down. But she pretends she doesn't hear me.'

'I'll go out to her.'

Mrs Peaslake looked like she might cry. 'Thank you, George. Father's off at the Bushfire Brigade meeting or I'd ask him.'

Georg doubted Mr Peaslake could get Mud to come down if she didn't want to. Neither could he.

But he could go up to her.

Samson looked up from the rug by the wood stove as Georg went out. The room felt breathless in the heat, despite the open door and windows. Delilah bounced around his heels, leading the way self-importantly to the pear tree.

Georg stared up into the branches. 'Mud?'

No answer. She sat with her back to the trunk, her arms around her knees, huddled like a koala like she'd been when she thought they wouldn't sing carols. But this was worse. Georg pushed his toes against the trunk and grabbed a branch, then heaved himself up beside her, but she kept her face resolutely turned away.

Two brothers facing the enemy, he thought, and one cousin who must be like a brother. And now her father was off to war too.

'It's all right to cry, you know,' he said at last.

'I'm not crying! I never cry!'

'I do,' he said.

She stared at him. 'Boys don't cry.'

'Maybe we pretend we don't, but we do. I cried for ...' He hesitated again to use anything other than his parents' real names. But he had no choice. 'When Daddy died. I cry for Mummy.'

'It ... it's worse for you too, isn't it?' said Mud slowly.

If only he could tell her how bad it really was, not knowing if Mutti was safe or hunted or in a camp; if Papa had really died there on the University lawn. 'I don't think it matters which is worse. Maybe it just gets so that it can't hurt any more … no matter how bad it is or how much worse it gets. But you've got to keep going.'

'Of course I'll keep going,' she flared. 'I can use a cross-cut saw as well as Dad and repair the fences.'

'I'll help. But Mud, I meant … your auntie is worried about you. Your mum will be worried too.'

'Why worry about me?'

'Because you're hurting,' said Georg simply.

Mud made a small sad noise. She knuckled tears from her eyes angrily, glanced at him again, then let them fall.

'Do you want to borrow my hanky?'

'No! Yes,' said Mud.

He handed it over, glad that it was clean and neatly ironed by Mrs Peaslake. Funny, he thought vaguely, to let children run about with dirty feet but make sure their hankies were snow white and ironed crisp.

'Come down and have some lunch.'

Mud scrubbed at her eyes with the hanky, then blew her nose. 'I'm not hungry.'

'I know. But it'll make you feel better. And your mum and Auntie Thelma.'

'I suppose it's not fair to make them worry about me as well as about Dad and the boys,' said Mud slowly.

Georg nodded. Convincing Mud that what her parents and auntie and uncle needed most was not to have to worry about her too made him feel better about leaving Mutti and Papa. A bit, at any rate.

'All right,' said Mud at last. She met his eyes. 'It's just … it's so big. The war, I mean. It just gets bigger and bigger.'

And makes us feel smaller and smaller, thought Georg.

'I'm going to load the hay bales this afternoon. All by myself. That'll show Mum and Dad that they don't have to worry, even if the land girls don't know what they're doing at first. City girls never know anything.'

Georg thought of the heavy bales of hay, of Mud's wiry arms tugging at the strings to get the heavy bales into the cart, then off into the shed.

'I'll come with you. We can lift them together.'

She didn't say anything. He could see when she realised how much easier it would be for two to lift the bales than one. He doubted even Mud's determination would be enough to bring in a paddock of lucerne hay by herself. But two of them could manage it.

'Thanks,' she said. Mud will never be pretty, he thought, not the Elizabeth kind of pretty, but she's sort of beautiful, when she smiles like that. When Mud thanked you she meant it from her heart.

'Friends help each other,' he said. He slid down the trunk, landing on his tough bare feet, and waited for her to join him.

Chapter 29

Bellagong

16 December 1941

My dear Alan,

I hope you don't worry at getting a letter written by your dad instead of Mum. We are all well, so don't worry, but it's easier for her if I write to you about all this, not her.

Your Uncle Don came home yesterday and told his family he had found a way to not get drafted into the army. Your aunt asked how and he said, 'I've joined the air force.' We are all proud of him, as you can imagine, but he is your mum's only brother, her 'little brother' too, and so of course she worries. More than five hundred blokes joined up just that same day. I only wish I were young enough to join up too. We'll let the Nips know that we have only just begun to fight.

I hope this reaches you as it leaves us. We are all well, and optimistic, despite the news. The sons of the empire will not be defeated, not by the Jerries nor by the Nips either.

Your cousins are all well and fighting fit if we are to believe their letters, and Johnnie Cooper's family had a letter from him last week too.

We old blokes left at home have turned the Bushfire Brigade into the Home Guard. I am the air-raid warden, but as it only takes ten minutes to check the whole of Bellagong I can pop out after dinner and be back in time for cocoa. Your mum and CWA are doing wonders with the camouflage nets. They can make a net in eight hours now, and did two last week alone, as well as the Red Cross work and the care packages. Mum even knits when she helps move the cattle. She was going to have a go at spinning wool but there's been an appeal for 'sheepskins for soldiers' so I tan the hides and send the fleeces there instead.

That's all the news from us. I know Mum will be writing to you next post, and probably young George too. Don't worry if you can't find time to put pen to paper, lad. Just know that you are in our thoughts every day.

Your loving father,
Dad

—⟊◎

It was a defiant Christmas this year. The Christmas pudding, the cauliflower cheese, the baked pumpkin, even the decorations hanging on the tree declared: we shall not be beaten. We will keep our traditions and our country free.

There were four empty chairs at the dining table now.

On Christmas Day the Japanese took Hong Kong.

Two days later Mr Curtin was on the wireless again, his words thundered in the newspapers too. England wanted Australia's soldiers and planes to defend England from the Germans, and to defend India from the Japanese.

For the first time an Australian prime minister defied the

English one. Australia had to defend itself. The United States was Australia's ally in the Pacific War now. '*Australia looks to America … free of … traditional links or kinship with the United Kingdom.*'

What did Aunt Miriam think in her office, far away in England? Georg wondered. Did she think Australians should sacrifice their country for England too? It was impossible to know. Aunt Miriam's letters didn't change, always calm and downplaying any danger. But he thought that when she signed them 'your loving aunt' she meant it.

Every night he and the Peaslakes sat by the big wireless in the lounge room to listen to the news. News broadcasts were too important to listen to on the small kitchen wireless now.

They listened as the Japanese pounded into Thailand, the Philippines and Borneo. The Italians took back dearly won Benghazi …

Part of him felt frightened, in a way that even Mud could never know. He knew what war was like. War wasn't real until you saw the flames after the bombs, the blood and glass scattered across the pavements.

Yet part of him was glad too, despite the change. Australia's hatred had turned from the Germans to the Japanese now. The cowardly Japanese, who had struck without warning; the treacherous Japanese, who had bombed before declaring war. Hatred had run through the town like the row of pennies the soldier had shown him, all falling down almost together.

Georg could share the hatred of this enemy.

This enemy wasn't him.

Chapter 30

Bellagong
26 February 1942

Dear Aunt Miriam,

I hope you are well. We are well here but we are worried about Mud's brothers. They are in Malaya and the Japanese are there, but of course you will know that. I hope the censor leaves that in about Mud's brothers because I do not think their being there is a secret that will help the enemy, and besides, Singapore is the best fortress in the world so the English and Australians will stop the Japanese there.

Alan Peaslake had a bad leg. I do not know what was wrong with it, as he did not say in his letter, just that he is back on duty and it is all right now.

I will not write more now as there is no news really. All the real news is on the wireless.

Your loving nephew,
George

Singapore could never fall. It had been said so often that everyone believed it — except the Japanese.

Georg sat on the lounge-room carpet, staring at the big wireless, the letter he had just finished forgotten. Delilah sat next to him, licking the scab on his knee.

Mr Peaslake stared too, as though it was impossible to believe what they had heard. Mrs Peaslake's knitting needles had stopped clicking.

Singapore had fallen. Singapore, the mightiest British fortress in the world.

Singapore was supposed to have made Australia safe. What could stop the Japanese invading Australia now, with so much of its army and navy still on the other side of the world, helping England?

'*And in other news* ...' said the announcer.

Mr Peaslake stood up and turned the wireless off. 'The boys will be all right,' he said heavily. 'Len and Ken ... they'll have escaped. If anyone can escape it'll be them.'

Mrs Peaslake said nothing, just looked down at her knitting and began clicking again.

How many Australian soldiers have been killed? wondered Georg. The wireless hadn't said. Surely they couldn't all have been killed, not the whole army. Soldiers could surrender, couldn't they? Maybe Mud's brothers would be sent to prison camps if they hadn't escaped. Prison camps were bad but people got letters from prisoners there. Mrs Purdon's husband had been taken prisoner in Crete and she had got two letters and a postcard.

He remembered with a taste of terror his own escape in the suitcase. There could be no suitcase escapes for Len and Ken. Maybe they could hide in the jungle, like boys did in adventure stories in the *Boy's Own Annual*, or find a boat.

Mrs Peaslake stood up. 'We'd better go over there.'

'Over there' meant Mud's place. Georg didn't ask what they would do there, or even if he should go too. He knew why they were needed: why he was needed too.

When things were bad you stuck together.

—❧○—

The women sat in the kitchen, talking quietly. Mr Peaslake glanced at them, then muttered something about 'filling the wood box'. He went outside. Georg heard the sound of the woodsplitter on a log.

There was no sign of Mud.

He walked quietly down to her room, and knocked.

There was no answer. He knocked again, then opened the door.

Mud lay on her bed. It was a girlie bed, with a pink bedspread with fuzzy tassels at the edges. There was even an old doll on the dressing table, next to a teddy bear with a chewed ear.

'Are you all right?' asked Georg. It was a silly thing to say, but he of all people knew that sometimes there were no right words, that just saying something was all that you could do.

'They've escaped,' said Mud. Her voice was hoarse, but there was no anxiety or anguish in it. Instead she sounded sure.

'How do you know?'

'I just do!'

'All right. Do you want to …' Georg searched for something they might do together. 'Help fill the wood box?' he said at last.

'We don't need more wood,' began Mud. Then she stopped, as though she finally heard the sounds of wood being split outside. She stood up and nodded.

They went to join Mr Peaslake at the wood heap.

Chapter 31

District Records Office
RAS Showground, Sydney
6 March 1942

To Mrs L Mutton
Red Gate Farm
Bellagong
New South Wales

Dear Madam,

I have been directed by the Minister for the Army to advise you that no definite information is at present available in regard to the whereabouts or circumstances of your son Corporal Ken Mutton 8th Division AIF and to convey to you the sincere sympathy of the Minister and Military Board in your natural anxiety in the absence of news concerning him.

You may rest assured, however, that the utmost endeavour will continue to be made through every possible source, including the International Red Cross Society, to obtain at the earliest possible moment a definite report, which, when received, will be conveyed to you by telegram immediately. It would be appreciated if you could forward full particulars to this office as quickly as possible of any information you may receive from any other source, as it may be of the greatest value in supplementing official investigations which are being made.

Yours faithfully,
HN Glass, Major, Officer in Charge, Records

—⁂◎

Mud sat dry-eyed in the stuffy classroom. Her eyes had turned to metal since her brothers had vanished in the fall of Singapore.

Both she and Georg knew all the kings of England off by heart now. Blaxland, Wentworth and Lawson crossed the Blue Mountains; Captain Cook discovered Australia; Columbus discovered America. What else was there to learn?

Nothing in the school textbook anyway, thought Georg. But it was time for the history lesson, so that was the textbook they had open.

Mrs Rose sat knitting at the front of her classroom, her face pale, the shadows dark around her eyes. She had heard the day before that her husband was a prisoner of war in Malaya. But she was still at school this morning, though she had set the littlies to work at their copybooks, practising perfect round letters, instead of giving lessons today.

Big Billy snoozed at the back of the room. He'd been shucking corn for cattle food by lamplight for his uncle the last few nights. School was the only chance of sleep he got.

Fat flies bumped at the window. Stupid flies, Georg thought. If they went to the door they could fly out.

Suddenly heavy footsteps sounded outside. Mrs Rose looked up in alarm. The children did too.

But it was Mr Peaslake. He panted like he'd been running. He was sort of smiling. Only 'sort of'. Georg had never seen an expression like that before.

'News,' he boomed. 'Mud, it's good news. They're safe. Both Len and Ken. Got the telegram just now. I said I'd run right over. Don't know where they are. But they're not prisoners. They're safe.'

'I knew they were,' said Mud calmly. She shut her history book and stood up. 'I'd better go to Mum.'

She ran out of the class. Georg wondered if he was the only one who had seen her face break into anguish, the tears pouring down before she had even reached the door.

Mr Peaslake looked after her, then back at Mrs Rose. 'Something else,' he said, quietly for him.

Mrs Rose clutched her knitting. 'What?' She was crying too: for Mud, for her husband, for herself, or maybe for us all, thought Georg. Little Susie down the back began to cry too.

'The Japs are bombing Darwin. They're bombing us now too.'

Chapter 32

Red Gate Farm
Bellagong NSW
29 March 1942

Dear Dad,

Here is a scarf I knitted for you. It was going to be socks but they didn't work so Auntie Thel changed them into a scarf for me. I am sorry about the lumps.

I know Mum told you about the letter from Ken and Len. I TOLD her they were all right. I wish they could come home on leave but I know that it is too far for them to come. Mum has stuck the letter on the dresser with a drawing pin so we can read it every time we go into the kitchen to remind us they are safe.

We got all the first cut of hay in and will have a second cut too. I drove the header all by myself except I let George have a go too. It's all right because he does really straight rows. His old hat was too small but the shop had a new one out the back. It still looks too new but I told him not to worry: it'll get sweat-stained and floppy by winter.

Everyone is furious about the Japs bombing Darwin and Broome and places. I am so angry I could bust. There are posters everywhere, even in the butcher's shop, about their treachery. I am glad Mr Curtin told the English that our men had to come home to defend Australia instead of fighting the Japanese in Burma. England already has most of our men and our planes and ships and it isn't fair that Mr Churchill wants more.

I called Mr Churchill a greedy pig at school. I was worried in case it made George angry, because England is his country, but he didn't say anything. I was glad because he is my friend and he helps a lot with the farm, you would never know he was from the city. He doesn't even talk posh now mostly.

It is good that the Americans are coming here and that Mr Curtin can work with General Mackarther. I am not sure how to spell his name, I need to look up the newspaper, but he looks good in the photo, not fat like Mr Churchill. If the Japs try to invade us we will be ready for them.

We got twenty-six pounds each for the stock at Friday's cattle sale. That is the best price yet. I told Mum we should keep all the weaners this year and fatten them as we will have enough lucerne even if we don't get much rain, and she agrees.

It was 106 in the top paddock today. I bet George we could fry an egg on the corrugated iron over the salt lick. I won, but the egg cooked solid and we couldn't scrape it off. It looks funny but when you see it you'll know what it is and not have to wonder.

Uncle Ron and the Bushfire Brigade were going to be a People's Army like it said in the paper, but now they are an official Volunteer Defence Corps. I wish I could join but there are no kids and not even any women, though it said in the paper women can be in the People's Army. I asked Mum and Auntie

Thel if we could form a branch of the People's Army here. They said no but if you write and say it is a good idea maybe they will say yes instead. Please write and say yes because we all have to stop the Japs now.

It is all right to tell me and Mum when you will be sent overseas. We will be careful that no spy finds out.

I hope your training is going well.

Lots of love,
Mud

PS I miss you.

—ᵒᵎᴼᴼ

Georg stood in Bellagong's small shop as Mrs Peaslake bought three yards of blackout paper. 'No, better make that four,' said Mrs Peaslake to Mrs Peters at the counter. 'We'd better cover Alan's bedroom window too, just in case he is posted back. I'd hate things not to be ready for him.'

Georg didn't think there was any danger of that. Even the sheets on Alan's bed were changed every Monday, just like all the other sheets in the house.

Mr Peaslake made plywood shutters for the bottom part of the bedroom windows. When the light went off the plywood could be pulled back to let in air, or left open during the day and only closed off when the lights went on. Lights that might lure the Japanese bombers to Bellagong.

Mrs Peaslake made proper blackout curtains for the lounge room and kitchen, pedalling the treadle sewing machine. It was hard to get the needle through the thick black leatherette. The curtains were so heavy it took the three of them to put them up after they'd been threaded on the rails. But when they went outside not a crack of light showed. Not a speck of light in the whole town.

The worst problem with the blackout was getting to the dunny at night. After one night when Mr Peaslake had put his foot in the chook's bucket (accidentally left by Georg on the path between the house and the dunny), Mrs Peaslake rummaged out three old chamberpots from the back of the shed, and crocheted cloths to put over them to cut down the smell.

It was a bit embarrassing to carry your chamberpot down to the dunny with you every morning, but better than tripping on your way there in the dark or, worse, sitting on a spider.

Only Mr Peaslake was allowed to use a torch outside now when he checked the town as air-raid warden, to see that no slice of light was visible. And even then, he could only use it in an emergency. But the pale dirt roads glowed in the starlight and, as Mr Peaslake said, he knew the town so well he could get around blindfolded — as long as no one left a bucket in his way.

Georg carried the rolled-up blackout paper as they walked back home with Mrs Peaslake carrying the flour and sugar and Vegemite in a string bag. He remembered Aunt Miriam's cans of baked beans and salmon, the string bag of bread. The world could vanish but Bellagong could feed itself from its gardens and paddocks almost without noticing.

'Going to be a storm,' said Mrs Peaslake, looking at the black bulges on the horizon. 'Good thing you and Mud got the hay in.'

Georg nodded. His hands had blistered at first, the hay-bale ropes cutting into them. But they were as tough as his feet now.

'Better get a move on,' said Mrs Peaslake, with another glance at the sky. 'Don't want to be out in it when this hits.'

The storm still hadn't come by dinnertime, though the air felt as thick as soup. Drawn by the last of the sunlight reflecting on the glass, big-winged moths flapped against the windows, till Mrs Peaslake drew the blackout curtains.

It was stuffed mutton flap for dinner tonight. Before the war the mutton flaps had been given to the dogs but now, even here in farming country, meat was more precious. Samson and Delilah slobbered over their bowls of chopped heart and liver, then wagged their tails and waited for the leftover mashed potatoes and gravy.

Georg went to bed straight after dinner and his bath; he had only three inches of bath water tonight as the house tanks were half empty. Mr Peaslake's cousin in Sydney had sent him down a whole box of old books she'd bought at a Red Cross jumble sale. One of them was even a John Buchan book he hadn't read.

The storm struck when he was on page 146: a scatter of hail on the tin roof like sheep pellets; and then the rain sweeping and pounding, the water gurgling down the pipes into the tanks.

A full bath tomorrow night, he thought, as he turned off the lamp. Green paddocks instead of brown. They might even get another cut of hay.

He wasn't sure how long he'd slept when the roar woke him. For a second he thought he was back in London, the bombs ripping through the streets. Then he realised it was only thunder.

It boomed again, but not frightening now that he knew what it was, like Mr Peaslake at a dramatic bit in one of his poems.

He was thirsty. The stuffing at dinner had been salty. He

slipped out of bed and opened the door. No need to turn the light on as someone was in the kitchen and there was enough glow from there to see.

He padded along the corridor and through the kitchen door, then stopped.

The table was covered in guns. Shotguns, rifles, a long grey pistol …

He stared at them, then at Mr Peaslake and two of Mr Peaslake's friends from the Bushfire Brigade.

'George, what are you doing out of bed?'

'I'm thirsty and wanted a drink.' He couldn't look away from the shotguns.

'Just giving them a clean,' said Mr Peaslake easily. 'What with the boys and Mud's dad being away next door. Need to be cleaned regularly, that's all.'

Georg nodded. He made his way awkwardly past the men and the laden table, ran water into a glass and drank.

'Good night,' he said quietly. He shut the door behind him, aware that the men stayed silent till he was halfway down the corridor, too far away to hear their words. He wondered if Mrs Peaslake knew they were there, or if she was asleep too.

Guns did need to be cleaned after you used them. But no one had ammunition to spare for hunting rabbits or roos these days, though he knew that Mr Mutton had collected used lead pellets to melt into moulds to make new bullets.

He supposed Mr Peaslake knew how to do that too.

But he didn't think they planned to hunt rabbits.

The war dragged on, dragging the year with it. A bad year, across the whole world. The Japanese had bombed Darwin again and again through February. They'd bombed Wyndham and Broome over in Western Australia in March. General MacArthur and American troops would be coming now. At last Australia no longer had to defend itself alone, but the Japanese Empire was so big now. Could even America be powerful enough to stop them?

Even the dogs were motionless when Mr Curtin spoke on the wireless now, as though they knew from their humans' silence that they must be quiet. '... *and we will advance over blackened ruins, through blasted and fire-swept cities, across scorched plains, until we drive the enemy into the sea.*'

The enemy was near.

Chapter 33

Dear George,

It was good to get your letter, mate. I reckon we eat 'sandwiches' here too.

I'm writing to Mum and Dad separately but give them a hug from me. I reckon they'll need it. I wish I could be back defending my own country but I reckon we'll have the Jerries on the run here soon, no worries about that, and maybe they'll let us come home then to share the job with all of you.

Give the dogs a hug from me too. I've got a good lot of mates here but I miss the dogs. There was a poor starved mongrel around a week ago. Some of the blokes and I gave him some tucker but I haven't seen it for a while. Maybe it likes the Jerries' sausage better. Doesn't know it's better off with Aussie corned beef.

It's funny the things you miss sometimes. Mum's roast mutton and her apple crumble, but mostly I miss the sound of the cicadas. Seems strange to be hot with no cicadas shrilling. I've been thinking that when this is all over I mightn't go to university like I'd planned, but to agricultural college, learn how to look after the

land properly so it doesn't erode away or go to the bunnies, put
my deferred pay into some decent land near Bellagong. But we
need to beat the Jerries and the Nips first, don't we?

Tell Dad from me to make sure he doesn't blow his false teeth
out when he sounds the air-raid warden whistle — but better tell
him when Mum isn't around. Tell him I'm proud of him and
every other bloke from Bellagong in the Volunteer Defence Corps.

Fly the kite high for me, mate, keep your chin up, and don't
forget those hugs.

Your loving foster brother,
Alan

~ ✿ ~

Overnight the road signs and the signs at the railway station
vanished so the enemy, if they landed, couldn't find their way
around the country.

At school Mrs Rose made them practise evacuation drill, in
case all the kids in Australia had to be sent to Alice Springs to
escape the enemy, marching back and forth across the paddock,
singing 'to keep your spirits up'. Singing '*Pack up your troubles
in your old kit bag, and smile, smile, smile ...*'

Mud marched with the rest, but Georg was pretty sure she
would refuse to leave her land to go to Alice Springs. He wondered
if he'd go this time. He'd been sent away twice, for his own good,
and to help keep those who loved him safe and worry-free.

But he was older now. Too old to be a parcel. Even for
Mr Curtin.

The newspaper said that already women and children were
leaving big cities like Sydney and Wollongong — a hundred
thousand children might be evacuated soon in New South Wales

alone. Georg remembered the child army with their labels around their necks back in London. At least here it sounded like the mums and kids would go together.

The newspaper photos showed buildings surrounded by sandbags in Australia now, in Sydney and Brisbane, and barbed wire on the beaches too. Georg and Mud ran down to the cliffs every afternoon straight after school, to see if *their* beach had been ringed with the stuff.

But it never was. Georg supposed there wasn't enough barbed wire in Australia for every beach. If the Japanese wanted to land they could easily find a beach with no defences. But he didn't say that aloud.

Summer stayed late, the heat pounding like a fist on the tin roof and the paddocks. The air shimmered like it was trying to get away. But every afternoon the southerly rolled in as though it had been watching the clock, sweeping away the heat and sending the dogs trotting back to the warmth of the stove.

'Pair of sooks that they are,' said Mrs Peaslake, grating apples for after-school pancakes. The orchard was rich with apples now: red ones and knobbly green ones called 'twenty ouncers' the size of footballs and striped ones and some an almost black-red called Democrats, that had to wait for winter to be picked.

Georg had learned how to flip pancakes now, to wait for the bubbles on top that meant it was time to turn them over.

'Pancakes!' Mud slammed the kitchen door against the wind.

'I reckon you can smell pancakes a paddock away.' Mrs Peaslake added lemon juice to the mixture to stop the apple turning brown. 'I thought you had to make the butter for your mum today.'

'Done it,' said Mud virtuously, nodding at the tea-towel-covered bowl in her hands. 'Here's yours and Mum says can she have two dozen eggs please 'cause she's making fruitcakes for the boys tomorrow.'

She grabbed a plate and held it out for the next pancake. Georg flipped it to her, then poured in more batter. Mrs Peaslake looked at him with fond approval. She poured herself a cup of tea from the pot that brewed on the stove all day, added hot water to weaken it a bit, and a splash of milk, then sat back with a sigh and picked up her knitting again.

She must have been planting cabbages all morning, bending over in the heat, thought Georg. There'd been six new long rows of them when he'd come home from school.

'Can't go wrong with a good fruitcake,' said Mrs Peaslake. She glanced at the new row of bottles of chutney on the bench. 'No need to say they're choko,' she said. 'What people don't know won't hurt them and it's for a good cause.'

'Which one this time?' asked Mud.

'Relief for Soldiers' Families,' said Mrs Peaslake.

'Did you hear about Mrs Cousins?' Mud spoke through a mouthful of pancake. 'She posted poor Mr Cousins rock cakes. He said they really were like rock cakes when he got them in Egypt. He said when they run out of hand grenades he can lob the rock cakes at the enemy.' She passed her empty plate to Georg again. 'Hey, I had an idea.'

'Hay is what horses eat,' corrected Mrs Peaslake while Georg asked cautiously, 'What?'

Mud rummaged in the pockets of the dress her mum insisted she wear to school, even though Mud mostly tucked the skirt into her bloomers so it looked like shorts anyway.

She pulled out an already grubby pamphlet. 'I found it at the post office. It's for schoolchildren! It says how to find a German spy.'

Georg froze.

'You have to listen to anyone who asks lots of questions,' said Mud, 'like where your dad or brothers have been posted, and then you have to ring this number and report them. It's got lots of other great ideas. Look!' She held it up.

Georg looked at the drawings. 'What's that kid doing?' He tried to keep his voice normal.

'Spying on suspicious characters. See, if you're behind a bush you have to keep your bum down —'

'Language,' warned Mrs Peaslake, not looking up from her knitting.

'Bottom then. The pamphlet says every school needs to have its own Junior Volunteer Defence Corps in case we're invaded.'

Is she really so brave the idea doesn't scare her? wondered Georg. Or doesn't she realise what it's like when enemies try to invade your home?

He watched her reading out more of the pamphlet in between bites of apple pancake. Knowing Mud, maybe a bit of both, he thought.

What would she do if she knew he was German? Would Mud — even Mud — think he was a spy?

'… and they say we have to think up our own ways of stopping the enemy. Like rolling garbage bins under tanks, but I think tanks would crush garbage bins, so logs would be better. We could wrap them in barbed wire so they stop the tanks from moving.'

Georg stared at her. Had she ever seen a tank, except on the Movietone News before the pictures up in Wollongong on her birthday?

He'd seen tanks in parades at home, years ago. He realised her idea might actually work.

'Time enough to start wrapping logs in good barbed wire if the Japs ever do land,' said Mrs Peaslake, her quiet voice suddenly sharp.

'We can use *old* barbed wire from the dump! And make stink bombs. You know those eggs Gertie was sitting on and then got off? We can mix those with dog droppings and tie them in balloons and —'

Mrs Peaslake's face relaxed. 'There'll be no mixing rotten eggs around here or you'll get sick to your stomach.'

She got up to stir the stew on the back burner of the stove, then opened the oven to check the Anzac biscuits. A slow-cooked Anzac biscuit lasted almost as long as a rich fruitcake if it was packed in enough old newspaper. Mrs Peaslake reckoned that if you could throw a package of biscuits at the wall and they didn't break, they were packed well enough to send overseas. 'Now if you have nothing to do I've got two old jumpers that need unravelling and rolling up again.'

'But we have to help the war effort!'

'Good-fitting socks in their boots will help our boys more than rotten eggs and dog droppings. The idea! Now off to the garden with you if you don't want to unravel the jumpers. There's the beans to be picked and the cabbage seedlings to be watered, and could you take some of the chutney down to Mrs Finister for the Christmas Box Appeal stall, and some to Mrs Aston for the Refugee Relief raffle, and a jar for your mum while you're at it, Mud.'

Mrs Peaslake took a tray of Anzacs out of the oven to cool before she packed them, and put in another. 'And then you can call in at the shop for another ball of string and roll of brown paper — my purse is just over there.'

'She's trying to keep us too busy to make stink bombs,' said Mud, as they took the baskets down from the laundry wall to put the beans into.

Georg thought of the bombers in the blood-red sky of London. 'I don't think stink bombs would make much difference to the Japanese,' he said.

'I've got a better idea anyway.' She gave him a sideways glance. 'Did you know Uncle Ron has a pamphlet called *Guerillas in Australia*?'

Georg shook his head.

'I looked up guerillas and they aren't the animals, they are people who hide in the bush and fight invaders. And he's got a new book called *Shoot to Kill* by a man called Ion Idriess.'

'He didn't show me.' Georg tried to keep the hurt from his face. Mr Peaslake shared all his books with Georg.

'He didn't show me either. I saw him take it down to the shed when the postman delivered it. Then I snuck in there after dinner. I don't think Auntie Thel knows he has it.'

'Why not?'

'Because it's about fighting the Japs if they come here. Real fighting. Not just stink bombs.'

'What sort of fighting?'

'There's how to make a thing called a Molotov cocktail to blow up tanks and armoured cars. It's like a bomb. You put petrol and kerosene and tar from the edges of the road in a bottle —'

'There aren't any tarred roads around here. And no one has any spare petrol either.' Plus, he thought, it sounded like something that would be more likely to blow up the person trying to use it than kill an enemy soldier.

'I got another idea from it though. A better one.'

'What?'

Mud grinned. 'You'll find out tomorrow.'

Chapter 34

Bellagong
21 April 1942

Dear Aunt Miriam,

I hope you are well.

Guess what? We have formed the Bellagong Junior Volunteer Defence Corps. We will start tomorrow. Mud is going to be the Captain but she says I can be her Lieutenant and Big Billy will be the Sergeant because he is the biggest even if he is younger than me and Mud.

I have not had any letters from you for two months, but I know not to worry as there is not much room for letters on ships now and that you are safe where you are in the country. But if you sent me any news in the last two months could you send it to me again in case it was on a ship that sank?

We have lots of pumpkins. They are drying out on the shed roof. It doesn't seem funny to eat cattle food now: it is very good. Mrs Peaslake makes a pumpkin fruitcake too, but I cannot send you one because it does not keep well like other fruitcakes.

Mr and Mrs Peaslake send their very best regards and Mud

says to send you her love. I do not know if this is right because you and Mud have not met, but Mud says it is because you are my aunt and she is my friend, so I send it anyway.

Your loving nephew,
George

~●~

The Bellagong Junior Volunteer Defence Corps stared at Mud from their desks. Though it was Saturday morning, all the kids had turned up — even Big Billy, scratching a mosquito bite on his leg. Most had also brought the broom or mop Mud had insisted on; and a bread saw or pen knife too.

'Right, I now declare this meeting come to order,' said Mud.

Little Sally put her hand up.

'What does that mean?'

'It doesn't *mean* anything. It's just what you say. Now, I've got a list here.' She held it up. 'I'm going to pin it on the door. Every Monday we have to bring in something metal that could be melted down to make an aeroplane.'

'What's metal?' asked Big Billy.

'Things like saucepans,' said Mud.

'We ain't got any except the one to cook potatoes.'

'Corrugated iron then. Old bolts. Tin cans.'

'We got those,' said Big Billy.

'Tuesday we collect old tyres. Ask at the other houses and see if there are any. Wednesday newspapers, Thursday bottles, Friday is jumble day, anything at home that can be spared that someone else might find a use for. On Saturday at eight o'clock Mr Henderson, the ambulance driver, is going to give first-aid classes at the church hall and everyone's got to be there.'

Big Billy brightened at the thought of another morning with no farm work.

'But most importantly,' Mud stared at the watching children, 'we've got to work out how to stop the enemy if they come to Bellagong.' She held up a 1932 *Boy's Own Annual*. It must belong to one of her brothers, Georg decided. He remembered the one that showed how to make an underwater spear gun in the library back in London.

'We're going to make our own bayonets,' said Mud crisply. 'Now, everyone got your brooms or mops?'

Little Billy and Sally held up theirs. Big Billy put his hand up. 'Don't have no mop left on my mop,' he said.

'Doesn't matter. It's the stick we want. Now, here's string and scissors. You've got to tie the handle of the knife to the stick in two places, like this. Now while you're doing that ...'

Mud reached down behind Mrs Rose's desk and pulled out a limp figure. It was a scarecrow, hay stuffed into old clothes and boots with a face drawn on an old stuffed pillowcase and an ancient hat on top.

Mud lugged the scarecrow into Mrs Rose's seat. 'Right, we're going to practise bayoneting just like they do in basic training. On the count of three you lift your bayonet, and then you charge.'

Georg stared, unbelieving. Mud had never seen anyone hurt by war. But he had. People bleeding, dying. Dead.

'One.' Mud lifted up a broom handle with what looked like a long carving knife strapped to it.

'Two —'

'What on earth is going on here? Mud! Put that down this instant! What has got into you?'

Mud put down her bayonet and glared defiance at Mrs Rose. 'It's the Bellagong Junior Volunteer Defence Corps.'

'I don't care what it is. You're not going to play with knives here. Or anywhere.'

'We're not *playing*,' began Mud angrily.

Mrs Rose's voice gentled. 'No, no you're not, Mud. But no knives. It's too dangerous — for the little ones,' she added hurriedly. 'There is plenty you can leave to adults,' she said softly. 'Things aren't that bad yet, love.'

She had never called Mud 'love' before. The other children put their 'bayonets' down uncertainly.

'George, can you take the knives off? Carefully,' added Mrs Rose. 'Mud, I know you're ...' She tried to find the words. 'This is a wonderful idea.' She glanced at the metal/paper/glass roster. 'But there are other things you can do.'

'Like what?'

'We'll work it out,' said Mrs Rose gently. 'Now, I think that's enough for today. Leave the, er, bayonets. I'll see they get back to your homes safely. And Mud,' she added, as the others began to file out.

'What?'

'Good show,' she said. 'It was a bit much, that's all. But it's a good show.'

Mud nodded briefly.

'Have you heard from your brothers?' Mrs Rose's voice was a bit too casual.

'Not for a couple of weeks.'

'Mail is unreliable these days. Nothing for three months sometimes, then five letters at once.' She bit her lip. 'I got a letter from my husband yesterday. He says he's safe and well in the prison camp.'

Everyone in Bellagong knew the news already. But Georg was glad to see the look of hope on Mrs Rose's face.

He made himself not count how long it had been since he had seen Mutti. Even one letter in all that time would have been like a miracle.

'Your brothers will be right,' said Mrs Rose, patting Mud's arm. 'Your dad too. Now you go off and play.'

—✷◎

'Play,' said Mud bitterly, as they headed up the footpath.

'I'm sorry,' said Georg. He didn't say, 'It was a dumb idea. You can't let kids like Sally and Little Billy play round with bayonets.' Instead he asked carefully, 'Do you mind?'

Mud shrugged. 'She's right. The littlies are too small to fight the Japs.' She looked him in the eye. 'I would though. If they try to send us to Alice Springs when the Japs come, I won't go. I'll hide in the hills if I have to. I won't let an enemy take an inch of Australian soil.'

She waited for Georg to agree: to say that he'd fight too.

George would fight, he thought. But he was *Georg*, who had run from Germany, had sailed away from England when things got bad. If he had pleaded would Mutti have let him stay, or would Aunt Miriam have worked out how to keep him with her? Was Mutti trying to fight the Nazis now? If he had stayed could he have helped her?

He didn't know.

And now? Now he felt hatred like a warm tide running through his body; felt it link him to Mud, to the whole town and country. He belonged now, because of hate.

'Yes,' said Georg. 'I'd fight the Japs too. And we'd win.'

266

The Bellagong Junior Volunteer Defence Corps met every afternoon after school, under Mrs Rose's watchful eye in case Mud experimented with bayonets again. They trooped from house to house, collecting for the war effort.

But it didn't take long to collect all the scrap from every house in Bellagong, and even from the farmhouses a bike or pony ride away.

Mud coaxed Mr Henderson, the ambulance driver, into giving first-aid classes one afternoon a week; how to support a broken arm or press a wound to stop it bleeding or use a cricket bat to make a splint, supposing there was a cricket bat around. She pinned up the air-raid precautions from the newspaper on the school door: Keep your head down. Upturned faces draw enemy fire. To avoid concussion, never lean against the walls.

At last the Bellagong Junior Volunteer Defence Corps was reduced to knitting squares at lunchtime to sew into blankets for refugees and wounded soldiers. Some of the squares were more hole than wool, and not quite square either. Georg hoped that those who got them realised that even small kids like Sally had worked on them: that they were made with love as well as holes.

He wished there was a way to send a blanket to Mutti too.

Chapter 35

26 April 1942

Dear Mutti,

I am going to put this letter in a bottle and throw it into the sea. I know you will not get it but when we meet after the war I want to tell you that I wrote to you.

I hope you are well and there are no bombs where you are. Aunt Miriam is safe. I got a letter from her at last yesterday. She said that there were no bombs in her part of the country. Her flat is still not bombed either.

I hope our house is not bombed but if the government has taken it maybe it is not ever going to be our house again.

I hope you have enough to eat. There is so much food here it hurts to think you may not have enough, but it said in the newspapers that many people in Europe are hungry. Mrs Peaslake sends lots of cakes to her son and to the Red Cross and to Mud's brothers and dad. I wish we could send cakes to you too.

I am working hard at school. I speak English all the time but sometimes when I am alone on the cliffs and the wind is blowing

hard I say some of Papa's poems in Deutsch. I do not forget them
or him or you either.

With oceans of love always,
Georg

—◊◊◎

Autumn turned the orchard gold and red, despite the stubborn greenness of the gumtrees. Mrs Peaslake made rag rugs from the old-clothes basket and cut down a pair of Mr Peaslake's old trousers to make into shorts for Georg for school. No need to waste cloth, she said, with him growing so fast.

The school room was in the middle of chanting the six times tables, Georg and Mud helping hear the youngest, when Big Billy yelled from outside.

'Missus! Mrs Rose! Come quickly, Missus!'

Mrs Rose ran out. The children poured out behind her. Had Big Billy been bitten by a snake? A big red-bellied black was supposed to live under the school room but only Mud had seen it. Or had he got a splinter in his foot?

Big Billy pointed at the sky.

Georg could hear it now — the stutter of a plane.

Bomber!

He peered over at the part of the sky where Big Billy pointed. There it was: only a speck, but undoubtedly a plane.

No plane had ever flown over Bellagong in all the time he'd been here. Don't panic, he told himself. It might be one of ours. No reason to think a Jap plane could be all the way down here, so far from north Australia.

The sound grew louder. His skin prickled, like it knew to be scared before his mind could take it in.

He gazed around. No underground station, like there had been in London, to hide in here, not even a cellar.

The plane drew closer.

'Cor,' said Little Billy. 'It's a Jap plane!'

'It can't be,' said Mud. 'The Japanese are miles away. Up north.'

Big Billy pointed. Now they could all see it: the round Japanese insignia under the wings. The plane was smaller than a German bomber, almost a big kite. You could imagine the wind buffeting it across the sky.

Enemy, thought Georg. The enemy had found him again, halfway across the world. Suddenly he wished that hatred could burn; that his thoughts alone could send that plane in flames to the ground.

The plane drew closer, and closer still. It was as though a rope was pulling it towards the school.

'It's coming here!' yelled Mud.

'Inside, now!' cried Mrs Rose. 'Under your desks!'

'No!' Georg shouted.

The children stopped. Mrs Rose stopped too. He fumbled for words that would convince them. 'Bombers aim for buildings. We'll be safer in the paddocks.'

He tried to remember the instructions pasted on the door. But Mud had taken over.

'Everyone get behind something — behind the fence. Lie down. Faces down.'

'Yes.' Mrs Rose was panting, as though she had already raced across the paddocks. 'Everyone behind the fence.'

They began to run. Sally stumbled. Georg hauled the child up and found that Mud had her other arm. Together they half dragged her through the gate in the paling fence between the school building and the paddock.

'Down,' ordered Mud. The child covered her head with her arms. The others were all lying down now, a line of bodies, their heads to the wall, their faces down. Elizabeth wouldn't have saved the little kids. The thought came from nowhere. Elizabeth needed a governess to look after her. But Mud took charge.

Mud pointed upwards. The plane was almost on them now, its engine like a monster's purr.

'It's coming here,' she whispered to Georg. 'For Bellagong.'

He nodded. One small town in a wilderness of bush and paddocks. The pilot was aiming for them.

He knew from the air raids in London that planes strafed, sending bullets from the sky, as well as bombs. Would whoever was up there shoot them all?

One bomb had brought down a three-storey block of flats. One bomb could destroy this small school and half the town too.

The plane was above them now. He peered up, trying to see the pilot's face through the cockpit. But the sunlight behind was too bright, gleaming off the glass.

Jap, thought Georg. Dirty rotten Jap.

'If it fires bullets at us we have to run,' he gasped.

Mud moved to cover Sally protectively. 'Try to make it to the trees?'

Georg nodded.

He waited for the bomb to fall, for the school to shatter just as the buildings had shattered back in London. The plane's shadow passed over them, a blackness on the ground.

Was the pilot saving his bombs for Bellagong? But as he watched the plane passed the town too, so low it almost brushed the treetops, then rose higher, and higher still.

He waited for it to turn back, to bomb or strafe them on the next go round. But it headed back into the blue towards the sea.

Its engine sounded like a washing machine now, not a roar, and then just a faint stutter in the distance again.

Mrs Rose stood up. She and Mud helped the smallest children to their feet, brushing off the grass. Georg stood too. He felt empty, as though his body might float away.

The enemy was here.

–⚬฿◎

'It was a Jap spotter plane, not a bomber,' said Mr Peaslake wearily, as Georg sat eating after-school bread and jam in the kitchen. 'I went down to the phone box and called the coast watch, but they already knew. They said not to talk about it.'

'But everyone saw it.'

'Only in Bellagong.' He shrugged. 'Government doesn't want people to panic, I suppose. Doesn't want everyone knowing there are Jap planes about.'

'But where did the plane come from?' Planes needed fuel. New Guinea was too far away for a plane to fly in one hop. And that one had looked so small.

Mr Peaslake hesitated. Mrs Peaslake turned from the stove where she was stirring apple sauce for bottling. 'He's seen worse in the Blitz,' she said softly.

'Rumour has it that there are Jap subs all along the coast. Big ones. Big enough to send out aircraft to scout the area.'

Georg sat still. 'The Japanese are going to invade here?'

He waited for Mr Peaslake to say, 'Of course not.' But all he said was, 'Probably not. Any invasion will come from the north. The Japs need supply lines to keep their army in food and fuel if they are to get here. MacArthur's Yanks are between us and them now. I reckon the Japs are looking for targets. Ships, factories to bomb or torpedo before they try to invade.' He gave Georg a half-smile. 'There are none of those in Bellagong, at any rate.'

'Thank you,' said Georg. He meant, 'Thank you for telling me the truth.'

The enemy was in their sea, that happy sea where he had learned to swim. It was in the sky, where they had flown their kites.

Nowhere is safe, thought Georg. The enemy can be anywhere.

Chapter 36

Dear Mum and Dad and George,

It's a sunny Sunday morn here. I've got Mum's socks on my feet and her fruitcake in me too and just smelled the gumleaf George sent me so I almost feel like I'm with all of you.

We had some good laughs at the concert last night. The VAD girls put on a turn with their blue frocks on back to front and gas masks back to front too. They did a burlesque of 'The Way the Army Does It', marching backwards then bending down and touching their toes, showing six inches of white skin between their stocking top and undies so we howled for more. (Maybe you'd better skip that bit, Mum. Oops, you've already read it.)

Rumour has it that there might be some Cairo leave (and Captain Censor, leave that bit in, won't you? The enemy has to know we're somewhere in this neighbourhood) coming on, so watch out, Cairo. Should be able to pick up something for you all. How about a mummy for Mummy? Maybe I'll send a camel back to see if the cousins can shear one of them as good as a sheep.

Well, I'd better go in case the war grinds to a halt without me.
Give my love next door and my special love to all of you, and a
hug for the dogs too, but only if they've had a bath. We're a fussy
lot in the AIF.

Alan

The very young and the old men left in Bellagong, including Mr
Peaslake, dug the school air-raid shelter later that afternoon. It
was just a narrow trench, about two yards deep, behind the
school fence, with steps cut into the soil to get down into it, and
logs propped across it to keep off the worst of the debris if a
plane came again and this time bombed the school.

The children watched. Little Sally sucked her thumb. Big
Billy ate Georg's leftover sandwiches. Mrs Peaslake always
gave him too many. Maybe she guessed that he shared them
with Big Billy.

'Needs corrugated iron on top,' said Mud. 'That's what they
have on top of Anderson shelters in England.'

'Got some left over from the old chook house —' began one
of the men.

'No,' said Georg quickly.

Everyone stared at him.

'I ... I saw a shelter once that was bombed. The corrugated
iron collapsed. It hurt one of the people ...' He didn't want to say
more. It wasn't needed anyway.

'No corrugated iron then,' boomed Mr Peaslake.

Mud looked at the work as though she wanted to help. 'I'm
going to become a plane spotter,' she said abruptly to Georg.

'What's that?'

'It's in the paper. I cut it out to show you.' She fumbled in her pocket. 'They say children can do it — you don't have to be grown up. We have to have a local spotting station — that can be the school — and we can spend the lunch hour searching for planes. If you see one you have to write down if it's an Oxford or Anson — you can tell by the wing shape — or what sort of enemy plane it is.'

'Mr Peaslake says the coast watch looks for planes.' And anyway, he thought, the whole district would look outside if they heard a plane now. 'There's the top paddock fence to mend,' he added instead tactfully. 'We were going to do that this Saturday. But we can look for planes as well.'

'I suppose,' said Mud. She gave him a swift, sudden smile. 'Thanks,' she added.

'What for?'

'Just thanks,' she said.

Georg trudged home with Mr Peaslake in the gathering darkness. No one stayed out after dark these days, unless there was a full moon, in case the enemy saw the torchlight.

It would be a half-moon tonight. Would that be enough to show the enemy planes where the town was? Georg looked at the pale dusty road. He thought it would.

He wondered what was for dinner. Shepherd's pie, maybe, made from chopped-up, leftover roast mutton with crispy potato on top. Maybe apricot pie from bottled apricots too, and custard.

Everyone would be getting their ration books soon, with coupons that you had to tear out when you bought rationed goods. Georg supposed rationing would be pretty much like it had been in England. Except that over there people really were hungry, and here there was still all the food you wanted. The only thing in short supply was tea.

Now Japan had occupied Malaya and other countries that grew tea there was hardly ever any in the shop. No one knew exactly what foods would be rationed, but Mr Peaslake said they would probably be the same ones as in England — sugar, butter, meat — the foods that were essential to send to troops overseas, and to England too. You couldn't fight if you couldn't eat. The only thing they'd really miss at Bellagong, though, was sugar, but Mrs Peaslake said she could make cakes and puddings sweet with fruit instead.

Mr Peaslake returned the shovel to the shed. Georg followed him as he opened the kitchen door and stared.

'Mother? What's wrong?'

Georg stared too. The house was silent. Even the clock tick seemed to have vanished. Mrs Peaslake sat at the kitchen table, not even knitting. Stranger still, Samson and Delilah lay with their heads down by the stove, not leaping and barking a welcome.

'No bad news?' asked Mr Peaslake sharply. Georg didn't know how there could have been any news they hadn't heard. Mud checked the casualty lists posted up by the shop every morning, in case one of the men from the neighbourhood had been hurt, and it wasn't time to listen to the news yet, and the whole town knew as soon as the telegram boy bicycled through the main street.

'What?' Mrs Peaslake seemed to finally see them. She stood up wearily, and that was strange too. 'No, I just feel out of sorts. Sit down; I'll put the dinner out. George, set the table after you've washed your hands: there's a dear.' She slipped on her oven gloves and pulled out the buttered baking tin. It *was* shepherd's pie.

'You sure you're all right, Mother?' boomed Mr Peaslake. Delilah whined.

'Of course I am. Just … just thinking about Alan, that's all.'

'Now don't you worry about Alan. We got a letter just this morning, didn't we? Right as rain.'

Or was when he sent the letter, thought Georg.

'I'll get you a nice cuppa,' boomed Mr Peaslake soothingly, reaching for the teacup. Mrs Peaslake kept the breakfast tea leaves in the pot on the side of the wood stove these days, letting them stew all day, and adding more water every time she poured a cup, instead of making a fresh pot. But it was unthinkable to end any meal or even have a conversation without a cup of tea, even if it was weak or bitter with so much stewing.

It was a strange meal. Georg described the plane again and Mr Peaslake talked about the new air-raid shelter. At last his voice died away.

Georg glanced at the dogs. Why weren't they sitting on their haunches drooling, or pushing their noses into his lap to persuade him to slip them some potato?

He washed up the dishes while Mr Peaslake dried and put away; and Mrs Peaslake packaged up the fruitcakes she'd made to take to the CWA 'comfort package' meeting in the church hall tomorrow.

She seemed more herself now, looking at the pile of cakes with satisfaction. 'Them Nazi nasties want to starve out England,' she said. 'We'll show them, won't we, George?'

The parcels went to soldiers, to refugees, to bombed-out families in England. Every fortnight she sent a fruitcake to Alan too, as well as a new pair of socks and another pair to give to a mate.

The packages to England contained canned fruit and tins of dripping and home-made sweets: luxuries for anyone in England in these years of war.

Georg wondered if England was trying to starve Germany too, as well as sending bombers across its skies.

Mutti, bombed. Mutti, starved. But he said nothing.

The dogs lay silent by the stove.

Chapter 37

MAY 1942

The Schools at War
A Message from the Prime Minister

You, the children of today, are passing through a terrible period in the world's history. I want you to do your bit for the safety of this wonderful country in which we live. As you know, we cannot waste food or clothing or boots, paper or ink or other school material. In fact, we cannot afford to waste anything.

Farther than that, we must salvage all the worn-out materials that can be again used in the war effort — such things as aluminium, rubber and paper. Each school, with your loyal help, can be made a salvage depot for freedom.

In addition, you can share in the sacrifice your country is making. By purchasing war savings stamps with your own few pence of pocket money, you, too, can make a real sacrifice for Australia.

With faith and trust in God, a spirit of service to your country, and obedience and cheerfulness in your homes, you can each help in the war effort and bring the days of peace much closer to us all.

John Curtin

Samson didn't eat his dinner, though Delilah did at last. He wouldn't eat at breakfast either.

'Poor old boy. Sickening for something,' said Mr Peaslake, patting the dog's ears.

Samson whined. Mrs Peaslake said nothing as she picked up their egg-stained breakfast plates.

'Maybe he found a dead cow in the paddocks,' offered Georg. 'I could pick him some grass.' He'd read that dogs ate grass if they'd eaten something bad and needed to be sick to bring it back up again.

'Could be. Alan's had that dog since he was a pup. Found him abandoned down at the dump. Couldn't bear to have to tell Alan if anything happened to him.' Mr Peaslake rubbed Samson's ears again.

Samson whined again. He didn't lift his head. Mr Peaslake stood up. 'If he hasn't picked up this afternoon I'll borrow the cart and we can take him to the vet's. Can't carry you all the way there, can I, boy? You're too big.'

Mrs Peaslake handed Georg his lunchbox and Thermos, and an empty jar as it was jar collection day. He shoved them in his satchel, and kissed her cheek. It felt cool, not warm from the stove as it usually did.

Neither dog tried to follow him out the door, to sit at the gate and watch him walk down to school.

The last flies of autumn buzzed sleepily against the windows as he and Mud were working their way through Chapter Eight of the Little Red Maths Book in their seats at the back of the classroom.

'Hey, Missus?' Big Billy bashed on the door, the branches he'd been collecting for firewood in the school paddock in his hands.

Mrs Rose glanced out nervously at the sky. But there was no sign or sound of Japanese planes. 'What is it?'

Big Billy wriggled his finger in his ear, looked at it to see how much wax had come out, then lowered his voice, though the whole room could hear it anyway. 'Telegram boy, he went to the Peaslakes'.'

Mud gave a small cry, instantly bitten off. Every other child was still. Telegrams might be good news: the birth of a baby; Mud's brothers safe; a soldier coming home on leave. But they could be bad news too.

'How do you know where he was going?' asked Mrs Rose sharply.

'Asked him as he rode past,' said Big Billy.

Georg found the room staring at him.

'George, I think you had better get your satchel and head off home,' said Mrs Rose quietly. 'Yes, Mud, you too. And George … if … if it's bad news, could you tell them —' Her voice broke. Georg realised that Mrs Rose must know Alan Peaslake. Everyone in the room knew him.

Except for him.

He didn't wait for Mud. He simply ran out the school gate and down the footpath, past the paddocks, the cows watching curiously, in through the faded red gate then round to the back.

It couldn't be bad news. It might be good — that Alan had been posted back to Australia maybe. Or had been wounded, but not badly.

He ran towards the kitchen door.

Then he heard the howl.

It sounded like a dog. For a moment he thought Samson had got his foot caught in a possum trap. The howl came again. It was Mrs Peaslake.

It was as though there was a wall between him and the kitchen door. He couldn't breach it. He couldn't walk into their pain.

He knew he had to.

He put his satchel down, then began to walk, one step, two steps, into the kitchen.

Mrs Peaslake sat with her head on the table, her face hidden, her hands limp in her lap. He had never seen them lying still before. Her breath came in strange sharp pants.

Mr Peaslake held her, his face expressionless, the tears falling from his chin onto his blue gardening shirt, his nose leaking snot unheeded. They must have been weeding when the telegram boy came. Mrs Peaslake would have given the boy a piece of cake to thank him for riding here. She would have waited till he was gone to open it.

The yellow telegram lay on the table. He glanced at it. *I regret to inform you that your son, Lieutenant Alan Peaslake ...*

No need to read the rest.

The empty space at the table seemed to get bigger until it filled the room. The dogs lay where he had left them this morning, their heads on their paws.

Had they known? Had Mrs Peaslake known in some deep part of her as well?

'I'm sorry,' he whispered. Would they want him to go? To leave them to their grief?

Mrs Peaslake looked up. She held out her arms. Her hands drew him close. And suddenly the three of them were hugging, crying.

Then Mud was there, and she was hugging too. Crying for so many things, perhaps: for her brothers in danger; just as he cried for Mutti and Papa, for the world he'd lost, for the hurt to those he loved now. It hurt more to cry together but at the same it was better too.

Chapter 38

28 MAY 1942

The vicar came on his bicycle that afternoon. Georg looked out through the window as the vicar leaned his bicycle on the fence and walked up the path. The Peaslakes sat side by side on the sofa, staring at nothing, or memories perhaps, the photos of Alan all around. There will never be another photo of him now, thought Georg. Mrs Peaslake's hands were still and empty.

Out in the kitchen Mud's mother bustled with the pots, getting a dinner that probably no one would eat, but desperate to do something, anything to help.

Georg answered the door before the vicar knocked. He looked tired. How many visits like this has he made in this war? Georg wondered. The vicar's daughter was a nurse up in Singapore, Mud said, and he hadn't heard from her since Singapore fell.

Did the vicar think of her every time he made a call like this?

'Good afternoon, George. I'm so very sorry for your loss.'

Georg nodded. 'They're in the lounge room,' he said. He led the way.

Mr Peaslake stood as the vicar entered. Mrs Peaslake stayed crumpled on the sofa. 'I am so sorry for your loss,' said the vicar again.

His words must have been used thousands of times. Millions. But they still sounded true.

'Thank you,' said Mr Peaslake dully.

The vicar reached into his pocket. 'Alan ... Alan was a fine young man. We will all feel his loss. The world is poorer for his passing.' Words that had been said many times too, yet still held truth as well.

He held out an envelope. 'Alan came to see me on his embarkation leave. He gave me this to give to you in case he ... well, he gave me this. He sent a postscript to it last month.'

Mr Peaslake's hand trembled as he took it.

'I'll come back tomorrow,' said the vicar softly. 'We can talk about the memorial service. The CWA will do all the catering and ... We'll talk about that later. George, could you see me out?'

'No, George, please stay,' said Mr Peaslake.

The vicar patted Georg's shoulder, then made his own way out into the hall. They heard the door click behind him.

Mr Peaslake opened the letter.

'Read it aloud,' said Mrs Peaslake hoarsely.

Mr Peaslake's voice sounded like iron. It sounded like Mutti's had three years before, though his was loud and hers was sweet.

Dear Mum and Dad,

I'm leaving this with the sky pilot in case the worst happens over there. If you're reading this, I hope that whatever happened was quick, but no matter how I got it, I'm going because I believe in fighting this war. Some of the boys around here enlisted for the adventure, but you taught me better than that, Dad. I know what war is, and what can happen to a man. I'm leaving for my country, for you, for everything I love.

I'm not saying I want to die. I don't. I want to live, to meet a girl one day, have kids, show them how to fly a kite like Dad's up on the headland, then eat Mum's apple pancakes. That will never happen now.

I think I just want to say that I know I might have to give my life for my country. I won't say don't cry for me, but when you remember me, remember this as well. I am proud to be going. I hope you are proud of me as well.

Give my love to the paddocks and the hills. Tell the sea eagle that no one will ever fly a kite higher than him. You are the best parents any bloke could ever have.

My love to you always,
Alan

The clock ticked on the mantelpiece. 'He always did have a way with words,' said Mrs Peaslake softly. She began to cry, not the fierce breaking howls of before, but gentle tears that trickled. She let them fall, wiping her nose.

'There's another bit,' said Mr Peaslake quietly. He handed another sheet of paper to Georg.

'For me?' This sheet was different from the first: pale brown, as though it had been stained with water and a bit crumpled too.

Georg glanced at the Peaslakes, then began to read it out.

Dear George,
I'm glad you're there for Mum and Dad. Give them a hug from me. Give them a hug every single day, mate. The train is

yours now. If you have kids, give it to them, and tell them it comes from me. Tell Dad to fly the dragon kite one last time, and then to let the wind have it.

Your loving brother,
Alan

It was only later that night, lying in his bed, the blackout shutters pulled aside to let in fresh air now the light was off, that Georg realised.

His country had killed the Peaslakes' son.

Alan Peaslake had been in Egypt, facing a German army. And the Italians too, perhaps. But it was Germany who had started the war. If Hitler had never yelled the orders, if his countrymen had never followed, Alan Peaslake would be alive. Alan could even be in the bed next door now, down on holiday with his parents.

Instead they had a German boy: a boy who lied. A boy who was the enemy who had killed their son.

The enemy was him.

Chapter 39

The whole town gathered at the memorial service. It looked strange as he and the Peaslakes rounded the corner to town: figure after figure all in black going up to the church like ants heading back to their nest. He hadn't known there were so many people in the district.

There was no coffin. Georg wondered what happened to your body when you died so far away. Did Alan Peaslake have a proper grave? He couldn't ask. He sat in the front pew with the Peaslakes on either side, and Mud's mum on Mrs Peaslake's other side, holding her hands tightly, and then Mud. Everyone from school sat in the back. Even Big Billy was in black today. Someone had found him a pair of shoes. He kept spitting on his hand and wiping it across his hair to keep it neat.

They took the kites up to the headland after the sandwiches, the lamingtons, the scones and jam and hoarded tea in the church hall after the service. Mud came too. Everyone seemed to take it for granted that Mud would be there, though her mum had gone back home.

The dogs had left the mat by the stove at last, had even eaten breakfast's leftovers. But they too knew this walk to the headland was different. They didn't snuffle after rabbits in the tussocks or pretend there were tigers in the stunted bushes. Instead they sat and simply watched.

They are on guard today, thought Georg. They can't protect us from the things that hurt us — not these kinds of things — but they know they have to try.

Mr Peaslake handed Georg the big box kite. He gave Mud the one he mostly used. It was heavy for a girl, but Mud was ... Mud.

He kept the dragon kite himself.

'Can't let the Nazis stop us, or the Japs,' said Mrs Peaslake, and she meant much more than flying kites. 'Alan was right.'

The wind roared and bit today, coming from the south. It tore the kites high above their heads, bit and spat at them.

Higher and higher they flew, till Georg wondered if they might almost reach to Heaven, so that Alan Peaslake could see them when he looked down.

The dragon kite bucked and taunted the wind. And then suddenly the sea eagle was there, appearing out of nowhere, or from under the cliff perhaps. Higher and higher it flew till it was above them, circling round and round as though it jeered at the human flights below.

Mr Peaslake gazed at the dragon blazing against the blue. He began to recite.

> 'Wrap him up with his stockwhip and blanket,
> And bury him deep down below

Tell the world that a stockman lies dead here
In the land where no gumtrees will grow.'

He was shouting at the sky now, at the wind, shouting as though his cry could be heard across the world.

It was almost the poem he'd read to Georg several times, *The Dying Stockman*. No one knew now who had written it long ago. But Mr Peaslake had changed it for his son.

'*... There's tea in the battered old billy,*
There are scones laid out in a row,
We'll drink to the next merry meeting
In the place where all good fellows go.

'*And oft in the shades of the twilight,*
When the southerly's whispering low,
And the darkening shadows are falling,
We'll think of our stockman below.'

He let the string go.

For a second the kite hung there. Georg waited for the wind to rip it away, or maybe let it fall. But instead it began to tunnel through the air, beyond the cliffs, over the sea, heading north with the wind.

The kite and the wind were partners now.

Mr Peaslake looked smaller, now his poem was done.

Mud began to haul her kite in. Georg started to haul his in as well. He wondered if the Peaslakes wished that Alan were there instead of him.

No. The Peaslakes weren't like that. They had love enough for both: for Alan and him too.

But the love was for the boy they thought he was: an English boy called George. Not a German, an enemy who'd lied to them for years.

How long had it been since he had used his real name? He was Georg!

Other kids had memories, stories about the day they started school, the flood that carried off the fences, the time they went to Sydney to the Show. He had memories, but none that he could share.

He could talk about things that had happened to a boy called George, in London and on the ship. But he could never speak of Georg and Georg's memories of Mutti and Papa, of gargoyles in the quadrangle and cream cakes and Tante Gudrun and Onkel Klaus and the horror of that graduation day and being folded up in the darkness of the suitcase …

Even today, when all around him were sharing their hearts in their grief, he could not.

I'm not here, he thought. I am like the wind. I make the kite move, I puff and blow. But no one sees me.

All they can ever see is George.

~卵◎

It was growing dark and late when they left the headland, as though none of them wanted to haul the kites down in this last unacknowledged sharing with the man who was gone, and the boy that he once had been.

They trudged back across the tussocks down to the road, the dogs leading the way. No traffic passed them now — petrol was too scarce for any but the most important journey. Mud left them at her place: a subdued Mud. She hesitated at the doorway, then ran out again. She hugged Mrs Peaslake, a sharp sudden hug, and then Mr Peaslake. She paused again, then hugged Georg too.

She was all arms and angles. She was gone before he could hug her back, the door closing against the autumn chill, no chink of light escaping to guide an enemy plane.

Their house was black against the starry night too. A year before a light would have been left on to guide them home, or they might have used a torch. Not now. But the gravel road was pale in the moonlight; and Samson and Delilah were indistinct shadows as they headed towards home and dinner. Impossible to stray.

Mrs Peaslake had pulled the blackout curtains before they left, so it was safe to turn the light on as soon as they went inside. Mr Peaslake went to put the kites back in his shed. Georg set the table, Samson pushing at his hands with his wet nose as though he wanted to help.

As though he is my dog now Alan is gone, thought Georg. But I can't be your master. I'm German, German, German. One day I'll be found out. One day I'll be gone.

Mrs Peaslake poked sticks into the fire to turn up the heat, and checked the stew she'd left slowly cooking on the edge of the stove while they were out.

'Tea's ready when you are,' she said wearily. 'Mrs Purdon left a rabbit stew. We'll have that tonight. Just get some potatoes from the scullery: there's a love. There's leftover bread-and-butter pudding for afters.'

Georg looked at the cake tin on the bench. There was a fruitcake in there; a smaller tin held a date loaf and another melting moments; and there was an apple pie in the food safe. Bellagong neighbours gave food instead of words when hard things happened.

Mrs Peaslake saw his look. 'Need to keep busy,' she whispered.

Georg nodded. He'd take parcels of cake and pie to Big Billy every day next week. Better for Big Billy to enjoy it all fresh than for the chooks to get it when it was stale. He had reached the scullery when he heard Mrs Peaslake scream.

⁓❀◎

Mrs Peaslake sat hunched by the kitchen wireless. Georg just had time to hear the announcer say, '... *it is not known if there will be further attacks. In other news ...*'

'Mother, what is it?' Mr Peaslake ran to her.

She stared up at him. 'Japs,' she said. 'Dirty stinking Japs. They've bombed Sydney. While we were mourning our Alan they've gone and bombed Sydney.'

Mr Peaslake glanced at the wireless as though he wished he could shake it to get the announcer to tell him the news again. 'Bombers? Over Sydney?'

She shook her head. 'Submarines. They didn't say how many.'

'Maybe they don't know. How bad was it?'

'I don't know. They didn't say that either. Maybe they'll tell us tomorrow.' She looked up at them helplessly. 'While we were flying kites for Alan the Japs were doing that.'

'Submarines,' barked Mr Peaslake and there was a note in the booming voice that Georg had never heard before. A sharp harsh edge. 'That's like the Japs. Sneaking in underwater. Think they can take over the world. Well, they can't. We'll fight them with pitchforks if we have to. Fight the whole German army if it comes to that.' Tears ran down his face, but he didn't seem to

294

notice. 'If I could get my hands on one of them! One dirty German —'

Georg looked at them. Helpless. Anguished, clinging onto hate to stop the pain.

His shell cracked. A shell made of terror, of distance, made even thicker by the Peaslakes' love. The shell that had kept Georg and George apart. It was like when you broke an egg and the inside fell out before you could even try to stop it.

'I am German.' It wasn't his voice. No, it *was* his voice, Georg's voice, the German accent back. It was the voice of Mutti and Papa's son.

Mr Peaslake scrubbed the back of his hand over his eyes. 'George, what are you playing at? This is no time for —'

'I am German! I was sent to England just before the war. I am Georg! I have been pretending I am English —'

'Look, boy.' The booming voice was flat and angry. 'I don't know what you're playing at, but you're upsetting Mother. This isn't the time for larking about —'

'I'm not playing! *Ich bin Deutscher! Deutscher! Ich bin Georg, George nicht!*'

'Stop talking nonsense!' yelled Mr Peaslake.

'It's not nonsense. It's German! *Ich bin Deutscher!*'

The second burst of German silenced them. Then, 'No,' whispered Mrs Peaslake. 'No, it can't be true.'

'I tricked you both. Tricked everyone!'

'You're a … spy?' Mrs Peaslake's voice was still unbelieving. 'Even the Jerries don't send children as spies, do they?'

'I'm not a spy. But I am German!'

'No,' said Mr Peaslake, more quietly than Georg had ever heard him speak. But he could see the big man thinking. No letters from English friends; the mother who was supposed to be sick, but who never wrote to her son. Only letters from an aunt, one who never put her real address. No photos of an English family to pin on his wall. No mention of an English school.

'You can't mean it! George,' Mrs Peaslake added pleadingly. 'George …' She stretched out her hands.

'There is no George!'

Suddenly he could take no more. He ran from the kitchen, out the door. The light shattered the blackout, but he didn't care.

He ran, hearing the shouts behind him. 'George! Come back here! George!'

But there was no George. Just Georg, his feet pounding into the night.

Chapter 40

Through the orchard, under the wire fence into the paddocks, stumbling on the tussocks, grey-gold in the moonlight. A mob of cows in the distance stared at him. He could dimly hear Mr Peaslake still calling.

He couldn't go back. Couldn't face the horror on their faces when he told them how deep and long his deception had been. He was their enemy, but had accepted all they had to give.

Perhaps if he just ran he could leave it all behind. Leave George and Georg, become a shadow in the night. It was as though his legs controlled his body now: Run. Run. Run.

He reached the trees before he stopped, slender gum trunks silver in the moonlight. He stood panting for a few seconds, then began to jog, more slowly now, slipping and dodging through the trees.

He didn't know where he was going. He didn't care. He simply moved, letting the rhythm of his feet drown out all feeling. He had come so far; from Germany to England; from England to here. Running from the enemy every time. Now the enemy was him.

Vaguely he was aware that the way was uphill now, steeper, then steeper still, dipping into a dark gully, scrambling up the other side, skin prickling with what might be nettle stings. He didn't care.

A mob of roos thudded into the distance. Somewhere a possum shrieked.

He ran along the ridge, the sharp stones glinting like earthbound stars. The trees were sparser here. It was easier to run. The ridge seemed to stop, so it was downhill now, more paddocks, meagre trees.

His legs felt like sacks of wheat, almost too heavy to lift, but somehow he kept going, staggering, leaning against trees to get his breath, the bark's loose fingers tickling him till he ran again. The stars wheeled fire overhead.

Time vanished. There was only the ground, the stones, the shadows, only the sky and him. Slowly it grew grey, instead of black, one thin finger of dawn pink above a small curve of horizon.

Then he heard the plane. It was a sound like no other he had heard, a stutter not a roar. But it came from the sky so that must be what it was ...

He turned to find it, but it was too late.

The sky exploded, a ball of fire as though a star had fallen, getting bigger as it fell. The noise hit him as though he had run into a wall. He put his hands to his ears as the colours pulsed before his eyes — red, blue, yellow, green all fusing into red again ...

Something else moved now. A white flutter in the sky, like a giant night moth coming to ground again with the dawning light.

But this moth was a man.

A man in a parachute, drifting slowly as the debris fell.

An enemy.

He pushed his body again, lurching through the trees as the white of the parachute vanished. Enemy. Enemy. Mr Peaslake's words sang through his head: 'If I could get my hands on one of them.'

He didn't think what he would do when he found him. He was beyond thought now too.

Then there it was: a crumple of white that looked like it had been dragged along the clearing, a tangle of strings, a man, half buried in the cloth. All Georg could see of him was his leather flying helmet, his face, the Oriental eyes.

Then he saw the blood. It welled from what looked like a crease on the man's neck. Georg had a sudden vision of bombed-out London, of flying debris that ripped through flesh. Of Elizabeth, the life seeping from her as they dragged her from the dirt.

The enemy didn't move, but he was alive. That's what they told you in first-aid books. If the blood flowed they were alive.

He could kill an enemy. Feed the hate inside him. Give a gift of hate to the Peaslakes, to Mud.

He looked around for a weapon. A branch. A rock.

The rock stared up at him, jagged, dusty, as though it had been put there for him to use. He lifted it, felt his hands grow big with power. He stepped towards the man. He held the rock high above his head, ready to smash it down.

The enemy groaned. It was a small sound, a whisper almost too soft to hear. It was a human sound, the first he had heard all the long night except his own panting and the thud of his feet.

Georg dropped the rock. For long seconds he stared at the crumpled body, like Papa's body on the ground, blood on the stones.

He kneeled, and pressed one hand to the man's neck, just as he'd seen the air-raid warden do, nearly two years before, with

Elizabeth. It wasn't enough. The blood welled about his fingers. He pressed his other hand down too, hard, then harder.

It hadn't worked for Elizabeth, but it worked now. The bleeding stopped, all but a gentle seep. It trickled down his arms, then dripped onto the white of the parachute. He pressed even more firmly.

The seeping stopped.

The man didn't move. Georg didn't know if he would ever move. Had the wound stopped bleeding because the man was dead, or from the pressure of his hands? He didn't care. Didn't care what would happen when they found him there: a German boy trying to save the life of a Japanese man.

If someone had kneeled by Papa, would he have lived?

Colours seeped into the world. The red grew redder, the leaves above became greener, the light almost too bright to bear. He felt his eyelids shut. He jerked awake, and pressed down hard again.

Someone would come. The coast watch would have seen the plane explode; seen the pilot's parachute too.

The world grew hazy. He felt hot then cold. There was only the man next to him, only the blood, his hands.

Someone would come.

Chapter 41

The sun had inched above the horizon when they found him. He heard yells, the beat of feet. Someone pulled him back. He fought them weakly with his bloody fists, trying to get his hands back on the wound, then realised that other hands were there, saw the red and white of the red cross on a first-aid kit.

'Is he the boy they're looking for? You, lad, what's your name?'

The words were far away. He could shut his eyes now. He could vanish, no longer George or Georg. I'm no one's enemy, he thought. I'm me.

Then black.

He woke strapped to a bed. For a few seconds he thought they had tied him down, imprisoned him already, then realised the pressure came from tightly tucked-in sheets: white sheets, starched, neat, a grey blanket. A strange smell. All he could see was white ...

'He's awake!' It was Mr Peaslake's too-loud voice.

'Shh!' said someone.

The white was screens. He turned his head, saw Mr Peaslake's face, black smudges below his eyes. He looked smaller, somehow, sitting there, his grey hat in his hands. A nurse stood next to him. She lifted Georg's wrist, felt his pulse, then nodded at Mr Peaslake.

'Ten minutes. And keep your voice down. There are patients trying to sleep in here.'

She left. Mr Peaslake's shadowed eyes watched Georg. Georg gazed back. I love him, he realised. Him and Mrs Peaslake and even Mud. The dogs and the paddocks and Mud's family.

Would they ever want to see him again when the war was over, when he was let out of the prison camp for Germans, this enemy boy who had let another enemy live? Maybe he'd have no chance. Maybe they'd ship him back to Germany straight away.

But he wanted them to understand before the officials took him now.

'I'm sorry.' The words scratched Georg's throat. 'I couldn't kill him.'

'Kill him? Kill who?' Mr Peaslake's voice sounded like straw on corrugated iron. 'George, we've been so worried. Why did you do it? I tried to follow you, then —'

'The Japanese. The pilot. I ... I —'

'You saved his life. But he wasn't Japanese, son. He was an Aussie.'

'But I saw his eyes.'

Mr Peaslake looked at him strangely. 'Name's Johnnie Chang. He's in the other ward. He'll be all right.'

'I thought he was Japanese when I saved him: an enemy!'

Mr Peaslake either didn't care, or didn't seem to think it mattered. 'You're a hero, son.'

Suddenly Mr Peaslake's face crumpled like the newspaper his

wife used to light the fire. 'I thought we had lost you. Vanishing out into the night like that. Then when they brought you here, your shirt, your arms, all red with blood. Oh, George.' He reached out a hand, took Georg's in his. 'The nurse's gone to get Mother. We've been taking turns to sit here all day, waiting for you to wake.'

Georg struggled to sit up. He pulled his hand away. 'Please ... you don't understand. I tried to tell you last night. I'm not George. I never was. I'm German. The enemy. I really am.'

Mr Peaslake knuckled his eyes. Again it was as though he hadn't heard. 'Couldn't lose you too. Not you as well.'

Suddenly he seemed to make an effort to hear again. He picked up Georg's hand, more firmly now. His voice quietened as he said, 'All right. You can tell me now.'

Georg did. Told him the whole story, the cries of '*Juden 'raus*', the bodies under the window, the tears Mutti couldn't cry, the suitcase, hiding in the London flat, practising with the wireless over and over, until he could be taken for a George.

Dimly he was aware that Mrs Peaslake had come in too and was knitting quietly; of the nurse who held water to his lips. He sipped, then kept on talking. It was like when he was running. It was impossible to stop.

When it was done, when every word was gone, he lay back. He looked at their faces, waiting for the horror to start, the anger, the hatred.

They didn't come. Instead they stared at him with love and wonder, and Mrs Peaslake stroked his hair. 'Our darling boy. Oh, George,' she said.

'Geh-org,' said Mr Peaslake, trying out the sound of the hard Gs. 'That's how you say it, isn't it, my boy?'

'Yes,' said Georg. It wasn't quite right, but it would do. He wanted to sleep again. Instead he said, 'I almost killed a man. But I couldn't. I saved him even though I thought he was an enemy. Does that make me a coward?'

Mr Peaslake blinked, as though he had no answers for this. But Mrs Peaslake took his hand. 'No. It means you're brave.'

'But Alan ...'

'A man's life is still a life to save, enemy or not,' said Mrs Peaslake firmly.

Alan killed enemies, Georg thought. So did Mud's brothers.

It was as though Mrs Peaslake knew what he'd been thinking. 'There're times you have to kill things. People. Animals. What matters is that you know there're only certain times you need to do it. What matters is that the rest of the time you're kind. Our Alan is a hero.' Her smile held tears, but it was a real smile too. 'Two heroes in our family now. If Johnnie Chang had been an enemy he'd have been helpless in a strange country. He'd have been sent to a prison camp.' She took a breath. 'And it wouldn't be a prison camp like our men are in either. I should hope we Aussies know a sight better than that.'

'Too right,' boomed Mr Peaslake. He looked at his wife and Georg with pride.

Georg nodded. It didn't quite answer his question — he wasn't sure he'd ever know what he should have done. But it was enough to go on with now. 'What happens now? When will they take *me* to the prison camp?'

'No prison camp,' said Mr Peaslake.

'But that's where the German refugees have to go. All Germans. All Japanese.'

304

'You're English,' said Mr Peaslake, still making an effort to be quiet. 'Shh, no,' as Georg tried to interrupt, to make him understand what being German meant these days, 'let me speak now. It's been a long day, son. Two long days and a long night. One of the coast watch gave me a number to ring. A high-up bloke. I asked him that very question, just in case what you said was true.

'If you've got a genuine English passport then it doesn't matter if you were born in Germany. Your dad was English, so you are too. We'll have to inform the authorities that your mum's probably still in Germany, but that's all.'

'Really?'

'We wouldn't lie to you,' said Mrs Peaslake softly. The jumper she's knitting looks just my size, thought Georg. 'If you were an adult it might be different. In a bigger town maybe there'd be some strife — people who'd only see the German, not the boy. But you're one of us now.'

'Will Mud hate me?' Somehow the thought of losing Mud's friendship was as bad as losing what he now knew was home.

'Mud?' Mr Peaslake gave a hoot of laughter, then shushed as his wife nudged him. 'Mud sticks to those she loves like, well, mud.'

'No prison camp?'

'No prison camp. Besides,' his smile was real now, 'you're a hero, remember. Young Chang's mum says she's going to bake you a cake.'

'I can bake all the cakes you'll ever want.' Mrs Peaslake gazed at him as though she didn't want to drag her eyes away, her fingers *click, click, clicking*. 'Georg.' She stumbled a little over the unfamiliar name. 'Do you think you might call me "Mum" now? And call Father "Dad"? We didn't want to ask before, not till you knew us well. But we think of you as our own son.'

'I … I already have a mother …'

'Auntie then,' she offered, undaunted.

Auntie Thel and Uncle Ron, the same as Mud? That felt wrong too.

'How about Grandma and Grandpa?' Mr Peaslake's boom was as quiet as it ever got. 'You got either of those?'

'No.'

'There you are then. You've got them now. That fit right with you?'

It did. It felt warm and solid, like the paddock rocks baked in the sun. The warmth comforted him as other memories came seeping back. The wireless broadcast last night. 'The Japanese!' How could he have forgotten? 'Have they invaded us?'

'What? No, calm down. It was just little subs in Sydney Harbour, that's all. Nowhere near as bad as people thought at first. Won't happen again. We're onto them now.' Mr Peaslake gave a half-smile. 'I'm not just saying that, laddie. Mud's brothers are up in New Guinea now, and their mates. Can you imagine the Japanese fighting an army of Muds? It's not going to be easy. Or quick. But we'll beat them.'

'And … and my mother?'

Mr Peaslake was silent.

'Do you … do you think she's dead?'

Mrs Peaslake met his eyes. 'Do you think she is?'

Georg was silent for a moment, trying to feel the thread that linked him to Mutti in his mind. For the first time he realised that Mutti might have changed as much as he had in the past few years. But somehow that small glow still lingered.

'No,' said Georg. 'Papa … I know they killed Papa. But I don't feel that Mutti is dead.'

'Then she isn't,' said Mrs Peaslake. 'If she's like her son she'll get through. And after the war is over she will be welcome here. But if you want to go back to Germany, well, you're family now wherever you go.'

'I won't go back to Germany,' said Georg. He hadn't known that he thought that until he heard his voice saying the words. But it was true. Sometime in the last day he had become Australian. Gumtrees were in his heart.

'You should sleep,' said Mrs Peaslake. 'We should all sleep.'

Yes, he could sleep now. Perhaps he could tell himself a story too, before he slept. Somehow he knew the stories would come again now. Good stories: of life and hope.

'Mud will be in later at visiting hours.' Mr Peaslake's voice was a boom again. The nurse glanced over at them, irritated. 'Her mum is coming too.'

And that felt right as well.

Mrs Peaslake bent and kissed him. 'Sleep well,' she said. 'Georg.'

He smiled as he shut his eyes.

Chapter 42

Dreams came, but it wasn't quite a dream, for he knew he wasn't asleep yet. There was the ship: not the ship he had sailed on but one much like it, still war-time grey, even though the war was over; men and women staring over the rail with limp hair from long days at sea, carrying cardboard suitcases; and children wide-eyed from too many years of fear, but excited too.

And there among the crowd was a woman. She didn't look like the Mutti he had left. She had a thin face that had forgotten how to smile, and deep-set eyes. No flowered dress this time; and short hair instead of the curls under a green scarf.

But it was as though a bit of string led from him to her. She saw him as she stood at the rail. He saw her face crumple as he waved; heard a sob in sympathy from his grandmother behind him.

'Is it her?' asked Mud urgently. Because of course Mud was there. Impossible to leave Mud out, even in dreams. Mud had helped him paint Mutti's bedroom, had knitted her a jumper that was, of course, more holes than jumper.

He nodded, still waving.

Mutti lifted a hand in a tentative wave. And then at last she smiled.

They had waited so long for this day: ever since the telegram from Aunt Miriam, and then the letters sent via the Red Cross. Mutti's letters had told a little of the camp where she had been finally sent after her years working with the anti-Nazi underground, and how she had survived it. But she spoke much more about those who had sheltered her, during the war and after: strangers who gave and who helped. If hatred was contagious, perhaps kindness was too.

Then there were no more letters because Mutti was on the ship, and the ship was sailing here, with other 'displaced persons'.

Would this continent ever be home to someone who had spent so much of their life in another one, even if that homeland had imprisoned them and taken what they loved? Could Mutti become part of a family just because it was already her son's?

They had both changed so much. He knew, though, that this wasn't an ending, but another beginning and a good one.

A small eruption at the other end of the hospital ward woke him. Mud's voice said urgently, 'I don't *care* if it's not visiting hours yet! I'm his *friend*!'

Her footsteps thudded down the ward. 'George! Why didn't you *tell* me? Do we call you Georg now?'

'Shh,' said the nurse. 'He's supposed to be resting.'

The dream faded. But it left him with a smile.

Epilogue

There is no true ending to this story. Lives go on. Children grow up and have children; those children live new stories of their own.

Enemies change. One enemy becomes 'just like us'; and new enemies are found. But the stories of friends, families and love continue too. So this book ends not where the story does, but with a glimpse.

It was a rainy day — grey sky, grey air — but welcome after too many blue days of drought. Umbrellas dripped in the university hall. No one quite knew where to put them.

The graduation ceremony was over. The young man stood in his mortarboard, his family around him. His mother, thin, with short white hair, defiantly bare shoulders despite the rain, despite the tattoo on her arm, which for the rest of her life she would refuse to hide. She was a student at this university too now, strong enough to accept that she was older, different from the others.

His grandma clucked like a happy hen. His grandpa stood like a proud rooster, a new Box Brownie camera in his hands. The young man's best friend strode over to them, her own mortarboard under her arm, wearing a black gown with different coloured lining, her parents and brothers hurrying in her wake.

'Let's have a photo of the both of you.' Mr Peaslake's boom rose over the chatter of the crowd. 'Mud, you stand there, and Georg.' Mr Peaslake waved his camera.

Mud smiled as Georg took her hand. That was how the camera captured both of them: smiling, hand in hand, two mothers and a father behind, an aunt-grandmother, and brothers on either side.

The camera clicked.

Later they would all go out, into the rain, to the restaurant table Mud had booked — a strange restaurant for Australia, where they served spaghetti and salads with things called olives instead of slices of orange and hard-boiled eggs — a place Georg and Mud had found in their first year as university students, and wanted to celebrate in now. A place where the cook and waiter had once been enemies, but now were ...

Us.

Author's Notes

The incidents in this book are based on real events, although they happened to many different people, from the graduation ceremony that ended with students thrown through the window, to the child hidden in a suitcase and the Japanese 'spotter' planes that flew above the towns on the New South Wales south coast in the months before and after the submarine raid on Sydney.

It wasn't until fifty years later that the public was told just how many submarines had lurked off the Australian coast, some large enough to launch small planes.

Of course the Japanese never did invade.

In late 1943 a news clip was shown in moving picture houses in Tokyo, showing Japanese bombers destroying Canberra and politicians running away in terror. The news clip said that Japanese forces had already taken over Australia, but it was a fake — a propaganda movie made in Japan. Back then, though, as the Japanese relentlessly conquered one country after another, it seemed inevitable that Australia too would soon be invaded.

Historians are divided on whether invasion was imminent when first the Australians and then the combined Australian and United States forces began to beat the Japanese army back in New Guinea: the first time in that war that the Japanese forces had been defeated. Perhaps the bombing of Darwin and other towns, as well as the attack on Sydney Harbour, were only to disrupt the supply lines to troops in New Guinea. At the time, however, the invasion seemed both near and real.

HEAD MEASUREMENTS

Racial Studies was part of the Nazi school curriculum. The idea that you can tell a person's race or intelligence or leadership ability by measuring their head is a myth. I have based the story of a Jewish boy who was told he had a 'perfect Aryan head' on an oral account from a survivor of the Holocaust. You too may hear it at the Jewish Museum in Sydney.

HITLER AND CONCENTRATION CAMPS

Georg's mother wasn't Jewish but she, like anyone who opposed Hitler, would have faced a concentration camp. The tattoo on her arm would have been the number tattooed on all the inhabitants of concentration camps.

By 1939, when this book begins, Jewish people had been forbidden to participate in many professions in Germany, including lecturing at universities. Nor would there have been Jewish university students. But many people in Germany back then whose grandparents or even a great-grandparent had been Jewish didn't consider themselves Jewish. They might have been practising Christians, or atheists. In some cases they may not even have known that one grandparent had been Jewish. But once the connection was discovered by the Gestapo or by fervent young 'Brown Shirts', the descendant was then classified by the German state as a *Jude* — a Jew. The radical Nazi students in this book who threw their classmates out of the window would have been hunting through the families of their fellow students, looking for Jewish ancestors.

Georg's father didn't consider himself Jewish. He was English and, like many Germans, would have been horrified by the campaign against Jewish people. But, as one man who had lived through those times told me, hating the things your government does is not a reason to abandon the country you love. Georg's father might also have considered his work as more important than politics. The worst horrors of the concentration camps were still to come in 1939, and even at their height from 1942 to 1945, many Germans or people in German-occupied countries didn't know of them, nor knew of a way to protest in a country facing the hardships and horrors of war and bombing.

Hitler — and his Gestapo — imprisoned or killed anyone in Germany or the lands they conquered who opposed him. The dictator wanted to make the (imaginary) German Aryan race fit and pure — a land of 'Supermen' or Übermensch. Anyone who was Jewish, Gypsy, communist, homosexual, had dark skin or was disabled was to be exterminated for the good of the race. Perhaps twelve million people were killed in concentration camps in Germany and the countries Hitler conquered.

POEMS IN THIS BOOK

Wandrers Nachtlied II by Johann Wolfgang von Goethe (a very loose translation by me — I tried to keep to the spirit rather than the words of the poem)

The Wild Colonial Boy, Anonymous

The Man from Snowy River by AB Paterson

The Night Before Christmas by Clement Moore or Henry Livingston, Jnr

Andy's Gone with Cattle by Henry Lawson

The Dying Stockman, Anonymous, and changed by me

GEORG AND MUD'S SCHOOL

This was typical of small country schools until the early 1970s, when 'one-teacher' schools were closed and children started travelling by bus to larger towns. Often these one-teacher schools were superb, with the older kids helping to teach the younger ones and teachers sending for textbooks to help gifted kids learn more about the subjects they loved. Other teachers, not so gifted or dedicated, left kids to read textbooks and do the exercises in each chapter. There was no help for kids with learning problems; like Big Billy in this story, they were often asked to do jobs around the school instead of schoolwork. Many kids left school not even knowing how to read the front page of a newspaper.

BRITAIN AND AUSTRALIA IN THE 1940S

At the beginning of World War II many people in Australia still called Britain 'home' — even if they'd never been there and even if their grandparents had been born in Australia. Australians travelled on British passports until 1949.

Even though the Georg in this book was brought up in Germany, he had a British passport because of his English father and so that made him British too — and, back in the 1940s, legally free to live in Australia. His Aunt Miriam, however, would have been correct when she worried that his German accent and name might lead to his being classified as an 'enemy alien'.

Australia's foreign policy followed Britain's too, until the threat of Japanese invasion, when Prime Minister Curtin made the decision that Australian troops should defend their home country, not Britain's colonies.

THE SCHOOLS AT WAR:
A MESSAGE FROM THE PRIME MINISTER,
JOHN CURTIN

This was published in *The School Paper*, a magazine for schoolchildren, in November 1942. I have changed the date in this book to make it appear in early May, when most of the action in this book ends, instead of November, as it so clearly expresses what kids were expected to do in that year of threat.

RATIONING

Severe rationing only came into force in Australia after the end of the main story in this book, in the latter part of 1942. There were also shortages of many foods, as fewer people were available to grow, harvest or process them — although 'land girls' and the women of farming families did take on most of the work, and many children in farming areas left school or didn't attend regularly, so they could farm too.

Even with rationing, most women loved baking cakes, usually on Saturdays. The Saturday cakes, pikelets, biscuits and pies were the family's major luxuries and a source of pride for many women too.

Once rationing began women swapped recipes for sugarless, butterless and eggless cakes. Even rationing wasn't going to put an end to cakes. Dried fruit was mostly kept to send to 'our boys' overseas, but there was plenty of fresh fruit to make cakes feel rich and moist — at least till they cooled down and became hard and crumbly.

Eggless, Sugarless, Butterless Apple Teacake

6 Granny Smith apples, peeled and thinly sliced and dipped in lemon juice so they don't turn brown

2 cups self-raising flour

½ tsp nutmeg, grated

1 cup 'top of the milk' (Before milk was 'homogenised', with the cream distributed evenly through it, the cream used to rise to the top of the bottle. Use cream instead or light sour cream.)

Rub a cake tin with dripping (the fat scooped off the pan after meat is roasted) or, these days, with butter. Dust with flour so the cake won't stick.

Mix all ingredients except the apples. Pour the batter into the tin. Slide in as many slices of apple as you can, pointed side down. The cake will rise up in the tin as you cram more and more apple in.

Sprinkle with nutmeg. Bake for forty minutes at 200°C or till the top is lightly brown and springs back. Eat hot — the cake turns gluey and crumbly when it's cold. But it is better than no cake at all.

War-Time Apple Pancakes/Pikelets (pikelets are just small pancakes, especially good for afternoon tea)
An experienced cook could have fresh hot pikelets or pancakes on the table by the time the kettle boiled to make the tea, served on an embroidered 'tea cloth', with lace or crochet at the edges. Pikelets could be made sweet with a topping of jam, which was made with only a little sugar in those war years, so it didn't keep well. But it was good.

I still make apple pikelets, but I add an egg to this mix. It gives the pikelets a better texture.

1 cup self-raising flour
1 cup grated apple
1 cup milk

Grease a frying pan with dripping (these days, use butter or half butter and half olive oil). Heat it on top of the stove for five minutes on a medium heat, then scoop in spoonfuls of the mixture in small rounds. When they begin to bubble turn them over with a spatula (this takes practice). Leave for about as long as the first side needed to cook, then use the spatula to take them out of the pan. Add a bit more butter (or dripping) and pour in more pikelet mixture till it is all cooked.

Butter and eat them while hot, or eat with jam and whipped cream, or, just as they were eaten back then, with fruit stewed down to a thick paste with just a little sugar to seem like jam.

Apple and Date Spread

My grandma made this in the war years to use on toast or scones instead of jam that needed sugar to make. It is so good my mother made it when I was young, and I still make it sometimes.

2 cups pitted dates, finely chopped
10 Granny Smith apples, peeled, cored and chopped
3 cups water

Simmer everything till the mixture is thick and goes *glop! glop! glop!* The dates will have dissolved into the apple to make a thick sludge. Keep it in the fridge for up to ten days, in a covered container. Eat on toast or scones or in a bowl with a good helping of natural yoghurt. Warning: don't let it 'glop' on your skin — it's hot. If a bit gets on your arm or hand put under the cold tap and run water on it till your skin is cool.

SPAGHETTI IN THE 1940s

Tinned spaghetti in tomato sauce and tinned baked beans became popular in the 1930s, especially hot on toast or cold in sandwiches. Kids at school would say 'swap you a beetle for a worm' — in other words, you take my baked bean sandwich and I'll take one of your spaghetti ones.

But few Australians ate spaghetti that didn't come from a tin till the 1960s, when the growing number of Italian restaurants made 'spag bol' popular enough to even feature in women's magazine recipes. Georg and Mud would have graduated in the early 1950s when Italian food was still strange to most Australians; even spag bol.

John Curtin

John Curtin was the prime minister who led Australia through the most dangerous time of World War II. He took office on 7 October 1941; and was a quiet, incredibly dedicated man, who walked to Parliament House every morning rather than be driven in a car.

Curtin fought fiercely and openly with Britain's prime minister Winston Churchill to bring Australian troops and equipment back to defend Australia. If it hadn't been for Curtin standing his ground, Australia would never have been able to turn back the advancing Japanese in New Guinea. Curtin also put the US General, Douglas MacArthur, in charge of Australia's defence forces, instead of relying on leadership from England.

Curtin declared that seven days was too short a week. He worked every day till midnight, even on Christmas Day, forcing his body to keep going even when he was ill.

The effort killed him.

Curtin died on 5 July 1945, just six weeks before the end of the war in the Pacific.

Kids evacuated

During the bombing of London and other major industrial towns and ports in England, many kids were evacuated out to the countryside. In 1940 some were sent as far away as Canada and Australia. One thousand, five hundred and thirty children were sent to Canada, 577 to Australia, 353 to South Africa, 202 to New Zealand and another 838 children were sent to the United States.

One ship of kids going to Canada was torpedoed, though all aboard survived, then on 17 September 1940 the SS *City of Benares* was also torpedoed by a German submarine. Seventy or seventy-seven of the ninety kids on their way to Canada drowned. The horror of their drowning, as well as the lack of destroyers to accompany the ships taking evacuees, meant the end of the official evacuation programme, though it seems likely that some children were sent on ships later in the war by their parents.

I've only been able to trace the records of two ships that brought evacuated British children to Australia. I have made the Georg of this book come on the second of them. I've been unable to find much detail about them however; and most of that detail is in this book. Georg's ship is based on the small amount I've been able to discover about the two journeys to Australia, including letters from a child sent here and one of the escorts, as well as letters from escorts and kids sent to Canada. While the latter voyages had escorts or were in convoy, there is a reference that indicates that at least one ship with children aboard was sent unescorted apart from the first few days out from England. It's possible that records with more detail about the ships and evacuees no longer exist.

Many children sent to Australia from Britain suffered cruelty and abuse in orphanages and other institutions. But the few records that remain indicate that unlike these children the Blitz evacuees had mostly good experiences, possibly because there were relatively few of them, so went to homes where they were genuinely wanted. However, I base that on the very few records I know to exist, and it is very possible that the stories of other evacuees on the ships to Australia, New Zealand and Canada were not as happy as the ones I have come across.

Australia had internment camps for any Japanese or German nationals living here. Even German Jewish refugees were sent to internment camps. Some Aboriginal people were also imprisoned in the north of Australia, as the government was afraid that they might help the Japanese if they were promised their lands back. By 1944, nearly 7,000 men, women and children were interned in eighteen camps spread across the country.

Prisoners of war were also held in Australia. By August 1944, there were 2,223 Japanese, 14,720 Italians and 1,585 Germans held in various camps in Australia. The biggest Japanese and Italian prison camp was in Cowra, in central western New South Wales.

Most of the Italians had been captured in the Middle East. They'd fought bravely but now they made the best of being prisoners. Soon the people of Cowra welcomed them. They worked on farms, made wine, played music at dances. Many later married Australian women and others returned to Cowra to live after the war, sponsored by the community.

Since World War II Cowra has become a 'Centre of World Friendship'. Japanese and Australians lie together in the Cowra War Cemetery. In 1979, battling drought and using faith and ingenuity to raise the money, the Cowra community opened Cowra's superb Japanese Garden, lugging water in buckets in the blazing sun to keep the trees alive.

This is a book about hatred. Although Georg is unable to kill a man he believes to be a helpless enemy, I also believe that Alan Peaslake in this book — who did attack and kill the enemy — was a hero, who died serving his country. If the German or Japanese armies of World War II had conquered our country many Australians would have been killed; all would have lived under a cruelly totalitarian regime. Sometimes you need to fight. But even then, it is worth remembering that an enemy can also become a friend.

Like many Australians, my different ancestors came from many countries. Some were Irish, Scots, Welsh, English, French, Native American, probably long ago Spanish and Danish too; and others were from many other places too far in the past to be remembered. Over the centuries the Irish have fought the English or the Scots; the Scots have fought the Danes; the English have fought the Welsh, the Spanish, the Danish, the Native Americans and the French.

I wonder if any of my ancestors ever dreamed that their descendants would marry their enemies. Less than a hundred years ago my Presbyterian grandmother was cast out of her family for marrying a Catholic. Now the two religions share services sometimes, to celebrate or pray for those in trouble or despair. Like their members, they are friends.

The world's hatreds are bitter, but in ten years, or a few hundred, they can be gone.

A Further Note from the Author

Sometimes many stories come together and become a book. More than ten years ago a story told to me in my childhood by a man — a kind man — who had once been a guard in a concentration camp, became the book *Hitler's Daughter*.

But there were more stories of that time. The whispered memory of a friend's father who had watched his fellow students thrown out a high window at a graduation day by a band of Nazis; the oral history of a Jewish boy who was told he had the 'most Aryan head' in the whole class; a neighbour who had escaped Nazi persecution in Germany as a small child, but then became a German enemy in England before finally — unexpectedly — discovering love and happiness in Australia.

All of these stories are in *Pennies for Hitler*, although altered. But the greater part of *Pennies from Hitler* came from a letter written to me by a fourteen-year-old boy.

This boy was in a class for children with special needs and *Hitler's Daughter* was the first book he and his friends had ever read.

His letter said:

Dear Jackie French,
*   What I have learned from your book is to be very wary of anyone who tries to make you angry.*

Yours,
James

I had never realised that message was in *Hitler's Daughter*, but perhaps it's the most important one there is.

So this book is for 'James'. It is about a boy who isn't there, who can't be anywhere, because wherever he goes he is the enemy. It is about how hatred is contagious, but it is also about how kindness, love and compassion are contagious too. In a world where there are still destroyers, like the Nazis, there are also loving people like the Peaslake family and indomitable friends like Mud.

You never know quite what you create when you let stories loose. *Pennies for Hitler* is an adventure and, in a strange way, a love story too. But I suspect that readers will find more in it than I knew I'd written, just as with *Hitler's Daughter*.

Acknowledgements

Pennies for Hitler has been a long time growing. My gratitude to those who created the foundations of this book should probably begin with the gentle neighbour who helped me with my German homework, late at night. He told me with shame and anguish the stories of his childhood in Nazi Germany, which years later led me to write *Hitler's Daughter*.

Since *Hitler's Daughter* was published over a decade ago, there have been hundreds, or even thousands, of requests for a sequel. Perhaps one day I will write one, but *Pennies for Hitler* is not that book. Instead it is a companion volume. *Hitler's Daughter* is about 'a girl who wasn't there', a foster child of Hitler who knows almost nothing of the vast tragedies around her, even though she lives in the heart of the Nazi world. *Pennies for Hitler* is about a boy who must remain invisible, existing only as the illusion he must present to the world. The questions and themes they both face, the hatreds they need to conquer, are each the other face of the same coin.

This book owes much to the continual reinterpreting and brilliance of Eva, Tim, Sandie and the casts of *Hitler's*

Daughter: The Play. Usually when a book is published I tuck it away as 'been there, done that'. Each new production made me rethink its themes, the times, the implications.

The Sydney Jewish Museum, and the inspiration of those who work and volunteer there, meant the scene of children measuring each other's heads to judge their racial worth was added long after I thought *Pennies for Hitler* was finished.

I owe an enormous debt too to my high school English teacher, Gillian Pauli, for the weekly piles of books she lent me, not only opening the door to possibilities of literature far beyond those I could have found myself, but who also trusted a teenager to read *The Protocols of the Elders of Zion* to see how contagious a lie and hatred can be.

To Kate Burnitt and Kate O'Donnell, so many, many thanks for your care and vigilance, and to Angela Marshall, as always, decades of gratitude for so many things.

Most of all, though, this book is due to the teamwork of Lisa Berryman and Liz Kemp. I gave them a short book. They demanded I fill the silences. Because of them I cried as I wrote versions two and three of *Pennies for Hitler*, but never doubted they were needed. Lisa may be the only publisher who can say 'can do better' with so much tact, support and inspiration to get it done. I owe you more than I can say.

Other titles by Jackie French

Historical
Somewhere Around the Corner • Dancing with Ben Hall
Soldier on the Hill • Daughter of the Regiment
Hitler's Daughter • Lady Dance • The White Ship
How the Finnegans Saved the Ship • Valley of Gold
Tom Appleby, Convict Boy
They Came on Viking Ships • Macbeth and Son
Pharaoh • A Rose for the Anzac Boys
Oracle • The Night They Stormed Eureka
A Waltz for Matilda • Nanberry: Black Brother White

Fiction
Rain Stones • Walking the Boundaries • The Secret Beach
Summerland • Beyond the Boundaries
A Wombat Named Bosco • The Book of Unicorns
The Warrior — The Story of a Wombat • Tajore Arkle
Missing You, Love Sara • Dark Wind Blowing
Ride the Wild Wind: The Golden Pony and Other Stories

Non-fiction
Seasons of Content • A Year in the Valley
How the Aliens from Alpha Centauri
Invaded My Maths Class and Turned Me into a Writer
How to Guzzle Your Garden • The Book of Challenges
Stamp, Stomp, Whomp
The Fascinating History of Your Lunch
Big Burps, Bare Bums and Other Bad-Mannered Blunders
To the Moon and Back • Rocket Your Child into Reading
The Secret World of Wombats
How High Can a Kangaroo Hop?

The Animal Stars Series
1. The Goat Who Sailed the World
2. The Dog Who Loved a Queen
3. The Camel Who Crossed Australia
4. The Donkey Who Carried the Wounded
5. The Horse Who Bit a Bushranger
6. Dingo: The Dog Who Conquered a Continent

Outlands Trilogy
In the Blood • Blood Moon • Flesh and Blood

School for Heroes
Lessons for a Werewolf Warrior
Dance of the Deadly Dinosaurs

Wacky Families Series
1. My Dog the Dinosaur • 2. My Mum the Pirate
3. My Dad the Dragon • 4. My Uncle Gus the Garden Gnome
5. My Uncle Wal the Werewolf • 6. My Gran the Gorilla
7. My Auntie Chook the Vampire Chicken
8. My Pa the Polar Bear

Phredde Series
1. A Phaery Named Phredde
2. Phredde and a Frog Named Bruce
3. Phredde and the Zombie Librarian
4. Phredde and the Temple of Gloom
5. Phredde and the Leopard-Skin Librarian
6. Phredde and the Purple Pyramid
7. Phredde and the Vampire Footy Team
8. Phredde and the Ghostly Underpants

Picture Books
Diary of a Wombat (with Bruce Whatley)
Pete the Sheep (with Bruce Whatley)
Josephine Wants to Dance (with Bruce Whatley)
The Shaggy Gully Times (with Bruce Whatley)
Emily and the Big Bad Bunyip (with Bruce Whatley)
Baby Wombat's Week (with Bruce Whatley)
Queen Victoria's Underpants (with Bruce Whatley)
The Tomorrow Book (with Sue deGennaro)
Christmas Wombat (with Bruce Whatley)
A Day to Remember (with Mark Wilson)

Jackie French is a full-time writer and wombat negotiator. Jackie writes fiction and non-fiction for all ages, and has columns in the print media. Jackie is regarded as one of Australia's most popular children's authors. She writes across all genres — from picture books and history to science fiction.

www.jackiefrench.com